people change

sara jafari

PENGUIN BOOKS

PENGUIN BOOKS

UK | USA | Canada | Ireland | Australia
India | New Zealand | South Africa

Penguin Books is part of the Penguin Random House group of companies
whose addresses can be found at global.penguinrandomhouse.com

Published in Penguin Books 2023
001

Copyright © Sara Jafari 2023

The moral right of the author has been asserted

Typeset in 10/15.2 pt Palatino LT Std
by Integra Software Services Pvt. Ltd, Pondicherry

Printed and bound in Great Britain by Clays Ltd, Elcograf S.p.A.

The authorised representative in the EEA is Penguin Random House
Ireland, Morrison Chambers, 32 Nassau Street, Dublin D02 YH68

A CIP catalogue record for this book is available from the British Library

ISBN: 978-1-5291-5755-0

www.greenpenguin.co.uk

People Change

Sara Jafari is a British-Iranian author and editor. She has contributed to the essay collection *I Will Not Be Erased* and the romance anthology *Who's Loving You*. Sara also runs *TOKEN Magazine*, a literary and arts print magazine featuring under-represented writers and artists. Her new novel, *People Change*, is the anticipated follow-up to her debut novel, *The Mismatch*.

Also by Sara Jafari

The Mismatch

For my late Maman Bozorg, Tahereh Esmailzadeh

Brixton

Now

They arrive at the house-warming party at 10 p.m. The Edwardian house sits squarely between Brixton and Herne Hill stations. Shirin Bayat does not particularly like going to Brixton because she feels complicit in the jarring, and ever-increasing, gentrification each time she is in the area. And that is likely because she is. She begrudgingly enjoys the overpriced coffee shops, with their excessive number of plants, millennial-pink sofas and rose-gold accents, spending money on various vegan dishes that even she can make at home for a fraction of the price. Every so often, to alleviate her guilt, she will go to the shops and restaurants that have been there long before the gentrification began, and she will buy something she might not even want. It never quite clears her conscience though.

There are clusters of people in the living room, some sitting on the three-seater sofa, others standing. The interior of the house could be sponsored by Ikea, the furniture white and familiar. There is a Malm dresser in the living room, and she is reminded of making said dresser many years ago and it eventually crumbling, the drawers breaking one by one. She remembers the many ways she tried to fix it because she couldn't afford another one, until in a fit of frustration she threw the planks of wood down the chute outside her East London flat.

Millie leads Shirin straight to the living room, like she has been here before, and kisses her boyfriend Henry on the lips in greeting. Millie is wearing red lipstick, and he rubs his lips after they kiss, to remove the stain. Millie has been with Henry coming up for two years now. Shirin dislikes Henry, dislikes being in the same room as him, and tries to avoid all gatherings he attends. It is difficult to be around them because Henry critiques most of what Millie does, due to his own sad insecurities. He has an air about him as though he is better than his girlfriend, although Shirin is not sure where his inflated ego derives from. He is the type to go on Twitter and reply to women's tweets that what they're saying did not happen, with his profile picture as an anime character. He will encourage debates about race or sexism, playing 'devil's advocate', though she suspects he believes the racist, sexist side. He is not quite an online troll but almost, teetering on the edge of what is acceptable online, though Millie cannot see this side of him. She is, sadly, too far gone.

Henry went to the same university as Shirin, and her first memory of him was when he added her on Facebook during freshers' week. She later discovered he had added more than fifty girls from university whom he deemed attractive, as though he were Robert Pattinson – or some other universally attractive man – and had a chance at sleeping with all of them if he so pleased. He was not and did not. He is best described as akin to a mole. Shirin does not mean to be derogatory to moles, but that it is the animal Henry looks most like. But her friend loves him, so that is that.

Millie returns to Shirin's side, looking off towards the connecting kitchen, and says, 'That's one of Dylan's housemates. I'll introduce you.' She lightly touches the top of Shirin's arm, before leading her towards the other side of the room.

Indeed, Shirin has gone to a house-warming party for people she does not even know. She found herself with nothing to do on a Friday night – an ever-increasing problem as she ages – and Millie reassured her that more was merrier, that it would be fun. The final push came when Millie added, 'You should have just stayed in Hull if you don't ever want to leave your flat.' Millie always knew the precise words to fire Shirin up and make her do something she didn't want to do – it was always like that at university, and Millie has only got better at it once her friend graduated and progressed in her career in public relations.

And that is how Shirin found herself here.

The man Shirin is being taken to meet has dark hair, short on the back and sides and long at the front. His shoulders are broad, his waist slender and he is tall. Very tall. It is curious that how much space one is able to take up is often seen as attractive in a man, but is seldom the case for women. She can only see him from the back, but he's wearing a black T-shirt in a soft jersey fabric.

'Kian, hey,' Millie says.

He turns around and then Shirin's breath catches. There is a painful feeling in her chest, an acute ache, from the surprise.

Millie had said that Henry's friend Dylan was moving into a flat in Brixton. She had said that he was moving in with three other boys. What she did not say, though, because of course she didn't know, was that Kian Rahimi went to Shirin's school and they have not spoken in ten years.

Someone I Used to Know

'Shirin,' Kian says, lips parted, his eyes squinting slightly, like he is wondering whether he is mistaken, whether it is really her. Shirin is also taken aback by the image of him before her. In her mind he is always sixteen, baby-faced but beautiful. His face has developed a sharpness to it that it didn't have back then – his jaw and cheekbones strong and well defined. It is the strangest sensation, to see someone you once knew very well as a teenager standing before you, matured, as though out of nowhere.

'Hi,' she eventually says. She has imagined this moment many times before and she always says something much grander than *hi*.

'You know each other?' Millie asks, looking from one to the other.

'Yeah, we went to school together,' Kian says. 'Back in Hull.'

Seeing Kian again after all these years makes Shirin regret coming here. Her gut, she knows, is usually right about these things, and she should have listened to it. Being so close to him now brings memories to the surface, up out of her belly, almost spilling out of her throat. Even him saying 'we' makes her heart thud wildly and pathetically.

'Oh. Small world, I guess?' Millie says, uninterested by this moment that is so monumental to Shirin. She tucks a blonde strand of her hair behind her ear, before continuing to say, 'Well, I'm sure you have lots to chat about ...'

And Millie is gone, returning to Henry, and Shirin is left reeling, thinking: Please, for the love of God, don't leave me alone with this person I used to know.

'Well, hello,' Kian says, beaming. It is an uncomplicated smile. The kind of smile Shirin cannot imagine having. She struggles to smile on cue, her face a permanent frown that she often tries, and fails, to soften. Like now, the tops of her lips are raised upwards, but the rest of her face is unmoved. The smile does not touch her eyes because, when she looks at Kian, she does not just see a person she cared so deeply for, she sees all of the shit from her childhood that she has worked so hard to leave behind.

'Long time no see,' she says, her voice cooler than she feels.

'What are you doing here?'

'I came here with Millie. I didn't know you lived here.' She scratches her neck to have something to do with her hands, and to mask that they are shaking.

Kian tells her that he sometimes hangs out with Henry – because Henry is Dylan's home-town friend – and that Dylan went to university with Kian. It is a too-coincidental and long-winded connection. What are the chances, she cannot help but think, that these two people from Hull have found themselves in a connecting friendship group ten years later? Isn't that the whole point of moving away from your home town, so that things like this don't happen?

'It's weird that we've not seen each other before, at parties and stuff, when I've come down to London,' he muses.

Due to her avoidance of Henry, it is not that weird. But the fact that Kian, of all people, is tenuously linked to her friendship group is. In the past, Shirin attempted to look Kian up on social media, curious to see what he was doing with his life. His Instagram, however, brandished no photos of him, instead showing landscapes lacking in filters so that they looked dull, or his paintings, which Shirin thought were impressive and experimental, almost dizzying if you looked at them for too long. She admired that he had continued with his art. She's realised how easy it is to lose sight of your passions, of who you were before adulthood kicked in.

'So, you've just moved here?' she asks.

'Yeah. I was living in Manchester before. You've been here a while though, right?'

She nods. 'I went to uni here, at Queen Mary's, and stayed since.' She pauses as though she is thinking. 'Where'd you go to uni again?' She knows already though, from her aforementioned stalking.

'Glasgow.'

She nods, then says, 'Right, nice,' a little too quickly. She did not pace her response correctly, and there is a short silence before she fills it by blurting, 'You've lost your accent?' It's not really a question, though she says it like it is.

He raises an eyebrow, laughs. 'I definitely haven't.' The side of his mouth twitches upwards as though he is deliberating about whether he will say what he wants to next. There is a glimmer in his dark eyes. 'Yours hasn't toned down, though, I see.'

Despite not living in Hull for eight years now, Shirin's accent has remained, just as strong as it was when she left. People she meets for the first time habitually comment on it, like it is a quirk of hers. Sometimes they do not understand her, sometimes it colours their perceptions of her – they see her as less intelligent because she has a soft drawl and elongates certain words. Kian's accent, by contrast, sounds neutral to Shirin, like it has been tempered through the years.

She narrows her eyes at him.

'It's a good thing,' Kian adds. 'It reminds me of home.'

She resists the strange urge to smile at this – the urge in general to pick up where they left off, which she is realising would be very easy to do. In her fantasies – or nightmares – of this moment, Kian is cold and bitter towards her. They argue. He is not friendly, and perhaps that is because it is harder to think of him as he was all those years ago. Perhaps she has needed him to be a villain to justify the things she said. Her gaze wanders past his shoulder, towards Millie's back as she leans into Henry, and other people Shirin does not know well, chatting together.

'What are you doing then? Did you get a job here or something?' she asks.

'I got a place to do an MFA in Fine Art at Goldsmiths.' His tone is marginally less confident and quieter when he says this. He clears his throat, covering his mouth with his fist.

Her gaze returns to his eyes and she cannot help the real smile then. 'That's amazing. Congratulations. I always knew you were talented.'

He looks away and presses his lips together. It is a somewhat embarrassed, uncertain expression. 'Thanks.' He then scrunches his nose, before adding, 'I know some people say Masters are pointless, but I think it'll be good for me. There's the potential to spend some time abroad, too, which would be sick – and it was partially funded.'

'I don't think it's pointless. It's your passion. It always has been.'

Kian's mouth is open, she thinks, to explain what he means, when Hana comes over, as though out of nowhere, sidling her way between them. She is wearing a black leather bustier and red flared trousers, her lips a wine-red to match her bottoms. Her skin is buttery smooth. Shirin has never seen Hana with a blemish, even in their late teens at university. Having witnessed Hana's skincare cabinet, though, she knows such faultless skin takes supreme effort. It somewhat softens the blow of how grey and lacklustre Shirin's own skin is, despite the various The Ordinary serums that she uses.

'I didn't know you were here yet,' Hana says to Shirin, almost accusatory.

'I just arrived.'

Hana looks at Kian pointedly, then back at Shirin, with an expression that reads, *What's going on here?* Shirin cannot help but feel a twitch of irrational irritation then, like Hana needs to know – or be involved in – every facet of her life.

'You said you couldn't come,' Shirin says.

Hana smiles, pleased with herself. Her sudden appearance is actually unsurprising, really. She likes to show up unannounced, declining invitations and then appearing suddenly.

At the start of their friendship Shirin found this energising and unexpected. Now, though, she perceives Hana's actions as indulgent, as though she always requires special attention, even at a party for people she barely knows. Shirin dislikes herself for thinking such things, now, about her best friend. She thinks there is an ugliness inside her sometimes, some kind of repressed anger that she takes out on other people in her mind.

'I live to surprise. You know me,' Hana says. She touches Shirin's hair gingerly. 'I like the colour. It's very 2015.' On a whim, the night before, Shirin dyed her hair a colour that Bleach London calls 'Awkward Peach'. Hana's words make her question her decision, given it is now 2018. She resists the urge to touch her very dry locks, which are coated in argan oil, in response. Her annoyance must show on her face because Hana backtracks and says, 'What I mean is it looks cool.'

The doorbell rings. Kian's eyes flick to Shirin's, hold hers for a moment, before looking back towards the door. 'I better get that,' he says, leaving them.

'So,' Hana begins once he has left. 'Aren't you happy to see me?'

Just looking at Hana, so immaculately put together, results in Shirin straightening out her geometric-patterned wrap dress, which by comparison feels frumpy – like Shirin is going to a garden party, and Hana to a club. Shirin used to dress edgy, though she'd never actually use the word *edgy*. She doesn't know when that changed. She tries not to compare herself to others, but often cannot help it. Especially when she gets the feeling her friend is also doing it to her, as she does now.

Hana perches herself on the armrest of the sofa and crosses one leg over the other. 'God, have you seen them? Could they get a room?' she says with derision.

Shirin turns to see that Henry and Millie are kissing. His arms are around her waist, and hers are wrapped around his neck. They are the same height, which makes the kissing appear more intimate.

She does not know what to say. Ordinarily she would join in, to appease Hana, but she is too wired, her heart beating too quickly. She feels a scary mix of wanting to take flight and freeze. Seeing Kian has made her feel so unsure of herself, unsure of anything. What are the chances of him being here, in her world, with her friends, after all this time? It's like she has reverted to being an unhappy teenager, and she needs to be alone to process it all. She knows that not even Hana, who she loves but who also sometimes annoys her, can assuage her anxiety right now. So she shrugs and says, 'I need to pee,' before leaving the room, allowing no time for her friend to reply.

She does a solitary tour of the house and finds herself in the kitchen, looking out onto the garden. People are smoking by the patio, and at the far end of the garden is a summerhouse. She opens her phone and sees that Uber has surge-charging and so she decides to stay.

Tonight is a balmy summer evening and the sky is black, pollution providing a mask over the night stars. She makes her way outside for some air. Voices from this party, and other people in other houses around Brixton having parties too, spill out into the gardens. Occasionally there are the sirens of ambulances and police cars, and it is only now that Shirin is alone, willing her thoughts away from Kian, that she notices them.

Unthinkingly she finds herself by the summerhouse. Phoebe, her friend from back home, has one and it has always struck Shirin as a middle-class addition to a house. The glass doors are left slightly ajar, the inside unlit. As she enters, her phone's torch illuminates the interior of the room. She shines it around the walls to find a light switch, and the bulb gives off a soft, dim light. It takes a moment for her eyes to adjust to her surroundings.

Against the wall is a white corporate-looking desk with grey legs, and a clashing pine chair. The desk is bare, except for a Sports Direct mug containing pens and pencils. Boxes are stacked against the opposite wall. She peeks inside one of them. It contains various vinyl records, and atop the pile is Fiona Apple, *The Idler Wheel Is Wiser Than the Driver of the Screw and Whipping Cords Will Serve You More Than Ropes Will Ever Do*. She runs her hand over the sleeve. It is covered in a thin layer of dust, which she brushes off with her fingertips and instantly regrets, wiping her now-dirty hand on her dress. She remembers listening to 'Every Single Night' on repeat one summer when she was still at university, with an unrequited crush and feeling as though she might die from the lack of attention.

'That's her best album,' a voice says behind her.

She jumps, dropping it. The record lands clumsily back into the box. She turns and Kian is standing in the doorway. He has put on a navy denim jacket, and she immediately thinks he is one of few people who wears double denim well. He looks as surprised to see her as she is to see him.

'Sorry,' she says. 'The door was open.'

'You not enjoying the party?'

'No, I am. I just needed a bit of a break.'

He nods like he understands. Stacks of painted canvas lean against the side of the desk.

'This is a really nice space.' She gestures around her.

'The landlord used to live here and was an author. This was her writing space,' he says.

'And you use it as a studio now?'

He nods. 'Dylan's parents bought him the house, and he's been quite sound in letting me use it for my work.'

'Of course they did,' she says, her voice thick with derision.

Kian's laugh is short and quick. She is struck by how different he seems now from the boy she used to skip class with, all those years ago. That boy was quiet, angry and wore his emotions plainly on his face. The Kian in front of her is so much more confident; he stands straight and laughs, so easy and carefree. Age has refined him, whereas she wonders if she has regressed. She had such passion back then, about everything. She gently chews her tongue to gain clarity, to remain firmly in the moment.

Above his desk is a painting of a woman, nude, lying on her front, her arm just covering her breasts, her hair in two space-buns. The subject is looking off into the distance, her eyes soft, as though they are about to flutter shut. Her expression is unguarded, like this is a shot between poses.

Her lips are parted, like she is about to breathe out a sigh. The brushstrokes are both soft and strong in places, the paint heavy, overlapping different shades to make her olive skin, which is textured and slightly pink on the tops of her cheeks. There are pops of colour in unexpected places, blended into natural tones. Surrounding her is a meadow, with bursts of pink, red and orange flowers in the background.

His style has evolved into Impressionism. There is an ethereal quality to these portraits, quite different from his older work on his Instagram, which is bolder and sharp in colour. When she goes to her friends' gallery launches she rarely sees art like this, though she is no real art enthusiast. Their works tends to be abstract or conceptual and she often does not get them, which makes her feel dense, because everyone around her seems to. It is not surprising, looking around now, that Kian is being funded to continue his work at one of the best art universities in the country. 'You're really good,' she says.

'Thanks.' His reply is quick. He does not take compliments well and visibly wants to move away from this topic of conversation. That this is still the case for him – that this hasn't changed over the years – is interesting to her.

'You're a proper artist now, you know, Kian. It's very cool – accept it.' She says this both because she means it and to make him more uncomfortable, so that they can both be uncomfortable, not just her.

He lets out a laugh again. He looks boyish, up close, more how she remembers him from school, his dark eyebrows softly framing his eyes. But now he has well-groomed facial hair, which shapes his face, creating more angles, making his high cheekbones more pronounced. 'I'm a proper artist, am I?' He shakes his head. 'It feels pretentious to say it aloud, to be honest.'

'Well, you are one, I'm afraid. Pretentious or not.'

She gives him a close-lipped smile, thinking she should go soon, when he asks, 'What was up with that girl talking to you earlier?'

'What girl?'

'The one wearing a corset.'

'Oh,' she says. 'Hana?'

'Yeah, her. The way she talked to you ... I mean, I might be wrong, but I don't know – it was weird. Does she always do that?'

She waves her hand in an *it's nothing* way. 'That's just Hana, that's how she is with everyone when she's in a mood. She's not always like that.' This is true; sometimes Hana is considered and caring. Other times, when she is feeling insecure, she takes it out on the people closest to her. She has difficulty hiding the ugly parts of herself, but at least she is honest.

Kian does not look convinced, which makes Shirin defensive. It is one thing for her to have the occasional negative thought about Hana, but not other people, not when they don't know her like she does.

'Well, you look really good. I like your hair,' he says.

She is still annoyed at him, so she looks at him blankly, even though his face is colouring ever so slightly. He does not backtrack, though, as she expects him to, as she would have done in his position.

15

In the end she shrugs, despite her now-quickening heart, which she wishes would shut up and get a life. 'I don't really take notice of what Hana says. I know she doesn't mean it anyway,' she says. The first part of what she says is a lie, but one she wants to be true. Perhaps if she says it enough times it will be. 'You should probably get back to the party. People will be wondering where you are.'

'Is it bad that I don't want to?' He is looking at his hands now, twirling the plain silver band on his right ring-finger.

It is rare to see men wearing jewellery. She is reminded of summers spent in Iran, with her Maman Bozorg taking her to jewellery shops and haggling with vendors to buy her gold. It is something that in England appears extravagant. But in her motherland, jewellery is an investment, like putting your money in stocks. Shirin keeps her jewellery in a box underneath her underwear drawer: thousands of pounds worth in her shabby bedroom. Today she is wearing a gold chain, which is textured like rope and shimmers in the light. Though it is 18-carat gold, it is such a bright gold it appears fake. Her Baba Bozorg gave it to her before he passed away.

'Why? Everyone is here for you,' she says. She understands why she might not want to return, but not Kian, whose party it is.

'It's a bit much in there.' He walks over to the desk, opens the drawer and retrieves a bottle of whisky. He smiles. 'You fancy it?'

The corners of her lips move downwards. 'Probably not.'

'See, you might have clung to the accent, but you've lost your Northern roots,' he jokes, raising one eyebrow.

'I'm trying not to drink,' she says, before pressing her palms against the wall.

'Oh,' he says, no doubt feeling like a dick and that maybe she's an alcoholic. Or that she's practising her religion – their religion. He is not, and she is not. She is on new antidepressants that do not mix well with alcohol.

'I'm just ... I'm trying to be good,' she says, not wanting to go into it.

He puts the bottle back in the drawer.

'Well, sit with me for a bit then?' he says. His hazel eyes are wide and hopeful, and she thinks she will disappoint him, but what comes out of her mouth is, 'Alright then.'

Later they are seated on the floor, their backs against the only wall that is clear of furniture. His shoulder is touching hers and she is acutely aware of it there. Fiona Apple is playing on his record player. They selected *Tidal* from his stack, and 'Criminal' plays now. Her voice is warm, the instrumentals both fuzzy and deliberate. They talk about music and Kian speaks about his favourite artists – so many that Shirin jokes they cannot all be his favourite, that you cannot have that many favourites or else the word is redundant; you must just like them, she says. He disagrees and is almost bashful as he tries to defend his point. He reminds her of a puppy in his enthusiasm now; it is an endearing, familiar quality.

And yet. Being next to Kian brings back long-buried memories. She is pushing them down, biting the inside of her mouth, to focus on that acute pain instead. It almost works, though it is like putting your hand over a leaking tap: small forgotten moments are at risk of escaping like trickling water, and there is only so long she can hold it for.

'Why do you have vinyl anyway?' she asks. Her voice is light and she surprises herself by how good a façade she can put on around people; how what she is thinking is often so different from what comes out of her mouth.

'Why not? It sounds better, doesn't it?'

'It's different,' she muses. 'Feels like more of an experience.'

He smiles at her. 'Exactly.' He leans over her to turn the volume up. They shut their eyes and sway slightly to the chorus, to the rises in Fiona Apple's singing. Shirin opens her eyes and watches Kian. His eyes are still shut, and he has a flicker of a smile on his lips. His head is bent back, and she thinks he is a man now; the years have made him at ease with himself, though there are glimmers of who he was when she knew him. She tries to erase such thoughts from her mind at the same time the song finishes. His eyes open and she looks away quickly. He turns the volume down.

'How long has it been since we last saw each other?' he asks.

Somewhere in the recesses of her brain she knew this would come up, that it was between them, hanging in the air, cramping the space in the summerhouse.

'I don't know,' she lies. 'It was just before we went into college, so I guess ten years, maybe?'

She is reminded of the days wearing polyester trousers that chafed, stiff white polo shirts and shiny black sweatshirts. Of being seated boy, girl, boy, girl in every class and of all the boys in her year being knobheads, calling her various names, all nasty with little consequence. Ten years have passed. So much time – and yet she feels herself being pulled back there so viscerally.

'Wow,' he says, and then turns to smile at her. It is a sad smile. 'What have you been doing with yourself then? You got out, like you always wanted to.'

Her throat is dry, but she gulps anyway. 'I work in publishing now.'

His expression changes at this; the slight sadness in his eyes is taken away and they are bright again, happy for her. He congratulates her on getting her dream job, on living the life she always said she wanted. 'Not that I ever doubted you would. You were always determined.'

'I'm assuming you did study Art at A-level then, in the end?'

He nods. 'I did it at uni too.'

'Did you? I don't know how you wangled that with your parents, but I'm very glad you did. I was being serious when I said you're very talented, Kian. Obviously.'

'I wouldn't have had the confidence to do it if it wasn't for you, you know.' His voice is quiet and his words make her feel very warm.

They are skirting around the obvious – around everything that is unsaid between them – and she is not sure what is worse: this feeling of being on edge in case it comes up, or just getting it over with. Both are unappealing. She is looking at the desk drawer, where the whisky is, wondering if she should have accepted his offer. This conversation would be easier if she had. She imagines pouring a shot into the bottle's cap, bringing it to her lips, the icy liquid spilling onto her dress, ever so slightly. She can taste it, sharp, warm, searing, burning her throat, warming her belly.

Memories of them being called in by their head teacher, of their parents getting involved, of cold words exchanged in the heat of the moment. Everything, and then nothing.

He leans his head back against the wall, his profile appealing, the slight bump on the arch of his nose familiar to her. His complexion is darker than hers, likely because his family are from a different part of Iran than hers.

'It's weird how we were the only non-white people in our year,' he says. 'I've been thinking about that more lately, how messed up that was. For us, anyway.' He shakes his head. He is giving her an opening. But it is okay for him, she thinks, he has had something to drink, whereas she is sober. And she talks about her race enough at work; she is part of too many organisations – labelled 'BAME' or 'POC' or 'under-represented', everything other than Iranian – and she doesn't want to do it now, not even with Kian. Especially not with Kian. She also doesn't want to leave. She wants to stay right here next to him.

She weakly acknowledges what he's said, murmuring something like, 'Yeah, it is weird.'

'I was sorry to hear about your parents, by the way,' he says. There is a slight frown on his face, and his eyebrows draw together once more, in concern or pity. He is so bold, she thinks, to bypass small talk and reach into her, bringing out all the things she would rather not talk about, things she doesn't even speak about with Hana, not really.

'It's a good thing, you don't have to say you're sorry.' Their separation was a long time coming. Her parents always fought – proper shouting matches and, growing up, she would put her headphones in, crank the volume as loud as it would go and stay in her bedroom until it was over. Often, then, she would wish they had left her with her grandparents in Tehran. She wonders if her life would have been simpler, if they had. Maybe she would have felt what it was like to be loved, rather than feeling like a burden her parents were obliged to love.

She wants to ask Kian about his family, about his brother and how he's doing now, but she hasn't the words to broach this subject after so long. She is not as bold as he is.

There is silence, in which they can only hear their breaths. They look at each other and it is like they are speaking without words. She is thinking she wants to kiss him, and she knows he is thinking he would like to kiss her. Like magnets, they move closer unthinkingly and they are soon inches from each other. She can feel his warm breath against her face now. A long-forgotten flutter in her stomach returning. It is so long forgotten that she wants to run away from it, to prevent any buried feelings from the past rising to the surface. Her eyes move from his hazel eyes to his full lips, which are parted.

'Maybe he's in here,' a posh voice outside says.

'Imagine if he's in there, painting at his own party,' another male voice says.

There is laughter.

21

It is the saving grace she didn't know she needed until it arrived. She moves away and stands up, smoothing her dress down. 'I best be going anyway,' she says quickly, slinging her bag onto her back.

He looks down for a moment, then up again, and there is something in his eyes she cannot quite describe but knows very well. It reminds her of the old Kian, the Kian from 2008 who got into so much trouble for her and who she barely even thanked.

'Right, of course. It was nice to see you, Shirin. Take care.'

'Bye, Kian.'

A Sentence

Then

Kian Rahimi was fifteen years old when he learnt how one moment can change a person's life for ever.

For the longest time he had wanted nothing more than to be like his older brother, Mehdi. He had always looked up to him. Two years his senior, Mehdi was brave in a way Kian never could be. He stood up for what he believed in, had the kind of charisma that is rare – so much so that everyone who knew him wanted to be close to him, so that Mehdi could rub some of his charm onto them and maybe they'd feel lighter, less restricted by their own self-doubt.

It was on the ride home from court, their dad silent in the driver's seat, his hands gripping the steering wheel so tightly his knuckles were white, their mum crying silent tears as she looked out of the window, that Kian realised he didn't want to be like Mehdi any more. That much confidence – such an abundance of it, at such a young age, as a brown boy in a white city – meant trouble.

He did not want to go to prison, like his brother.

It started small. Sneaking out of the house in the early hours, taking Mum's car (never Dad's) even though he was underage, or smoking weed at the back of school at lunch.

It wasn't any of these things that got him sent away. Comparatively they were minor, though they added up. Soon the police knew Mehdi Rahimi, he was a recognised name, a notorious troublemaker. No one ever asked *why* he wanted to make trouble though. Why *anyone* would want to make trouble.

People are not born inherently bad or rebellious. It comes from somewhere. Kian still wonders, sometimes, whether he could have had the power to stop what happened to Mehdi all those years ago.

Back then, they lived in Kirk Ella, on the wealthier side of Hull, East Yorkshire. Their driveway could fit four cars if they wanted. Their house was detached, three-storey. They were new-money, that much was clear to everyone. They stood out on their street. His dad's impractical convertible sat out front, barely used. It was like his dad forgot they lived in England, in the North, and that the good weather only lasted four months of the year if they were lucky. 'This country,' his parents would begin, 'it's nothing like back home. Always rain, rain, rain.' Kian often wanted to retort, *Well, why did you move us here?* But he never did.

Every Sunday when he played footie with his friends it would pour down and they would play anyway, their feet sliding against the mud. He longed for the sun on his face, felt his mood perceptively lift when it did. He wondered if this longing, this need for sun, was in his blood, and whether his body knew he wasn't from England, not really, not biologically. That Iran, with its scorching summers, was the climate that his physiology was accustomed to – even though he had only been there a handful of times and was not fluent in his own language.

His dad pulled into their drive that day and they got out of the car. Betty, their opposite neighbour, gave them a sad nod as they returned as a three, and not a four.

His mum, who was often so chatty, always luring her sons into the living room to watch TV and spend quality time with her, said nothing the whole car journey. She went directly to her bedroom and shut the door with a barely audible click.

'I'm going for a drive,' his dad said, picking up the key to his convertible from the side table by the door.

'Now?' Kian said. 'Mum's upset.'

His dad looked at him, sharp-eyed, raising a furry eyebrow. 'We're all upset.'

'Can I come?' As he said the words he knew they were wrong. But he didn't want to be alone in this big house, not when Mehdi wasn't in it and his mum was upset.

His dad shook his head and left. He didn't even bother to shut the front door properly; it was left ajar.

Two years in prison.

Mehdi's face had crumpled at the news. His usually smooth face, quietly confident, broken.

'The sentence can be halved with good behaviour,' their lawyer told them afterwards. 'So one year, really. I know it's not what we wanted, but it could have been much worse.'

Kian imagined his brother in prison, as it's portrayed on TV, being forced into a gang, or beaten up in the showers or something. He imagined Mehdi lonely, wanting his family. He felt his eyes prickling, so he slapped himself hard across the face and focused on that pain instead. He tried to think of anything other than his brother being incarcerated for one whole year.

Book Launch

Now

They are handed lukewarm wine in small paper cups. Shirin requests Shloer. It is sickly sweet but mostly resembles Prosecco, which is what she really wants. The room is buzzing with chatter and subdued laughter, and people are spilling out onto the pavement outside. It is a July evening and everyone is clinging to summer, to the light and sun and warmth, to the jubilation of it all, which they will inevitably long for again, come winter. It has been five days since Shirin saw Kian.

Hana guides Shirin now through the crowd to Abigail Underwood. Shirin and Hana were friends with Abigail at university but, since they graduated, slowly they grew apart, as many people do. They are now more like acquaintances who see each other at events, and who like each other's Instagram pictures. They go over to Abigail to congratulate her on the release of her debut novel.

'It's such a gorgeous book,' Hana says to Abigail, clutching said novel, *My Corner Shop*, as though it is something very dear to her. Ten minutes earlier both Shirin and Hana had complained that it *is* spendy at £17.99, and they had wondered whether they could get away with not buying one, whether Abigail would notice and be offended. In the end it was the guilt that they should support their peers, and small businesses – like this independent bookshop in Peckham – that propelled them to purchase a copy each.

'Thank you,' Abigail says. Her eyes are bright and her movements skittish. Despite these telltale signs of nerves, she puts both her arms around Hana and Shirin and says something patronising like, 'We're all doing so well since uni. I'm so proud of us.'

Shirin and Hana look past Abigail's shoulder to each other and exchange A Look. They ask Abigail to sign their books, which she does, writing a different inspirational message in each one. In Shirin's she says, *I hope this encourages you to follow your dreams.* It is mildly insulting because she *is* following her dreams and believes herself successful in such aims.

People are hovering around Abigail to speak to her, so Hana says she is going to have a fag, and Shirin keenly follows. Outside the air is cool, with a welcome breeze. They stand by the side of the shop, in the small outdoor seating area. Shirin is wearing a pink midi dress and mules. While she enjoys her outfit, she cannot escape the fact that her sense of fashion is influenced by her colleagues at Hoffman Books. They all wear mules in the summer and thick gold jewellery, as she is tonight. Following Hana's previous comments, she washed out the peach colour in her hair. It is now bleach-blonde, cut into a long bob, and she is in desperate need of a root-bleach, with her dark roots peeking through. She has pinned her fringe away from her face with gold hair-clips and is in two minds about cutting her fringe back shorter or letting it grow. It is a constant battle every six months, as she inevitably succumbs to the curious lure of the full fringe.

Hana is wearing a kimono crop top and high-waisted black trousers. A thin strip of her stomach is showing and the skin there is smooth and tan. She customised the top herself and makes a point of telling people it's okay when she does it, because she's half Japanese. No one ever asks, but it is information she is keen to share, presumably to shame others for appropriating her culture.

Shirin has been friends with Hana since their first year at university. They met at the student union. Hana was sitting alone at a picnic table in the smoking area, her long dark hair partially covering her face. She looked like a goth, and Shirin had thought that was a cool, admirable look. In fact she still thinks that, though Hana no longer dresses as a goth. Shirin asked if she and the two people she was with could sit there for a bit. Hana let them, and an hour later Shirin's hall-mates had left to dance, while Hana and Shirin were embroiled in conversation about some celebrity – likely Justin, and whether he was back together with Selena. It turned out Hana wasn't at Queen Mary's, but Central Saint Martins. She'd come to the student union with her friend, who did go there. Said friend had got with someone, leaving Hana behind. Shirin thinks it was fate that brought them together. That if Hana's friend hadn't got with someone that night, so much of their lives would be different. For their three years at university they were a duo, they went to every party, every event, together. They were inseparable.

Hana arrived in Shirin's life when she needed her most. When Shirin and Kian had stopped talking, she'd acutely realised how much she had been holding her breath around her home-town friends, that there were certain subjects she did not broach because it would be uncomfortable, and potentially painful. With Hana it was never like that. Though, despite her early realisation that with Hana she could speak unrestrained and be truly accepted, Shirin did not tell her about the things that happened to her during her school days. In fact, she hasn't told anyone she's met in adulthood about that time, adopting the approach that if you don't speak about something, it never happened.

There are clusters of people around them now, making connections and introductions. Shirin and Hana are not included in this. They lean against the shop window, and Hana lights up. 'I can't believe Abigail wrote a book,' Hana says. 'Who has the time for that?'

Shirin looks at the inside cover, at the blurb there. The *Guardian* has praised it as being a 'Superb future classic', and the *Independent* as 'A shrewd look at being working-class today … a breathtaking debut.' Shirin reads this aloud, to annoy Hana.

'Is she really working-class, though?' Hana asks. She is not quiet when she says this, and Shirin tells her to *shh*. 'At uni she was all about wearing vintage Burberry that was her mum's, or that Prada backpack that she says she got cheap, but how cheap can a Prada backpack really be?'

'You can wear designer clothes and be working-class,' Shirin says.

Hana turns to her, blows a puff of smoke out of the right corner of her mouth, away from Shirin. 'That makes no sense.'

'It's not black and white,' Shirin says, though she does not quite know the parameters. She does know that what Hana is saying is likely incorrect, with envy clouding her words.

'Maybe I should write a book,' Hana muses. 'About all the fuckboys I've met. I can set it in Japan. That'd get publishers excited, right?'

Shirin snorts. 'Yeah, right. Since when did you want to write a book, anyway?' Hana has always wanted to be a stylist. She studied Fashion Communication at Central Saint Martins, though partway through her course she came to the realisation that she didn't want to be a journalist. She would put off writing essays until the night before, eventually producing something quick and scrappy. She left university with a 2.2, with minimal effort. She is intelligent, but refuses to put work into things she does not care about, which Shirin thinks might be smarter than people who put too much of their time into things that add little joy or value to their lives.

'Well, I have a lot to say,' Hana retorts. Her face is tight now. Shirin does not doubt that Hana has enough stories to fill a novel. Despite them being close friends for so many years and divulging everything about themselves to each other, there are still things Shirin doesn't know about Hana. She has never been to her family house, where she currently lives, in Woolwich – a temporary measure until she finds full-time work. Hana says her family are weird about people visiting. Shirin has never questioned internally what that means, let alone out loud.

'You could write a really great book,' Shirin soothes. 'A novel for the millennial times.' She moves her hand ahead of her as she speaks, as though the words are written in the stars, or the equivalent newspaper headlines.

'I'm going to do it one day.'

'I'm not doubting it,' Shirin says, doubting it.

Hana will forget about this new-found dream of hers tonight, or when the shininess of Abigail's launch party has worn off. Shirin has seen this happen many times; Hana's mind flip-flops between dreams and goals because she is easily influenced by others. She shuts her eyes and inhales Hana's smoke.

'Why did you leave the party on Saturday so early, anyway?' Hana asks. 'You never said.'

'I had a headache,' Shirin lies, badly.

Hana takes another long drag, before saying, 'Right, sure you did. Does this have anything to do with the guy you were talking to?'

Shirin sips her Shloer. The bubbles tickle her throat and the sugar clings to her teeth, but she drinks for as long as she needs to, to think of what to say next. 'No,' she finally says.

'Shirin, we lived together for two years and have been friends since we were eighteen. I know when you're lying.'

She sighs. 'Fine. The guy I was speaking to – Kian – that wasn't the first time I'd met him. We went to school together. In Hull.'

'Okay …'

'I got a bit freaked out, seeing him at the party. Like, we haven't spoken in ten years and we kind of ended our friendship on bad terms. It was very weird to see him. Then we chatted in his summerhouse and it became quite intense, so I got out of there. I'm sorry I didn't say bye.'

'What happened with you both?'

Shirin shrugs. 'Just school stuff. It's silly now.' The words come out with difficulty because that's not how she feels at all, but she can't dredge up the past; she doesn't want to. So she smiles, waves her hand in front of her and says, 'Honestly, it's nothing. It was bizarre at the time is all.'

Hana drops her cigarette on the floor and puts it out with her heeled boot. 'If you say so,' she murmurs. That's the thing about Hana; she knows when to drop something. Well, except when she adds, 'He could be at Jasper's gig on Monday. I'm just going to leave that there.'

The past four times Shirin has had an excuse for not going to their friend Jasper's gigs, and while Hana has a legitimate reason for not going to this one – a Hinge date – Shirin can't justify producing yet another fake excuse. But gigs just aren't her thing.

'I don't really have time to think about it. I'm so busy with work ...' She doesn't really consider her words, and a flicker of irritation shows on Hana's face, but it is too late. Shirin is so attuned to Hana; she can tell exactly what she is thinking, and instantly regrets bringing the subject of employment into their conversation.

'How is work, anyway?' Hana asks, her face now apparently devoid of any emotion other than mild curiosity.

Shirin has been working at Hoffman Books for more than two years now. It was a long adjustment, but she finally feels settled in. The marker for this is that her anxiety doesn't spike in every team meeting when she has to speak. Instead of saying this, though, she quickly replies, 'I mean, I'm still an assistant. The majority of my day is spent doing admin, or working on other people's projects, not my own. It's not, you know, the ideal or anything.'

Hana nods, relief plain on her face that Shirin is apparently unhappy, as she is too. 'Graduate life, eh?'

They graduated five years ago, but when Shirin is with Hana, they always move backwards to their university days. Time is divided into pre- and post-university. It is a marker Shirin feels finally ready to move past now, though she is not sure how to tell Hana this.

'How is the job hunt going then?' she asks Hana gently.

Hana closes her eyes. It is the kind of expression none of her other friends would consider pulling; it is theatrical and does not look at all natural, but maybe for Hana it is. 'Let's not talk about it. I'd really rather not,' she replies. There is a short silence before Hana says, 'Your eyeshadow is perfection, by the way.'

'Thanks,' Shirin says, a strange glee within her at the compliment, at the validation from Hana, which she realises she craves more and more. It is like she needs it, sometimes, to feel good about herself.

Despite this, her mind lingers on Kian. Her dream had always been to live in London and work in publishing – to put her past behind her. So it's strange that now she has everything she wanted, she cannot stop thinking about whether she made the right decisions all those years ago – and whether seeing Kian again means something in relation to this.

She even considers asking Hana what she thinks, when Abigail appears before them wanting to take a picture together. They raise their copies of the book in the air, in something like jubilation, as she leans in towards them to take a selfie. Abigail's hand is pressed against Shirin's back as she tilts her head and smiles for the photo. Afterwards she asks if they're having a good time, and they lie and say they are.

'Your time will come soon, don't worry,' she says, like she is a bride and they are single women desperate for marriage. Shirin has her mouth open to say actually they're good, but then Abigail is already off to talk to other people, and she isn't given the chance.

'God, she's bloody annoying,' she says.

Hana lays her hand heavy on Shirin's shoulder, looks her dead in the eye, a solemn expression on her face. It is so solemn, Shirin becomes worried. 'Don't worry, your time will come,' Hana mimics, in Abigail's nasally Irish accent.

Hoffman Books

In Shirin's peripheral vision she can see Florence Ainsworth. She is looking at Shirin through the gaps between their computer monitors. Shirin pretends she cannot see Florence looking, but her presence across from her is inescapable, like she's a snake peeping through woodland foliage, watching, waiting.

The editorial team's desks are joined together in five rows of three. They often joke that they are battery editors in the open-plan office, squished together like hens, expected to produce perfect manuscripts one after the other in quick succession. If she holds her arms out to the side, Shirin will be touching Poppy, a quiet editor from Australia, on her left, and Joanie, a dry-humoured and often hot-and-cold commissioning editor, on her right. Her manager, Lilian, is seated behind them, at her own separate desk, as though she is an island, with a short bookcase between her and her employees.

The office is situated inside the Shard; the walls are all glass, with a view of London that is expensive and surreal. Lustrous light shines in most days, providing them with much-coveted and needed doses of vitamin D. Since working as an assistant editor at Hoffman, Shirin's seasonal affective disorder has drastically improved; she no longer yearns for daylight, compared to her previous dingy office jobs, where she saw the sky for merely half an hour on her lunch break.

Shirin is not fond of Florence, who is still looking at her now. Florence is from Hertfordshire and went to Cambridge, like most of her colleagues at Hoffman. Her father, Tom Ainsworth, is the MD of the one of the biggest publishers in the UK. Her mother, Robin Joyce, is a successful novelist and writes the kinds of literary novels not many people truly understand, but everyone pretends to. She recently wrote a long feature in *Vogue*, which Florence brought into the office. There were multiple spreads of Robin in Gucci, Prada and Givenchy, as she attempted to convince the public that she is just like us. Her latest book is about an interracial relationship and has been heralded as 'The only book you'll care about' and '*The* book about race and relationships.' Robin is a white woman, married to a white man. Privilege aside, it is not for these reasons that Shirin does not like Florence. It is for the fact that they once had a heated argument, across tables, in which Florence declared that 'paki' is not a derogatory term, but a shortening of a place. Exchanges such as this happen regularly with Florence, though Shirin can tell that, despite this, Florence likes her and wants them to have a connection, even though Shirin makes it clear she is not interested (by never returning her stare).

Hoffman Books was founded by David Hoffman eight years ago. David is a man who is a multimillionaire by birth, but who never mentions this in press interviews about the quick rise of the publisher, which is reported to give the big five a run for their money. Shirin's closest friend at Hoffman is Mariam, a marketing executive, who sits across the office from Shirin, but is still close enough that they can see each other from their seats. This proves useful when they need to exchange quick glances, though they usually spend the day messaging each other on Microsoft Teams. Mariam has been at Hoffman only four months longer than Shirin, and very quickly they banded together. She messages her now:

Shirin: *Book bin???*
Mariam: *1 min*

Shirin gives it a few seconds, then picks up her half-drunk mug of coffee and walks in the direction of the kitchen. Instead of going inside, though, she continues walking around the corner towards the post room. Toby is sitting on the stepladder by an industrial-sized blue bin. He is on his phone and when he sees Shirin, and then Mariam close behind her, he gets up, asks if they're alright and leaves his seat. Toby does not have a desk in the office; he is just expected to float around, continually dropping off and collecting parcels. Shirin feels for him, but then every time she gets a new ASOS order he will make a comment like 'You again' or 'I knew this would be for you', and then her sympathy dissipates.

Shirin peeks inside the bin and thinks how sad it is that these works, which take years to write and edit, are now in a literal bin, some of the covers bent or damaged from people lobbing them in. When she first started at Hoffman, Mariam gave her an unofficial tour of the land. The first place she showed her was the book bin. Tucked away by the post room, it is not officially advertised as the place where staff can get free books, but that is essentially what it is – otherwise they get pulped. They tend to pick a couple of books to take back to their desk, even though they know the likelihood of reading them is slim, because they enjoy the aesthetic of books sometimes more than actually reading them. Shirin thinks most people in the publishing and bookish world do, they just don't like to admit it.

It is a spot – along with one of the storage cupboards – where Mariam and Shirin go to speak privately. Mariam tells her she has an important pitch meeting for a book she loves and asks Shirin to distract her from the nerves. Mariam fidgets, adjusting her hijab, and then shaking her body as if to forcibly shake the anxiety off her. Shirin cannot help but admire her make-up, despite her constant moving. Her eyeliner is always sharp, drawn with precision, her cut crease impeccable, and looks so effortless it makes one think it is easy to achieve. Shirin wears the same shimmer eyeshadow, a touch lighter than her own eyelid tone, and heavy mascara combo daily, very firmly staying in her lane when it comes to make-up.

'Florence is staring again,' Shirin says. She leans against the bin and the hard plastic digs against her shoulder, but she doesn't move or adjust her stance, just lets it continue digging.

'I think she wants to be your friend,' Mariam says. 'It's actually quite sad, if you think about it.'

'Doubtful, when we're both competing for the same job now,' Shirin says.

'How do you mean?'

'Poppy's leaving in four months to go back to Australia, and Lilian told me they'll be hiring a new editor soon. Last week she handed three authors over to me, which I'm assuming shows she thinks I'm ready for the next level ...'

'You've been an assistant editor for two years now – if anyone should get it, it's you,' Mariam says. 'This is excellent news, my friend.'

Shirin waves her hand, not liking the attention being on her any longer. Sometimes she is so desperate to be seen, but then when she is, she feels her skin crawl and wants to divert the attention elsewhere. She asks Mariam how her housemate situation is going, which sets Mariam off. She tells Shirin all about her nightmare housemate, Kesha, who appeared kind and timid in their SpareRoom interview, but who since moving in leaves passive-aggressive Post-it notes all round their flat. She ruined Mariam's dinner party on Saturday by telling them to keep it down, at 9 p.m. It is a rite of passage, Shirin has recently come to realise, to have at least one terrible housemate in a flat-share. She has certainly experienced it enough times, and now lives in a house with three other women who don't speak to each other. She knows what they sound like climaxing – or pretending to – through the thin walls, but not exactly what their jobs are.

Shirin and Mariam disperse when Toby comes round again, realising they have been talking for a touch too long. On her way back to her desk, Shirin sees an article up on Poppy's computer. A familiar, haunting face, looking back at her. One she constantly tries to forget about, but, due to his steady climb to fame over the years, it has become harder and harder to do so. In the picture he is blond-haired with ginger stubble, his features generic, though less pretty than they were at school, his nose much bigger, his eyes the same bright blue. He has his arms held wide, and it looks like he is onstage at the Apollo. She imagines the applause he must have received after spewing his racist and sexist jokes, all in the name of free speech. He always told similar 'jokes' at school, but she never thought he would become so big or inescapable.

At her desk she types his name into Google. The first news article that appears is:

WODEHOUSE PUBLICATIONS TRIUMPHS IN
10-WAY 7-FIGURE AUCTION FOR MEMOIR BY
COMEDIAN ROB GRAYSON

'Jesus,' Shirin mutters, her hand shaky on her mouse as she closes the webpage. He is encroaching on her life, in her industry. Not only that, but he is being allowed to spout dangerous verbiage – and is being paid millions for it. Around her she can hear her colleagues chatting, but her mind is in tunnel vision. An encroaching anxiety in the pit of her stomach is threatening to overcome her – because while she escaped school ten years ago, it is coming back to haunt her more and more lately. She doubts that he'll mention in his memoir what he did to her – and to Kian. He will be lauded, as so many terrible men are.

She picks up her phone and has this urge to message Kian, like it is something she has done in her adult life – though of course it isn't. She remembers Jasper's gig is tonight and the possibility of Kian being there. What does he think to Rob's rise to celebdom? She actively avoids discussing it with her home-town friends; they forget the wrong he has done and instead are awestruck at how a working-class boy from a ordinary Northern city has become an international comedian. They forget how racist he was at school, and how racist he is in adulthood. The reason for this is simple: they do not care because it doesn't affect them. Back then, it only affected Shirin and Kian.

Camden

The venue smells distinctly of bleach and beer, the combination familiar and not wholly unwelcome. As Shirin walks deeper inside, her Doc Martens stick to the black floor. Along the back wall is a bar area, and a thin crowd has already formed. This surprises her for a Monday night.

Jasper is a copywriter for a department store by day, and the guitarist for an indie band by night. They were in university halls together in their first year. He is more friends with Millie and Henry, though he is always friendly towards Shirin – and everyone he comes across, for that matter.

Someone is calling her name, and she turns to find Millie in the far corner, waving at her. Shirin walks over to the group. Her pulse is quickening now and she chews on the inside of her mouth to focus on something. She keeps her gaze on Millie, her neck flushing more and more with each passing moment. Millie almost hugs her, but stops halfway, laughing. 'Sorry, I forgot: you hate it when people hug you.'

She says this every time they greet one another. It isn't necessarily that Shirin dislikes hugs, but she thinks they're overused. They are intimate, and it does not make sense to her that people greet each other with hugs when not much time has passed since they last met. She did not hug her parents, growing up, and only when her Baba Bozorg died did her mum hug her.

Shirin laughs. It is hollow, but she knows that if she squints her eyes when she does it, no one will know the difference. 'Yeah,' she says. 'Hate it.'

She notices Millie turn her head to jokingly roll her eyes at the group behind her. She does this to stay in control of the situation, it being preferable to rejection. Shirin is the unreasonable, strange one. She finally looks to the group and her stomach flops with relief – and oddly, also, disappointment. In the group are Jasper, Henry, and a man she vaguely recognises from the party. What a waste of an adrenaline rush and nervous sweats, she thinks.

'Thanks for coming,' Jasper says, giving her a toothy smile. He brushes his floppy hair away from his face.

'Wouldn't miss it.'

Millie lets out a short laugh. 'This is literally the first one you've been to in years.'

'Well,' Shirin begins, 'I've just never been able to make it before is what I mean.'

'I get you, bud,' Jasper says, slapping his hand on her shoulder reassuringly, before telling them he needs to go onstage to set up.

Shirin goes to the bar and considers ordering a white wine. It is not even her favourite alcoholic drink. Wine often gives her headaches and crippling anxiety the next day, but it is the cheapest option – bar beer, which she categorically cannot stand the taste of. She is feeling sorry for herself now. She realises that while she had been dreading seeing Kian again, a part of her had also been clinging to the idea of seeing him; as though if they spoke he could assuage the confusing emotions she's feeling now. He's the only one who can truly understand how she's feeling about Rob Grayson's book deal.

For a fleeting moment she considers going home, and leaving without telling anyone. The idea is appealing. She can say something came up, that work emailed her asking for an urgent read. She can blame her boss – and the publishing industry as a whole – for not allowing her a work–life balance. She can then get the Tube home, make pasta, and return to the comfort of her small bedroom.

'Hey.' The voice comes from next to her, and she only turns when there is a pointed silence, which makes her realise it is because the person is addressing her.

She pivots, her arm still resting against the bar, until she is face-to-face with the speaker. He is tall, South Asian, with beautiful black thick hair. She remembers, then, that he is one of Kian's housemates – Dylan.

'Hello,' she says slowly, her eyes shifting automatically from side to side.

'You excited for the show to start?' he asks, a hint of a smile on his lips, like he is not excited for it, but rather the opposite.

'Obviously – can't you tell?' she says.

He laughs and leans against the bar, before running his fingers through his hair, which comes just past his ears. She is not sure it is a look many people can pull off. His dark hair is so shiny that the light overhead reflects from it.

'Yeah, you look dead excited,' he says. 'You were at our party the other week, weren't you?'

'I was, yeah.'

'Did you have fun?'

She nods. 'Your house is really nice.'

He smiles. 'I mean, that doesn't really answer the question, but sure.'

She thinks he'll order his drink and leave now, but he continues to lean against the bar, looking at her, saying nothing, waiting for her. Impatience – because she has no interest in small talk – makes her ask, 'How do you know Kian then?'

His brows furrow, ever so slightly. 'We went to uni together in Glasgow. I pretty much came back to London as soon as I graduated though. Glasgow was nice and all, but it doesn't really compare to here, you know.'

She nods, like she can relate, even though she has never been to Glasgow.

'How do you know him?' he asks.

She bites her bottom lip, though not in an alluring way, more like she is chewing it off. She angles her body slightly away from him, looking out at the pub, which is now filling with more people, before answering. 'I don't really,' she lies, her voice breezy. 'We went to school together, ages ago.'

Henry makes his way towards them and she can't help but mutter, 'Oh, fucking great.' Dylan looks surprised, but then Henry is before them, wearing an ill-fitting T-shirt, pint in hand.

'I wouldn't bother trying to get with her, mate – Shirin is picky,' Henry says, winking at Shirin.

Dylan clears his throat, visibly embarrassed, and says, 'We were just talking.'

Henry slaps his hand on Shirin's shoulder, jolting her. His hand stays there and she hates it. It is like, with his touch, he is weighing her down, tarnishing her in some way. She knows from the outside, though, it looks like they are friends. That is what Millie always sees, anyway.

'Piss off, Henry,' she says lightly.

He laughs like she is joking, and Millie comes over to them and asks them what they're talking about.

'Shirin's love life,' Henry says. 'Or lack thereof.'

'She's just picky,' Mille says, echoing Henry. 'She could have someone, if she wanted. Couldn't you, Shirin?'.

She notices Dylan looking at her and thinks: Are normal people humiliated daily by their friends? 'I'm not picky. I'm just not desperate,' she says. 'Men are often disappointing. No offence.' She looks at Dylan for the last part.

'Not *all* men,' Dylan says. 'Surely not all of them.'

Shirin opens her mouth to counter his comment, but Millie puts her hand between them. 'I can't be arsed for the inevitable debate that is about to happen here. Before they come on, I wanted to check you're all on for the barbecue at mine on Saturday? For the England-versus-Switzerland match.'

Dylan says he and Kian are down to go, and Shirin's ears prick up at Kian's name. She is about to say she can't come any more, even though she has been planning on it. Then she feels this twitch of irritation, like she is being shooed out of her own friendship group. Yes, a friendship group she often finds annoying, but it is hers, nonetheless.

'Yeah, I'll be there,' she says.

The lights begin to dim and a woman appears onstage, announcing that the gig is about to begin. They go and sit down, apart from one another. As she watches Jasper play the guitar onstage with his band, red spotlights overhead, their indie-rock beats radiate around the room. It is loud and it swells, and people are swaying. The music is good; much better than she expected. They sing about the first time they met some girl, and it gets Shirin thinking about the first time she saw Kian when he moved to her school.

North Oak

Then

Mehdi had been in prison almost three months when Kian was told he would be changing schools. The summer holidays were nearly over, and it was supposed to be his final year at Foxview before he went to college. It was his mum's idea. She said Foxview was the reason his brother had ended up the way he had. 'The teachers,' she said. 'They all hated him. And they'll hate you too.' Kian argued, pleaded with her to let him continue at Foxview, where all his friends were. When that didn't work, he tried to reason with her. 'Just because the teachers didn't like Mehdi doesn't mean it'll be the same for me.' He raised his voice at his mum, panic mounting in his chest. He had never shouted at her before, but it was unfair. He was being punished for something Mehdi had done – something Mehdi had done *for him*, but it wasn't like Kian had even asked him to do it.

He missed his brother so much it hurt. He wrote to him. Every week. Sometimes he would send two, even three, letters in a row, before he got Mehdi's response back. He needed to tell him every little thing, like when his mate Teddy had eaten ten double cheeseburgers from McDonald's, one after the other, on a dare; and how his face had gone all yellow afterwards, and he'd taken a sip of his milkshake, which had tipped him over the edge and he'd had to run to the toilets before it was too late. They'd all laughed, Kian included, but all the while he'd been conscious that his brother was in prison and his mum was always red-eyed, his dad stressed and distracted. His unabashed laughing had turned to guilt, and he'd stopped.

But despite all this, with his parents' increasing strictness – the way Kian was expected to be perfect, so he didn't end up the same as Mehdi – he felt something chipping away at him. The day his mum told him that he would be moving schools she had her back to him. She was dusting the fireplace, like she didn't care that she was ruining his whole life because of something his brother had done.

They were in the front room, 'the guest room' his mum called it, their sofa white leather, bulky, curved and thick on the arms. In the middle of the room was a glass coffee table, with gold Iranian ornaments on it, and a large empty fruit bowl that his mum would fill with at least five different fruits for visitors. On the shelf beneath the coffee table: intricate glass plates, small fruit knives. The floor was covered with a large red Persian carpet that they'd imported from Tehran. His mum was always ready for visitors, but they barely had anyone round any more. Over the past year the room had been used only for lawyers and police.

And when his dad came in, presumably having heard Kian's tone increase, he glanced from Kian to his wife, a stern look on his usually soft face. His dad had let his stubble grow into a beard. It was thick and dark, and made his face appear much rounder. He had been dedicating himself more to Islam since Mehdi had been taken away, though in doing so he had become more reclusive. He spent many evenings after work in the mosque, returning home late and going straight to his office before bed.

'Enough, Kian – it's been decided. And don't talk back to your mother,' he said in Farsi, in a harsh tone that was unusual for him. It was easier for Kian to argue with his mum, but with both his parents on the same side, he knew none of his pleading would be of any use now. Little did he know, though, that moving to North Oak would be what led him to Shirin Bayat.

North Oak was divided into two sites, one for years seven to nine, and one for years ten and eleven a mile away in another building. Kian was in the latter. It was a shabby school; most of the classrooms were in huts intended to be temporary, though they had been there since the late nineties. The science block, however, was newly built, with underfloor heating and silver-speckled tiling. It was there, Kian would soon discover, that people congregated in winter to keep warm during lunch.

The uniform they were made to wear was basic: black trousers, white polo shirt, black sweatshirt. Because he'd enrolled at the last minute he didn't have the North Oak badge on his sweatshirt, and his mum rang up reception to explain that the shop was out of stock. They told her a plain one was okay for the first few weeks, which she told Kian, relieved – like he cared.

He began year eleven knowing no one. As he walked through the entrance and along the long tarmacked strip leading to the main building, he noticed that everyone was together in clusters. It was only really then that he realised how lucky he had been at his old school that he had never felt this acute aloneness. No one was brown or Black here, but that was unsurprising. Foxview had more Asian students; his best friends, Koyer and Ahmed, were Pakistani and Bangladeshi. They had been friends since primary school and were like family to him now; he couldn't ever imagine not having them in his life.

Eyes were on him: some enquiring gazes, some hateful stares. Kian thought he heard someone walking past say, 'Fucking paki', but he didn't know if he was imagining it. He probably wasn't.

A boy shoved past him, knocking his backpack off his shoulder. Ahead of him, the shover turned, his face pink, his blond hair gelled up at the front. 'Look where you're fucking going, dirty paki,' he said to Kian and spat, inches from where Kian's backpack was. The friend he was walking with began singing a mock-Bollywood song at the top of his lungs. People around him stared – and then laughed.

Instantly Kian thought about turning round and going back home. His jaw was tight and angry. He considered punching both boys in their faces, but knew he was so weak he'd only end up getting beaten up himself. He used to practise boxing with Mehdi, and the impact of his punches had always made Mehdi belly-laugh.

'Is that all you've got?' Mehdi would say, lifting the pads. 'Come on – give it your all now.' Kian would punch with all his force, and only then would Mehdi say, 'Better, but you need to practise.' He wished he had practised after all. He imagined beating the prick up and getting carried out of school, rejoicing, arms in the air. Instead he collected his bag from the floor and put one foot in front of the other.

When he was nearer the entrance he heard someone say, 'Hey. You alright?'

Kian turned to see a boy with short mousy-brown hair and acne on only the right side of his face. His facial expression was earnest, but Kian still didn't trust him. He didn't know what to say in response, so he shrugged.

'You're new here, right?' the boy said. Kian nodded. 'I thought so. Don't let it get to you; they're dickheads to everyone.'

'Great,' Kian mumbled.

'I'm Connor,' the boy said.

'I'm Kian.'

A girl approached them, looped her arm into Connor's. She had her polo T-shirt tied in a knot on the front, so that her stomach was showing. There was a mole above her belly button and when Kian noticed it, he quickly looked away, embarrassed for some reason.

'What's going on?' she asked.

Kian took this as his cue to leave, but then Connor said, 'Jordan and Rob are bothering the new kid.'

She rolled her eyes and turned to Kian. 'A bit late to move schools in our final year, isn't it?'

'It's a long story,' Kian said.

'Mysterious,' she replied. 'Well, if you want any advice from us: avoid those two. I don't think they're right in the head.'

'I mean,' Connor began, 'they're bad, but you're being a bit dramatic.'

'Didn't you hear what they did to Shirin? She had to go to hospital.'

'It was an accident, wasn't it?' Connor said.

'Well, you shouldn't be throwing mud balls at people in the first place – that's what my mum said when I told her.'

Connor turned to Kian. 'Becky over-exaggerates things. You'll be fine here.'

Kian wasn't so sure, but said, 'I know I will.'

When he went to his first class and sat in his designated seat, head bowed, scratching at the skin around his nails, it was the word *paki* that he couldn't get out of his head. It was so often thrown around, sometimes casually, sometimes affectionately, mostly with malice. The way Jordan had said it – like it was so repulsive he needed to get it out of his mouth quickly. Kian hated how his head continued to spin long after the moment, and how he couldn't stop his internal berating for not defending himself. He wished he had done something to show everyone that they couldn't just push him around or treat him like shit on their shoe. He detested how weak he was, how confrontation frightened him. It reaffirmed that he had learnt nothing from Mehdi going to prison, that even after months of rehashing the event that got his brother sent away, he still wasn't able to defend himself.

Then the classroom door opened and a girl walked into the room. She asked the teacher if he had any whiteboard markers they could borrow, because Ms Brewin's had disappeared from her classroom. His teacher chuckled and said her whiteboard pens *always* disappeared. The girl laughed, an obligatory laugh more than anything else. She stood awkwardly, her jumper sleeves pulled down over her hands, balancing one foot on top of the other as Kian's teacher bumbled around to find her some markers. Her gaze remained down and her dark hair covered her face, until she tucked a front strand behind her ear. Her lips were a pale pink, and the colour struck him because he had never seen someone with lips that shade before. He knew he was staring, and that was fine, until she looked towards him and they locked eyes. This continued for three beats before they both looked away quickly. His heart was beating suddenly, and it was both peculiar and embarrassing. Her eyes were hazel, so distinctly Iranian and beautiful. He doodled on his workbook until she left, and it was only when the door clicked shut and the teacher began the lesson again that his heartbeat steadied to a normal rhythm.

World Cup

Now

It is outside Millie's front door that Shirin begins to reassess her life choices. She had niggling doubts in the morning, and as she walked with Hana from Peckham Rye station to Millie's they only became more pronounced. She didn't even scold Hana when they saw Abigail's book in the window of the Review Bookshop and Hana made a gagging sound, because all she could think about was that Kian would be at the barbecue.

Millie's house is just off Bellenden Road, the side of Peckham that is village-like, with artisanal coffee shops and clothing boutiques that are always empty. Millie lives with one other woman who is the live-in landlady, though she is rarely in the flat. So Millie effectively lives alone in a well-furnished, spacious flat, in Zone 2, with a garden. It is every Londoner's dream and Millie is loath to ever let it go, despite Henry wanting them to move in together.

Steps lead up to the front door, which is emerald-green with a gold knocker, where they are standing now. On the doorstep is a potted plan that is gagging for water, the leaves crisp and brown.

'Maybe this is a bad idea,' Shirin says to Hana. She shifts her weight between both her feet and looks desperately to her friend, like she is her salvation.

'Girl, please,' Hana says, before pressing her forefinger to the doorbell in one swift movement. So swift that Shirin has no time to stop her. 'I'm the true victim in this situation; I hate football,' Hana says. 'But I'm here for you.'

'You said yesterday you had nothing else to do.'

Hana waves her hand in the air. 'Same thing.'

'And why do you have an England top on? Where'd you even get it from?'

Hana is wearing a white tennis skirt, with a white England T-shirt that she cropped, and pointed white kitten heels. She was catcalled numerous times on the walk over, and each time she told the men to 'fuck off and get a life'. One van stopped when she said this, so for the last stretch from the station they power-walked.

'A guy I was seeing left it at mine. It felt right to give it an outing for the occasion,' Hana says.

When Shirin sees a figure approaching the door, she clutches the straps of her backpack tightly. This seemed like a good idea in theory, but she hasn't actually considered what she will say to Kian. Every time she's tried to plan in her head what she would say, her chest would go tight and she'd have to divert her thoughts elsewhere. But these are her friends, it's her life. What is she meant to do? Avoid everyone now?

It is difficult to distinguish her anxiety from her depression at times. They come and go, passing each other in waves, settling together to make her life a sometime misery. She is reminded now of why she seldom puts herself out there. Her pulse is racing – embarrassingly, because this is arguably a mundane experience – as they wait for a door to open, and then her stomach flops when the door is opening and it is too late for her to change her mind about coming here. She quickly smooths down her black summer dress and presses her lips together to even out her lipstick, just in time for Millie to appear before them.

Millie has on a white crop top, denim cut-off shorts, and is bare-footed. They greet each other and take their shoes off by the door. In the entryway Shirin can hear chatter, and low, humming football commentary coming from the TV. It reminds her of her dad; every Saturday evening he would watch *Match of the Day*, when she and her mum wanted to watch a movie. He had the monopoly over the remote, so they were never able to watch anything if it cut into his 10.30 p.m. slot. He still has a monopoly over it in fact, but now, instead of Shirin's mum arguing with him about it, it is his new partner, Karen.

The hallway is carpeted and it is satisfyingly plush. Various framed artworks decorate the space, though none of it is Millie's. She says sometimes it bothers her that she isn't able to decorate her own home, but it is something she is willing to accept in exchange for an affordable, nice flat.

They enter the living room and greet Jasper and a girl he is seeing, whose name Shirin promptly forgets. She is pretty, with red, shiny hair and bright blue eyes. But Jasper is always with a different woman; he is a serial dater, believing each girl to be the one, until she isn't.

The TV is mounted on the wall, and underneath is a console table with various snacks in coconut-shell bowls. At the back of the room, joined on to the living room, is the kitchen, with a sliding glass door leading out onto the garden. The doors are open, letting in a gentle breeze.

'The others are outside, trying to start the barbecue,' Millie says, rolling her eyes.

'The others?' Shirin repeats.

'What Shirin means is who specifically,' Hana adds, hands on hips. Shirin bumps her with her hip.

'Just Henry and Dylan,' Millie says. Shirin exhales a breath she did not realise she was holding. 'Oh yeah, and Kian, too. He seemed particularly excited, Shirin, when I said you'd be coming.'

She notices Hana looking at her, and she knows the expression will be deeply annoying. 'Oh, really,' Shirin mutters. 'Can I use your toilet?'

'Sure,' Millie says.

She goes to the bathroom, shuts the toilet lid and sits there for a moment. She stares at the towels hanging from the back of the door. She doesn't know how to feel – and that's the problem with all of this. She is constantly teetering between excitement at the thought of seeing Kian and then complete abject horror at the prospect of actually speaking to him. Her rejection of Hull was deliberate – she rarely goes back for a reason. The version of herself back then is one she wanted to leave behind, and with Kian here, she feels her former self coming back too.

After a few more minutes she leaves the bathroom and enters the living room. The boys have come in and numerous conversations are happening at once. Dylan and Hana are talking on the sofa. Millie, Henry, Jasper and his date are in the kitchen, leaning against the countertop and discussing the logistics of the barbecue. She goes out to the garden, saying hello to Dylan and Henry as she passes. Her feet are moving, but she is not really thinking about where she is going, or why, until she is outside.

Kian doesn't turn round immediately. His head is bent low as he works to start the barbecue. It is black and rusty, though much bigger than one she has ever used.

'Hi,' she says.

He looks up and smiles, wiping his hands on his shorts. She briefly notices his tanned, small-muscled biceps against his white T-shirt. She quickly looks away.

'Hey,' he says.

'Are you okay there with the barbecue?' she asks.

He pulls the sides of his lips down in a gesture to mean *No, not really*. 'Do you know how to use one?'

'I do not,' she says. 'It was an empty offer.' She leans against the brick wall, and it feels like as long as there is enough distance between them she is safe. Though safe from what? From getting too comfortable? From saying the things she wants to say?

'Well, I appreciate the offer, even if it was empty,' he says. 'I think we need to get more charcoal. I have my car with me, so I might just drive down to get it.'

'You drive in London?'

'Yeah. I don't know how you people live without a car.'

'You people?' she says.

'Londoners.'

'Oh, I'm a Londoner now. I see how it is.'

He smirks. 'I don't make the rules. You never come up to Hull, so your Northern card has been revoked.'

She was smiling, but now she stops and looks out at the tiny, desolate garden. There isn't much to look at, so that doesn't help. She focuses her gaze on a crack in one of the paving stones.

She hears someone approaching and then Millie appears. At first she doesn't notice Shirin because she's standing to the side of the doors, and Millie does a little jump when she sees her. 'You scared me,' she says. 'Kian – are you still okay to get the charcoal?'

'And some beers,' Henry shouts from inside.

'And some beers,' Millie repeats. 'It'd be a real help, with your car and all. The corner shop didn't have any.'

'No problem,' Kian says.

'Amazing, thank you.' Millie goes back into the house and Kian goes after her. As he passes Shirin he asks her if she wants anything, and she says no, thank you, and adds, 'If you need any help getting stuff, though, I can come.' The words spill out of her, and it is like her own mouth is betraying her.

'That would be great, actually,' he says. 'If that's not an empty offer too.'

She smiles, a very small smile. 'No, I'd be happy to help.'

*

Kian's car is pristine. It is 24 degrees today, and he opens all the windows to let the dead, dry air out.

'It's only a five-minute drive,' he says before turning the engine on. Blink-182 immediately blares from the speakers, and he turns it all the way down, chuckling. 'Sorry about that.' He seems so at ease, while Shirin is sweating profusely – only partly due to the summer heat – and trying not to look over at his thighs, because she knows his shorts have ridden up since he sat down. She is not sure when she became such a pervert, but it is a side of herself she is not enjoying.

'That's fine,' she says. 'Do you sing in the car then?' He is pulling out of his parking spot on the road, but still manages to give her a quick quizzical glance. 'The music,' she explains. 'I thought it might be loud because you were singing or something.'

He laughs. 'No, I don't. Is that something you do though?'

Her cheeks flush stupidly. She sounds like a ten-year-old. 'I had a car for a few years when I first got my licence, and I used to love driving around and singing loudly. I managed to keep my car for a bit while I was away at uni, until my dad said the insurance was too much and if I wanted to keep it, I had to pay for it … Needless to say, we got rid of it.'

'I think I saw your car, you know, in Hull. It was a rickety red Ford Fiesta, no?' he says, smiling.

'It was not rickety, but it was red, so maybe you did. When did you see it?'

He shakes his head. 'I think it was just before we all went off to uni. You were maybe at the Humber Bridge with your friends or something.'

'I didn't see you there,' she says.

He shrugs. 'It was a long time ago.'

She knows exactly the day he is referring to. Just before she left to go off to Queen Mary's to study History, she went to the country park by the Humber Bridge with her friends Phoebe and Carmen. They went there to get one last look at Hull before they left for university. Which was a bit dramatic, since Phoebe came back straight after her degree, and it wasn't like they would never return during the holidays anyway. What Shirin didn't tell her friends, though, was that it wasn't solely for that reason that she wanted to go there. She didn't even admit that to herself.

'What you thinking about?' Kian asks.

'Not much.' She stretches her legs and looks out the window, at the terraced houses they pass on their way, many with England flags on their windows. He makes a sound between a chuckle and a scoff, and she diverts her gaze from the passenger window straight to him. 'What?'

'I can still tell when you're lying,' he says.

She crosses her arms, relieved when they enter the supermarket car park. Because what Kian said isn't right: he didn't always know when she wasn't telling the truth, and that was the problem all those years ago.

They walk in the supermarket at a leisurely pace, at first close together. But then Kian's shoulder brushes Shirin's and she takes a large step to the side, to prevent it happening again. The charcoal is at the front of the store, and next they make their way to the alcohol aisle. Overhead is a tannoy reminding customers of their offers on picnic food, beers and burgers, all perfect for the summer weather and the football.

'Did you bring yourself a drink?' Kian asks. 'A soft drink, I mean.'

Her throat feels tight and she attempts to clear it, brushing her hand along the fabric detergents they pass on the way to their designated aisle. Instead of speaking, she nods a tad too enthusiastically.

'Right, good,' he says. She thinks that's the end of it but he continues, 'I know it's rude to ask, but is there a reason you don't drink? There doesn't have to be, obviously. I'm just ... Tell me to do one if you don't want to say, and I won't be offended.'

He is clutching the bags of charcoal to his chest and gives her a sidelong smile. Perhaps in other circumstances she would be annoyed by the question, but she chooses not to be and instead says, 'I'm on medication that doesn't go well with alcohol. I know, from experience, that it's best when I don't have it.'

'Oh, I had no idea ...' His face is awkward, which makes her realise she has been more aloof than intended.

'They're for my anxiety.' She cannot bring herself to say they're antidepressants. It would signal, she realises, that while he has clearly progressed into a well-adjusted adult, she is exactly the same as she was at school: often sad – only now sad, worried and empty.

He nods like he understands. 'I was on antidepressants at uni for a bit. I drank the same as I normally would, to begin with, and it completely wiped me out. So I get you.'

She really looks at him then. 'You were?'

'Yeah. I'm off them now, but they helped. And I stopped smoking weed – that really messed me up; I kept having panic attacks.' He shakes his head as though to wipe away the memory and the overshare.

'You don't have them any more?'.

'No, thankfully. What are you anxious about?' he asks. 'If there is anything.'

It is so direct she is taken aback. She blinks and refocuses her attention ahead of her, on the various aisles filled with glossy goods that briefly divert her attention.

'I don't know,' she says, though it's a lie. Her issue is that she always thought once she got the things she longed for in life – to live in London and work in publishing, to be so far away from her sad life in Hull – she would be fulfilled and content. But she feels just as empty, though in a different way because she has nothing to hold on to, no imagined future to project on. This is it; this is life.

'You can tell me, you know,' he says, as though he is reading her mind.

'Why are you being so nice to me?' she whispers.

He stops walking, so she does too. They are down the snacking aisle, filled with various multipack crisps, nuts and chocolates. There is a woman and her small child at the far end, but it is otherwise empty. Kian looks down at her, his eyebrows furrowed.

'Why wouldn't I be?'

She clenches her jaw and breathes deeply through her nose. This is exactly the conversation she didn't want to have, and yet she is the one who provoked it. 'We stopped speaking ... we stopped being friends.' She hopes that he will understand what she means, that she doesn't need to spell it out.

'It was a while ago,' he says.

'I always thought you didn't like me any more. And now you're here, hanging out with my friends. It's just weird.'

'Maybe it's fate?' he says and she gives him a look. 'Oh, come on, I'm joking.'

She picks up a packet of nuts next to her and weighs it in her hands, for something to do, something to distract herself with. 'I don't like to think about Hull or school. I know it makes me sound like a crazy person, and I want us to be able to be friends or at the very least friendly, but ...' She breathes out, accepting that she will have to sound like a crazy person. 'On the condition that we don't speak about school. Ever.'

He laughs, until he realises she isn't joking. The bags of charcoal are put on the floor, and he weighs up what she is saying in his mind. While he is no longer laughing, he has the glimmer of a smile in his eyes. 'I can tell you're still as strange as ever, but okay. I'd like to be friends, so no school talk.'

They begin walking again and turn into the alcohol aisle, and Kian picks up a pack of beers, attempting to balance it atop the bags of charcoal. Shirin offers to hold the beers, which he reluctantly takes her up on.

'Okay,' she says. 'Can I break my own rule for one second? Have you been following everything with Rob?'

Kian stands straighter at this, perhaps a reflex, and narrows his eyes at her. 'How do you mean?'

'Just the fact that he's a celebrity now.' She looks away at a bottle of wine and the recommendation card underneath, paying far too much consideration to a bottle of Shiraz that she will not be buying.

'I try not to pay attention to it,' he says, his voice strained.

'It pisses me off,' she says, still looking at the card. 'And no one gets it. He even got a book deal. He's crossing into my space.'

Kian puts the bags down between his legs and places one hand on Shirin's shoulder. It surprises her, so she turns to him suddenly, her lips parted, about to question what he's doing. 'I get it,' he says gently. 'But we can't let it bother us. We're both doing our thing; what he's doing doesn't matter. It shouldn't matter.'

She is so conscious of his warm hand on her shoulder, of how all her nerves are hyper-aware of it. She looks up at him. 'When did you get to be so wise?' she says, one eyebrow raised.

He pushes her jokingly. 'I don't know – I guess I just grew up,' he says. 'We both have.'

She nods, though she's thinking she's not all that different from when she was a teenager, not really.

The Author Party

'How are you?' Shirin's dad asks over the phone.

She makes her way unsteadily down the bus stairs, balancing her mobile between her ear and shoulder. 'I'm okay, how are things with you?' she says.

He sighs deeply. 'It hasn't been a good week.'

She leaves the number-8 bus at Shoreditch and begins her journey along the busy road, dodging people as she goes. 'Really, how come?'

A drunk man staggers towards her and Shirin quickly jumps out of the way and onto the side of the road. She mutters something under her breath before continuing at a brisk pace.

'I've been feeling so anxious. I can't sleep at all – only a few hours a night. Karen is annoyed at me, too. She doesn't get that it's my anxiety, that I can't help it. I wish I could feel better. I wish Allah would just let me be better. I sometimes ask Allah: Why me? Why me?'

She can feel her breath quickening, her mind a fog, as it always is when these subjects are broached by her dad. Before her parents' divorce, her dad did not believe in anxiety or depression. When Shirin was at university, in her second year, her world was black and white and grey, and she often thought about how she would kill herself, though she did not tell anyone this. When she came home for Easter, she spent most of the break in bed, eyes wide, all day. She often overheard her dad saying to her mum that he did not understand why she acted the way she did; that she had everything and was still, allegedly, unhappy.

'Maybe have less caffeine and see if that helps?' she suggests. 'You always feel worse when you drink coffee. Have you been drinking it again?'

'Yes, but it's not that,' he replies. 'My counsellor says my mind is too busy, that I need to take care of myself. But Karen's always complaining about everything I do. And your mother doesn't even want to talk to me.'

Shirin feels her mind drifting elsewhere. They have had this conversation many, many times before. He rants and tries to get her attention, though she does not know how she can help him. She listens and gives advice, though she is not a therapist, and she is not the person to come to for mental-health advice, when she herself is struggling. She is his child and wishes so deeply that she were not always required to parent both her parents.

For the first four years of her life Shirin's Maman and Baba Bozorg brought her up in Tehran. Her mum and dad moved to Italy when she was two for a brief period, before settling on England. They left Shirin in the care of her grandparents while they travelled around Europe to see more of the world, and to find the perfect place for them to go to university and to ultimately settle down. Objectively, she knew that being raised by her Maman and Baba Bozorg was no bad thing. While her mum and dad quarrelled, and sometimes more than that – with full-blown arguments that Shirin thought would mean they'd finally leave each other – her grandparents provided her with enough love. She was never left wanting, never unsettled with them. Her parents wanted parenthood to be a part-time endeavour, and their resentment that it was not was palpable, growing up. Now, while she might understand their perspective, her relationship with them continues to be both strained and distant. At twenty-six years old, she has no desire to remedy it.

Her dad quickly moved on from her mum leaving, with Karen. He was strict with Shirin, so she wouldn't be someone like Karen when she is older, and now he is engaged to her. Karen has two children with two different men, and both of them live with their dads because they do not like her, and she swears that said children are 'little bastards'. Karen is thirty-eight and her dad is sixty. Karen is very obviously only after her dad's money – and he isn't even wealthy, which makes it all the sadder for them both. Shirin is not sure how they met, though she imagines through online dating. Or perhaps at their local shopping centre. Her dad wanders the shops when he has nothing to do, especially after her mother left. She imagines Karen in their family home, watching TV on their sofa, sleeping in the bed her mother slept in, her children in what was Shirin's bedroom when they visit, and it makes her heart beat quickly, angrily.

'Sorry, I'm on my way to a work thing, so can't really talk right now. But take care of yourself, okay? Just take it easy?'

There is a short pause before he replies. 'Fine, okay, darling. Take care.'

When the call ends she feels guilty. She always feels guilty. If she indulges the conversation, she feels guilty that she did not set her dad straight about his behaviour, or that she isn't on her mum's side. And if, like now, she doesn't indulge the conversation, she is a bad daughter who is leaving her dad all alone. Even though he has a counsellor – and Karen. It is Shirin who is all alone, but because she does not shout like him, no one hears her.

All that remains is irritation now. Her heart beats out of time, her fists are clenched. She shakes her hands as she walks, takes a deep breath and quickens her pace. She cannot remember the last time her dad pressed her for more information about how she is feeling. And she is sure he does not know what she does for work, in London. He does not care about her as an individual, but sees her as an extension of himself, like a growth that he needs to tend to occasionally, with phone calls like this. He does not see that she too has a life, has problems, has feelings.

Though while her dad calls to vent, her mother does not even reply to her emails. Shirin hasn't heard from her in a week, though she posted an Instagram story of herself with friends in a café in Tehran yesterday, so Shirin knows she is okay.

As she approaches the venue in Old Street, she texts him:

I'm sorry I couldn't speak more. Do you want to call me tomorrow?

He sends the thumbs-up emoji in response.

*

Every year Hoffman has a summer party to celebrate its authors. This year it is in a basement bar space, and the stairs leading downwards are mirrored, as are the walls, with a gold banister and a chandelier. From the outside, the venue appears worn down, but within it is beautiful and decadent.

Down the stairs Shirin is met by a member of staff dressed in a sharp suit, who shows her the cloakroom, and soon afterwards she is given a tall glass of Prosecco with a raspberry in it. She did not ask for one, but takes a sip anyway, figuring that one glass will not hurt. In fact, following her call with her dad, and the sinking, guilty feeling within her, she thinks it's needed.

Mariam catches her as she enters the main room and touches her arm lightly. 'There you are,' she says. 'I was looking for you.'

'Well, this is quite intense, isn't it?'

Mariam's mouth is open to continue speaking when a group of authors approaches them. One of the authors Shirin recently started working with is among them, Leila Campbell. Leila has lived in Egypt for most of her life, and her memoir has won Hoffman awards, though it has sold few copies.

Leila tells Shirin and Mariam that she is so glad there are people of colour rising up through the ranks in publishing, and tells them to continue even if it's hard – that they are the future. They both thank her, say she is so kind, and that yes, the lack of representation is really not good enough, is it? Though all the while Shirin feels a heavier sinking within her; the conditions in which people of colour are placed in this industry are so stark, compared to their white counterparts. There is the sense that it *will* be hard for them and they just have to be strong enough to deal with it. That they must, otherwise nothing will change from within. Normally Shirin shakes the heaviness off, but it sticks tonight, holding her down.

Later in the night the mood is merry. Shirin is also vaguely merry from the Prosecco, though she is avoiding another one of her authors, who goes by the pseudonym Georgina Barlow-Wallows. She is really called Sally Smith. Sally has written a series of books about impressive women in the Regency and Victorian eras. She is a large woman, with short highlighted hair cut just underneath her ears. Her laugh radiates around the room, and she reminds Shirin of the dinner ladies at her school – which is not an unkind comparison, because those women were lovely to Shirin. But the comparison ends with her outward appearance.

Earlier in the evening, in a group of five – Shirin, Sally and three other authors – Sally detailed her trip to Cuba over the summer. She was describing the long flight, and in her description of how awful and cramped the flight was, she mentioned a Black woman who was sitting next to her, and how her hair was 'invading her space'. 'So I told her to put her hair away,' she said. 'It was everywhere. I mean, I'm not being funny, but it shouldn't go over to my side of the chair.' Sally's cheeks were pink and she was smiling, and Shirin felt so outside herself, so reminded that this is a space she most certainly does not belong in.

'What did she say?' one author asked, also with a slight smile on her face.

'Well, to be honest, she kicked off, used the race card – it's not a race thing, obviously, it's a space thing. Anyway, I complained to the stewardess and we got upgraded to first-class, so … result!' She grinned and the others laughed and said how lucky she was, how things like that never happened to them. They asked her what first-class was like and she said it was 'fabulous', and Shirin stood there, looking off past their shoulders, a second glass of warm Prosecco in hand. She was mute, and she hated herself in that moment for being mute. But it was not the time, the place, the person, to say something. In any other circumstance she thinks she would have, but here she was rendered silent. It was so at odds with her body's reaction, which wanted to fight rather than freeze.

When she left Hull at eighteen, she thought she was leaving all of this behind her. But now she is wondering whether the publishing industry is any different from being at school. There is often this impression that the South is much more civilised than the North, but here she is at an industry party, putting up with racists. There isn't all that much difference – and it is a depressing realisation.

Time slips further away. She is enveloped in various conversations, her glass topped up without prompt, and her face hurts from fake smiling. She is pretending to laugh constantly, so much so that she no longer thinks she can call what she is doing laughing, but rather making a strange sound at everything the people around her are saying. When she realises this, she excuses herself to go to the bathroom, where she sits in a cubicle, her face stony and tired. She sits on the toilet and goes on her phone.

She has an Instagram follow request from @KianRahimi. It has been three days since the barbecue and while she has of course Instagram-searched him since, she has resisted following him first. She goes to the request, her finger hovering, lingering over the accept button, before she taps down on it.

> **@KianRahimi**: Hey, it was really nice to see you at the BBQ.
> **@ShirinInTheCity**: It was nice to see you too.

She clicks on his stories, finally, because she has wanted to do that for a while. He only has one post and it's of a book by an author Hoffman publishes – A. K. Hosseini – and he writes how much he enjoyed it.

> **@ShirinInTheCity**: We publish his books, you know – I could get you a proof of his new one if you want.

She is not even entirely sure she can easily do it, but types it anyway. He replies almost immediately.

> **@KianRahimi**: Seriously?? That would be awesome.
> **@ShirinInTheCity**: No problem!
> **@KianRahimi**: Maybe I could buy you a coffee to say thanks?

She types different responses and is supremely conscious that she is sitting on the toilet, so eventually she simply likes his message and says: *Sure! x*

She receives a text:

Hana: *I'm on a date with a guy who just said he's not read a book before. From, like, start to finish. I even asked him what about school, and he said he always pretended. He's hot tho, so . . .*

Shirin: *But does that mean he wouldn't read a book YOU wrote?*

Hana: *God, you're right, but look . . .*

She sends Shirin his Bumble profile picture, and Shirin immediately replies with:

Ok, fine, I won't judge your decision either way.

Eventually she exits the cubicle and takes time washing her hands, relishing the quiet, the warm water and expensive soap lathering her hands. She smooths down her dress, which is black and tight on her waist, flowing down to her calves. The straps sit in a Bardot style, and she wears a blue crystal Swarovski necklace she was given for her twenty-first birthday by Hana. She observes her blonde hair, which she has clipped back with crystal hair-grips, away from her face. She wonders for the first time whether her dyed hair is her way of assimilating, whether it even suits her. And then she thinks of Kian, who said he liked her hair – who she might be seeing again – and in addition to the confusing stirring of many conflicting emotions, mostly negative, right now is another one at this thought: excitement.

At 10 p.m. Mariam yawns into her cranberry juice. Shirin has both elbows on the standing tables, her body away from the dance floor that has formed. Mariam gets her phone out and scrolls through it, before pausing, putting her glass down and tapping Shirin's hand. 'Oh my God,' she says. 'That small man is at it again.'

Shirin stands a little straighter and says, 'What small man?' Mariam is five foot ten; in her eyes, most men are small men.

'That shite comedian Rob Grayson.'

Dread in the pit of her stomach appears so suddenly that Shirin is theatrically breathless when she asks, 'What now?'

Mariam hands Shirin her phone, and Shirin scrolls through a tirade of tweets attacking various people. He is far-right in his views, and says that England has turned to dirt because of all the foreigners who have entered and stayed. It is not what he is saying, necessarily, that is most surprising, but the overwhelming agreement with his words under each post. He says Shamima Begum, the girl from east London who left England for Syria after being groomed, should not be allowed back in the UK, that she should rot in Syria. People reply with crude memes, and it is not new, but it is still shocking to see the way people who look like Shirin and Mariam are so othered, as though they are not human beings. It is not just white people in agreement with him, but some Black and brown Twitter users are proclaiming that 'enough is enough', as though he is not attacking them, too.

Rob's comments are in response to calls for his book deal with a major publisher to be revoked – he says he will not back down. A quick scroll through and Shirin discovers he recently performed a racist comedy sketch about migrants, which began all of this. As she scrolls, new tweets come in thick and fast. He retweets supporters saying that freedom of speech is a human right, not seeing the irony of such a statement, given the context. He retweets supporters from America who say they need to stick together. Though against whom?

It shouldn't all be shocking – but it is. Shirin wants to think Rob hasn't changed since school, but that wouldn't be true. He is more overt in his racist views now, whereas back then he was more secretive about it. Now he has hundreds of thousands of people agreeing with his poison, and that only makes a person bolder.

She returns Mariam's phone to her, speechless for a moment. 'Fucking hell.' It's all too much. They entered publishing because they enjoyed reading. They assumed their industry would be a gentler world, that they would not have to confront racists regularly, that they would help publish books that make a difference. But more and more she is noticing there is only talk about doing better and less action – which prompts the question: why is Rob being published in the first place?

'At least *we're* not publishing him,' Mariam says, as though she can hear Shirin's mind. Mariam mock-shudders – and she does not even know half of what Shirin knows about him. And Shirin is keen to keep it that way.

Cross-Country

Kian had been at North Oak for two weeks when he finally spoke to Shirin, in the most unexpected of places: during cross-country running. They were to do two laps of the field, with both boys' and girls' classes mixed. The PE teachers stood at different points around the running course, faux-encouraging in their deep bellows as the students passed them.

Kian began at a steady pace, but while he was one of the best at Foxview, he was middling at North Oak. Halfway through the first lap they had to go up a mound, which he thought might finish him off. The girls' PE teacher, a blonde Swiss woman with a mole above her lip and eyebrows that naturally cast downwards, told him to 'hurry up', clapping her hands as he passed her. He pegged it down the mound with a stitch in his side. Just before PE he'd eaten a cheese-and-bean baguette from the canteen. Knowing he wouldn't be one of the first to finish wiped out any motivation he had to push himself.

Out of sight from the teachers, Kian jogged away from the track, towards a line of trees. He planned to lean against one of them to catch his breath and soothe the ache in his side. He was thinking he'd sprint the rest of the way, to not lag too far behind, but for now he would give himself a moment to steady his ragged breath.

At first he didn't see her. The ancient tree trunk was so wide it hid her from view. But when he looked behind him, at a certain angle, he caught a glimpse of her leg. Then he walked around the tree and she was there. Hair thrown into a bun on the top of her head, she wore a baggy blue polo top and long navy shorts. The other girls wore more form-fitting PE kits; hers looked like it was two sizes too big and made her look petite.

Shirin's head whipped around to Kian, momentary panic plain on her face, until she realised it was just him. Dangling from her ears were the wires from a pair of pink headphones, which she slowly removed, her eyes narrowed at him. She didn't say anything though, and he broke his frozen stance by saying, 'What are you doing?'

She looked from side to side, like his question was stupid. 'What does it look like I'm doing?'

He kicked a bit of bark in front of him, and it jumped over the grass two times before landing pathetically not too far away. 'Why aren't you running?'

She shrugged. 'I needed a break.'

He frowned. 'You'll get a really shit time, though, if you stay here.'

'Who said I care about what time I get?'

He was taken aback by the sharpness of her tone. From what little he had seen of her in the corridors, Kian had created an image of her in his head that was at odds with how she actually spoke. He thought she would be shy and timid, bullied, and not the kind of girl to be sacking off cross-country to listen to music.

'Alright then,' he said, about to turn round.

'Sorry,' she said. She reached into the waistband of her shorts, produced a lime-green iPod Nano, and paused her music. 'Phoebe was meant to meet me here, but she must not have been able to get away from the teachers.'

'What do you mean?'

Shirin looked off behind Kian, gestured for him to get closer to her and out of view. He took two steps forward, and she gently put her hand on his shoulder to guide him behind the tree. 'I thought I saw Miss Kemp,' she said, before finally looking him back in the eyes. 'We worked out that if we hide here for a bit, we can pretend we've already done one lap and come out, when no one's looking, to finish the race.'

'That is so lazy,' Kian said, smiling.

'What they're doing is cruelty; no one wants to do this. They get to relax while we struggle to breathe, going up the mound.' She shook her head. 'Nah, no thank you.'

Kian leant against the tree. 'What are you listening to, anyway?'

She gripped her iPod tighter. 'This and that.' He raised an eyebrow. 'Blink-182,' she said. 'And Mary J. Blige. I have varied taste, before you say anything.'

'I wasn't going to say anything.'

'Keep it that way,' she said. 'You're new here, aren't you?'

He nodded. 'Yeah.'

She wrapped her headphones around her iPod and tucked it back into the waistband of her shorts. 'So, how do you like North Oak so far?'

'It's a bit shit,' he said. 'I liked my other school.'

'Oh. Why'd you come here, anyway?'

He shrugged. 'My parents thought it would be better.'

He somehow knew she knew about his brother. There was something in her eyes, in the way she looked down when he said this and didn't push it further. 'Don't you all wear proper suits at Foxview? Like, a tie and everything,' she said.

'Yeah.' He couldn't stop the small smile from growing on his face.

'I think your parents were right. It's too posh there. Why are they making you dress like you're businessmen or something?' she said, smiling back.

'There were more people like us there,' he said.

Her head tilted to the right, and her eyes narrowed ever so slightly. 'Like us?'

'You know what I mean: Asian. But I didn't know any Iranians there. You are Iranian, right?'

'How did you guess?' she asked.

'Your eyes,' he said.

They looked at each other a beat longer than was normal, and then Shirin looked away, cleared her throat. 'Yeah, well, North Oak is pretty white and racist. So, welcome.'

'I heard you were in hospital after something someone did?' he asked slowly.

She was quiet for a moment, frowning. 'Jordan thinks it's hilarious to throw mud balls at some of us. He said he does it to everyone, but he only got me in the face, and there was a piece of metal in it. I'm fine now, so it's like, whatever ...'

'Jesus.'

They could hear a whistle in the distance and a teacher shouting, 'One lap left!'

'Okay, give it a minute, and when Miss Kemp is out of view we need to run,' Shirin said.

'I was really good at running at my old school,' Kian said, because it was true and he wanted her to impress her. What he didn't realise, though, was that this was not information that would impress her.

'Do you want me to give you a round of applause?' she said, and then her face lit up. 'Okay, I'll race you the last stretch, and whoever wins has to give the other a quid.'

'I mean,' he began, 'I'm obviously going to win.'

'Well, let's see.'

Shirin looked ahead, saw the coast was clear and began to run. He didn't realise she meant right now, so he was a little behind her. He had to really leap as he ran to catch up with her; she was quick. In the end, she completed the run two seconds ahead of him. At the finish line she had her hands on her thighs for support, her face a tomato red. In front of everyone who had already finished, she didn't acknowledge him. In fact she turned her body away from him while she caught her breath, and then went over to Phoebe, presumably to find out why she hadn't met her as planned. Phoebe had her blonde hair in a high ponytail and was about three inches taller than Shirin. He thought he heard Phoebe say that Miss Kemp wouldn't bloody leave her alone.

When Connor had completed the run, he said to Kian that he hadn't seen him on the course for ages. 'You must have been quick,' Connor said. Kian mumbled something about him not kidding when he said he was good at running, deciding to keep what he and Shirin had done between them.

Once everyone had finished, the boys and girls started to make their way back to their changing rooms. As Shirin passed Kian to go into the girls' room she whispered, 'You owe me one pound.'

Speak Up

Now

Hoffman Books prides itself on having a 'speak up' culture. They require their employees to undertake online training dedicated to it. If you do not do the training within thirty days, you will receive daily reminders urging you to partake. If you don't do it after three months, they will contact your manager. In the training they show examples of scenarios in which you should speak up if you think something isn't quite right. Racist colleague? Tell your manager. Sexist boss? Tell HR. It is every employee's prerogative, and duty, to speak up about goings-on that are morally questionable, and in turn make a change. This is the first time Shirin has done so at Hoffman Books.

Lilian sits across from her in one of the narrow meeting rooms that is angled in the shape of a triangle. Between them is a coffee table that holds both their green teas, and a conference telephone that Lilian is never able to work herself.

The walls are navy and there is a quote in silver from one of Hoffman's bestselling children's books that was subsequently turned into a blockbuster film: *There is nothing more magical than believing.* It is in a whimsical font and is surrounded by stars. She thinks the quote could be applicable to many things, including religion, but the book is about a girl who befriends dragons who carry her around a magical world as she goes on various quests. So, not quite the same.

They have spent the past half an hour rattling through Shirin's tasks for the week ahead, when Shirin says, 'I have something I need to speak to you about.'

Lilian looks at her more attentively with those words, closes her notebook and nods. 'Of course.'

Shirin recounts Sally's story at the author party. 'It was racist,' Shirin says. 'I'm not sure we should continue publishing her.'

Lilian's eyebrows draw together and she leans back, looking off to the side. 'It's a sad truth that in this industry we won't always work with people we like. Sally's books are never problematic – in fact they are very empowering to women – so I don't think we can, as you say, not publish her any more because of an offhand comment she made at a party. Do you understand?'

'I just think if we ignore this, it sends the wrong message. We talk a lot about being more inclusive in our publishing and welcoming everyone, so to have an author who openly says the things she does ...'

Lilian initially seems taken aback, but then she smiles at Shirin with her teeth. 'It was an offhand comment, Shirin, by an author in a small group at a party. Please do not think any more of it.'

And that is that.

'I do have something exciting I'd like you to begin working on, though. There's a Diversity and Inclusion team being created within the company. As it's something you're *clearly* interested in, I thought you'd be keen to be the non-fiction representative, but I obviously wanted to check with you first.'

When Shirin asks Lilian what it would entail, she says Shirin would help the team create a booklet about things to look out for from an editorial perspective, in terms of the language used and essentially how not to be racist (though this is not how she phrases it). This is contradictory to the conversation they've just had, but Shirin is defeated and so tells Lilian, 'Right. Okay, yes, of course.'

She leaves the meeting dejected, with an excess of performative work, on top of her actual work. In reality, it is futile to speak up.

Home Friends

Shirin is on the phone to Phoebe, her friend from back home. Phoebe is married to George, who they both went to school with. They live in a house around the corner from Shirin's family home and are in the process of adopting a dog. Phoebe's a social worker, and Shirin thinks she's her only friend who has her life together – at least in the way everyone thought their lives would look, when they were teenagers imagining their mid-twenties.

It is not that Shirin wants Phoebe's life – because she doesn't. Though the ease of Phoebe's life is something Shirin sometimes envies. While Phoebe owns her house, Shirin shares a rental with three women – Chloe, Anna and Jane – in a block of ex-council flats in Bow. The three women are all in their twenties too, and are relative strangers. Their flat is small, though two-storeyed, and they share one bathroom between them. Sometimes it is like there are seven of them, when their boyfriends are round, and everything is either broken or breaking. The electric shower routinely stops working every six months. Each new shower that is installed is cheap and so is never worth fixing, resulting in a new cheap one being fitted, and thus the cycle continues. The rent is reasonable though, for London. They opt for cheaper rent so they can eat out, buy new clothes, and pretend their home life is less bleak. The landlady, a well-meaning Bangladeshi woman who once lived in the flat with her husband until they separated, responds promptly to their emails when things break, but Shirin senses she is overwhelmed by each email about something new going wrong. It is clear she did not want to be a landlady; this was not her ambition for the flat. It leaves an aura around the building.

Shirin mentions that she has plans to have coffee with Kian, to which Phoebe says, 'Kian? As in Kian Rahimi from school?' Before Shirin can reply, Phoebe continues, 'Hold on, let me stalk him.' Shirin can tell she has been put on speakerphone while Phoebe looks at his social-media profiles, because her voice is now distant. 'Why does he have no recent pictures of himself?'

'It's annoying, isn't it?'

'Very. I sometimes see his parents in Morrisons, you know,' Phoebe muses. 'It was so sad when his dad got sick.'

'Wait, what?'

Phoebe explains that four years ago Kian's dad was diagnosed with prostate cancer, and he underwent aggressive chemotherapy. She says that she used to see Kian around Hull a lot more during that time, visiting his dad, and that his mum always looked so tired when she passed her in the supermarket. Shirin forgets how small Hull is sometimes.

'Is he okay now?' Shirin asks, thinking of how hard Kian's family life already was, with everything that happened to his brother.

'Yeah, last I heard it worked and he's back to normal now,' Phoebe says. 'Anyway, is it a date, your coffee?'

The switch surprises Shirin and she quickly says, 'What? No. It's just a friendly thing.'

'You were always close at school. I always thought you liked him.'

'Yeah. Ten years ago. And we were only ever friends then, too.' She is aware she doth protest too much. 'And we hadn't spoken since school. Since … you know.'

'Oh, yeah, since he went psycho, you mean?'

That isn't how Shirin would phrase it, but perhaps if she hadn't seen Kian again she would have accepted this version of what happened; perhaps it would be easier to see him that way. Now, one corner of her top lip twitches in irritation. 'I mean, *they* were the psychos, not him,' she says steadily.

She doesn't want to say their names, but Phoebe has no such qualms. 'Jordan, yeah – I will agree with you there. He's in prison now, did you hear?'

'He is?' Shirin puts Phoebe on speakerphone and google-searches Jordan Young. She knows she shouldn't, that she should put boundaries in place with Phoebe, as she has with Kian, on what they can talk about. Though she can never imagine saying this to Phoebe. Her friend would say she needs to get a grip, perhaps rightly so.

The first webpage that comes up is a *Hull Daily Mail* article detailing Jordan's conviction. It says he had a string of previous offences and it was racially aggravated battery that put him away. The boy he beat up was only eighteen; he had come from India to study at Hull University for his undergraduate degree and had allegedly pushed ahead of Jordan in a takeaway queue after a night out. The pictures on the webpage show a stock image of a splattering of blood on white-tile flooring. Shirin curses under her breath.

'Tom has really turned his life around though,' Phoebe says. 'George has mutual friends with him.'

Tom always hung around with Jordan and Rob. He very rarely would start something on his own, but in a group setting he did whatever they told him to do. Shirin's lip twitches again now; it is an automatic response. Having even three degrees of separation from a racist smells racist to her. She has sometimes wondered whether George is low-key racist. Whether, on a night out, he might slip up. She's seen it, the way drunk people switch; and she thinks if that is what they act like drunk, they are clearly thinking it sober, too.

'And obviously Rob is like crazy famous now. He bought his mum a huge house in Kirk Ella, you know. She used to live near me in a tiny terraced house. My mum is always asking why I didn't become a comedian or something, like him, and buy her a house.' Phoebe is laughing, while Shirin clenches her fist. She is not an angry person, but she wants to hit something. Instead, she squeezes the pillow on her bed tightly for a few seconds.

'They're *all* awful people,' Shirin reminds Phoebe through gritted teeth. 'They were quite nasty to me.' She is playing it down. *Quite nasty.* Jordan once pushed her down the stairs and she sprained her arm. He denied it, said he accidentally knocked her, and Shirin even doubted herself in front of the teacher, wondered if she was imagining the malicious intent. When she faltered, said it might have been an accident, it was swiftly branded an accident, nothing more. When the teacher turned his back, Jordan winked at her. It was the day before she was supposed to perform her solo in the school orchestra, and she had practised her flute every evening for the past few months. Instead, she watched them play from the audience, her arm in a sling, bitter and sad. That was just the start, anyway. And for all of Jordan's physical violence, it was what Rob said – and subsequently did – to Shirin that she can never forget, or shake, even after all this time.

'Oh, really?'

There is a long, unpunctuated silence. This happens some-times when they mention school. Phoebe was in most of the same classes as Shirin, and yet she somehow did not see what Shirin experienced. She is reminded why she chooses not to speak about it.

'Anyway,' Shirin says slowly. 'How's George?'

'Fine, nothing new to report really.'

Shirin can tell Phoebe has something more to say, by her tone.

'What?' Shirin says.

'What?' Phoebe repeats back to her. Shirin lets the subsequent silence drag on because she knows Phoebe will fill it. 'Oh, fine,' Phoebe concedes. 'Don't tell anyone, but … we're trying for a baby.'

'Oh, wow. That's amazing!' Shirin lets her voice go high-pitched, but she is straight-faced and all the enthusiasm resides in her tone. She is lying on her bed, looking up at the ceiling, and can hear two different housemates having sex on either side of her room.

She does not know what questions to ask because this is the first time a friend has said this to her, and objectively, while it sounds like it would be a thing one would find exciting, to Shirin they still feel like children themselves. She looks at babies in coffee shops, or when her colleagues bring theirs in on their maternity leave, and she thinks they look ugly and not cute, but says 'Aw' when their mother or father looks for validation. She cannot imagine Phoebe with one – or pretending to find Phoebe's baby cute.

'How long have you been trying?' she finally asks.

'Only a month now – it could take ages, but I had to tell someone.'

'That's so, so exciting,' Shirin says.

When they end the call, the flat is quiet, bar the footsteps of people coming in and out of the bathroom, post-sex. She puts on the sound machine next to her that blasts white noise. Then she retrieves a packet of Night Nurse from her bedside table. It is expensive and she rations out her use of it. Tonight she pops one capsule in her mouth with a large gulp of water and turns her lamp off. It doesn't stop the intrusive thoughts though. Her mind is so busy – more so lately. In the daytime her thoughts flicker from worry to worry, but at night it is existential emptiness that consumes her. She wonders at the pointlessness of life. Or her life, more specifically. At the fact that she strives continually for things that she thinks will bring her happiness and yet she is never happy. She wonders if it is her that is the issue in all of this. Whether her work, her friends, her life – all of it – should be enough for her. Whether there is something inherently wrong with her that means she will never be happy. This thought remains until the Night Nurse kicks in and lulls Shirin into a heavy sleep.

Shirin hands Kian an advance reader's copy of *You People* by A. K. Hosseini. To get said copy she had to beg Mariam to ask her friend in another department for a proof. At lunch Mariam said that they didn't have any spare, which led to Shirin sneakily taking a copy from the publicity cupboard. When Kian's eyes light up and he says she's the best, she simply says, 'It's no problem – they were giving them away.' She does not condone stealing, but when it is from a multimillion-pound company that still pays its entry-level staff £18,000 a year, she can justify it. With that, and since her conversation with Lilian about what Sally said at the author party, right now Shirin has no affinity towards a company that does not value good morals.

They are in New Cross, in a coffee shop just down the road from Goldsmiths. Kian said that he was visiting his studio space there, and it is seven minutes on the train from her office, so she said they could meet here. She has never been to New Cross before and is initially taken aback by the sheer number of people walking along the pavements, the liveliness of the area, with its strip of pubs, takeaways and cafés. In the distance she can see a tall grey building with a squiggly metal sculpture atop it. She imagines it has something to do with the university, though it contrasts with the other buildings, which are rundown and graffitied.

She is not sure coffee past 5 p.m. will be good for her, or her sleep issues, but asks for a soya latte anyway. Kian gets up to order their drinks, and while he is away from the table she quickly smooths down her hair. Old-school R&B plays over the speakers, and there are several students seated around them, working on their laptops. There is art on the walls made by local artists in the area. She studies one of them. It is a painting of a woman with her legs open, exposing her labia. It is painted in different shades of pink and red. The woman is smiling, her teeth sharp and pointed. Disturbed, Shirin looks at her phone instead.

Lingering in her mind are questions about what she is doing here. Is it a date? It feels too casual to be one, but what Phoebe said has her thinking. They were never close romantically as teenagers, but in adulthood she is not sure they can maintain the same kind of relationship. She is not sure she wants that because being near Kian now, she feels awkward and excited, which is to say that she thinks she likes him as more than a friend. But they are stuck in this place of knowing each other but not really knowing each other, not any more. She isn't sure how to get to know Kian again for the first time, or whether it will be difficult trying to.

When he returns, she can smell his aftershave; it is fresh and ever so slightly fruity. A marked change from the Lynx Africa of his youth. He is wearing a long-sleeved striped T-shirt and navy Nike shorts, and she is also wearing a striped top and a tennis skirt. She debates making a joke of this.

'What I need to know,' she says instead, 'is how you went from your parents not letting you study Art at A-level to doing an MFA in it?' She has been thinking about this, after the initial shock of Kian returning had dissolved from her mind. It is so at odds with the Kian she knew, who loved his art but was so cautious about taking it seriously.

Something in his usually soft face changes then. His eyebrows furrow together, and she notices his jaw tighten ever so slightly. Shirin knows she is perceptive of how other people are feeling; a psychic told her she has a third eye, which she took very seriously. It is a curse in some ways because, like right now, she cannot ignore that something has shifted, that Kian is annoyed by something she's said, when she thought she was asking an innocent question.

He scratches his chin, then says, 'I saw my friend Ahmed earlier at the mosque and he asked the same thing. Well, he told me it was stupid to spend years studying it further and that it'd be better for me to get a real, well-paid job.' He shrugs. 'He's probably right, but here we are.'

Everything he says is loaded. She has so many questions and he didn't even answer her original one. 'Ahmed from Hull? He lives here?'

Kian nods. 'He was always the clever one; he's a lawyer now and lives in Greenwich with his wife and son.'

'Wow, okay. I mean, for what it's worth, to me what he said sounds like rubbish. If you love something, why not pursue it? And also, not being funny, but would you want a wife and kid right now?'

The last part makes Kian scoff, like the thought is unimaginable. Their drinks are brought over and set down on the wooden table. The latte art is impressive, and Shirin gazes at it briefly before using her teaspoon to stir the rosetta away. Kian leaves his as it is and takes a long sip. His hands are large and make the teacup look especially tiny.

'It's fine,' he eventually says. 'It's not like my parents haven't said the same thing to me. So, to answer your question, I just did what I wanted, even though they didn't like it. It was easier at uni, because when my brother came back from … you know … they were so busy wanting to fix his life that they focused less on me. At least I was going to uni, you know? At least one of us was. But now, doing a Masters in Art, they don't get it. They think it's a waste of money and time.'

'What do you think?'

He looks up at her, surprised by the question. 'I think I need this. In Manchester I was only working admin jobs while I did my art on the side. If I was lucky, I'd be involved in tiny exhibitions, but because I was so tired from work, I never felt like I focused on my art. And now I'm excited,' he says, and she can see it in his eyes. 'For the first time in ages, I'm excited by the future. Jesus, I sound depressing, don't I? But it's true.'

She smiles. 'We're old now, Kian: it's okay for us to be depressing. I do need you to back up a bit though – since when do you go to the mosque?' She wants to say, *You never used to*, but ten years have passed; of course he's not the same boy as back then. People change.

'My dad got cancer just when I graduated from uni. So I moved home for a bit and it really shook me up. It made me realise that we're all going to die. And the thought of nothing happening after – it fucked me up. That my dad would simply be gone if his treatment didn't work. So, as a family, we started going to the mosque. I'm not perfect, obviously, but it really helped me get out of a dark time. I like to go sometimes even now, to balance myself, I guess.'

'I'm sorry you went through that with your dad,' she says, looking away from his eyes to his ear, because she is never good at comforting people, even people she cares about. 'How is he doing now?'

'He's recovered, touch wood.' He knocks his knuckles on the table and smiles. 'Sorry, I've offloaded on you for the last fifteen minutes. I bet you think I've not changed at all,' he says, the tops of his cheeks lightly pink, like he is embarrassed.

Her heart begins to beat quicker and she takes a long sip of her drink to give herself some composure time.

'Don't be silly,' she says. 'I'm interested. And you have changed. The Kian I knew at school definitely wouldn't be going to the mosque. Nor would he be doing a Masters in Art.'

'Do you ever go to the mosque?' he asks, bypassing her comment completely.

The waitress returns to bring them a slice of lemon cheesecake and two spoons, and she is glad of the interruption because questions like this remind her of her mild identity crisis. She often feels this way around her friends who are Muslim. Shirin's relationship with her religion is confused. In fact it always has been, but the gulf between her saying she is Muslim and her actually doing what Muslims are supposed to do has only got bigger. Her parents were never strictly religious, though they warned her to stay away from boys and to cover herself – fairly standard stuff. If she ever told her parents she was scared of dying one day, something she keeps to herself now, she would be scolded that a true Muslim knows what will happen next: God will protect us. She is not sure God will protect her, though, or whether she deserves protecting.

'No, not really,' she says, thinking Kian might push it, but instead he nods. Because he says nothing – and because she dislikes the silence – she continues. 'It feels too late for me now – to try and go to the mosque, I mean.'

The one thing she doesn't want is for Kian to preach at her. Or maybe she does. Maybe she is saying this to see what he will do – to see whether he is the same as he was when they were younger: kind and solid. She walks the fine line with Mariam, but it's not like that with every friend. Mariam is patient with her, never tells her what she should or shouldn't be doing. It is refreshing, and Shirin knows not everyone is like that.

Her warmth towards Kian is almost threatened, but then he says, 'It's never too late. And it doesn't make you any less of a good person, you know, that you don't go.'

God, even now he knows exactly what she is thinking. She feels this stinging in her eyes and it is humiliating. She bites the inside of her cheek hard, letting her incisors really dig into her stupid fleshy mouth. It helps to focus the pain elsewhere. She waves her hand in the air dismissively. 'It's fine,' she says, echoing him.

'I want to know about you,' he says. 'You always said you'd get the fuck out of Hull and be a big-shot editor – looks like you did it.'

She scoffs, loudly. 'Hardly. I'm an assistant editor – still.'

He shrugs, taking another spoonful of the cheesecake. 'You still got out.' The way he says it, though, is like it's an accusation – like she abandoned him. Or maybe that's just because she's always felt guilty for the way they left things. And because, in some ways, she knows she did abandon him when he needed her most.

When they've finished their drinks, Kian offers to show her his studio. On the walk there, she asks him about his brother. There is warmth in Kian's eyes when he speaks about him now. It is so different from before, she realises. His brother and his imprisonment at such a young age brought Kian so much pain; he shouldered the burden, even though it wasn't his fault. Though he would never accept that.

'I've got into mindfulness,' Kian confesses, giving Shirin a cautious sidelong look.

She bursts out laughing and then apologises. 'That's very Zen of you.'

They have gone down a side street, with terraced houses, which upon further inspection belong to the university, with placards proclaiming them as the counsellor's room or the history office. It is typical of London universities, whose campuses are spread far out – not really a campus at all.

'Hey, it helps. I'd recommend it. You know, since you mentioned that you struggle with anxiety.' He says this last part quieter – and Shirin remembers she told him and immediately feels irrationally pathetic. She thinks he might see this on her face because he says, 'But who am I to talk? I'm pretty fucked up myself.'

She turns to him and frowns. '*You* don't seem fucked up at all.' And she means this. Kian appears emotionally intelligent – a trait very few men, Shirin has realised, possess – and he has coped with so much, while seemingly appearing much more stable than Shirin, who thinks about death every night and perpetually has an existential crisis, and she has had minimal tragic life events thus far. She is the one who cannot bear to think about the past – about the specific moment when she and Kian stopped speaking. If Kian is fucked up, what does that make her?

'Well, we haven't actually spoken in ten years, so I don't think you're the best judge of that,' he jokes, and she is reeling, thinking: How can he make a joke of that? She is so taken aback she lets out a pathetic little laugh, and then clears her throat.

As they walk further down the street, the car horns and hum of motor engines become more and more distant. When they round the corner, they walk through gates to the silver building that she saw all the way from the station and wondered at. He tells her this is the Ben Pimlott Building, where the art studios are, and that people call it the 'Squiggle' building for short. He taps his pass onto a metal sensor by the doors, which automatically open. The entryway is sparse, with cream floor tiles and white walls. They climb two flights of metal stairs, until they reach his corner of the studio.

'You know what I realised recently?' she says.

'What?'

The lights are automatic and turn on one by one as they make their way further down the floor.

'That work – and by work I mean publishing – is no different from school,' she muses. She has been thinking about this earlier in the day.

The walls are all glass, and outside the sun has gone down, the sky a hazy pink. She is sure when she opens Twitter there will be numerous pictures of the sky, with the same captions, by different people. She looks at it briefly, uninterested, when she thinks she should be more interested. The problem is, next to Kian, she feels herself on edge – not in an unpleasant way, but like this small moment is so significant, though she doesn't want it to show in her own body language. She never thought they'd see each other again; never thought they'd speak so casually, like no time has passed. She certainly did not think she would be telling him passing thoughts again, like she is now.

Kian pulls a face. 'I mean, that is very concerning. What makes you say that?'

'Well, I went to an author party last week and an author said something questionable—'

'Questionable?'

'Racist,' she amends. 'And I spoke to my manager about it and she was quite dismissive. I always thought life would be much different. But it's like that song "High School Never Ends".'

'Oh God, I hated that song,' Kian says, attempting to lighten the mood.

'It's a brilliant song,' Shirin says, taking her phone out of her pocket, as though to put it on.

Sara Jafari

He puts his hand over hers, lightly, and says, 'God, no.' His hand on hers feels particularly intimate – perhaps because it is Kian's hand on hers. She is unusually excited by it, her face suddenly feeling hot. She looks up to see him looking down at her, smiling, his teeth white and straight, his face decorated with slight laugh-lines now, but it is his eyes that are the same – he is the same Kian from back then, after all.

'Okay, okay,' she says, lightly shaking him off because this is all too much and she won't let herself indulge in it any longer. 'I won't put it on.'

'Thank you. Anyway,' he says, arms out in exaggeration, 'this is my space.'

It is a small area of the room, with tall white panel dividers, which give some semblance of privacy from the other artists he shares the room with. Tonight they are the only ones there. His desk looks out the window, and on both sides of it are numerous plants, mainly cactuses of various sizes in mismatched pots.

She wanders around the small space and notices some painted canvases that are stacked against the wall. When she looks up at him, she realises he is staring at her. He quickly looks away and clears his throat.

'Can I?' she asks, to which Kian nods.

She flicks through them. They are portraits of people, each one utilising a different colour palette. There are more of the girl she saw in the summerhouse, and something dawns on her then – something illuminating that takes her momentarily out of body.

'Is this your girlfriend?' she asks, not looking up at him.

108

She can hear a laugh; it is distant in her ears, less confident than she's sure he wants it to be. 'No,' he says. 'Just a friend.'

She turns to him and manages to smile, though she knows it does not look genuine. 'She's, like, naked in some of them.' The key is to keep her tone light, she reminds herself, though that in and of itself is difficult.

He leans against his desk and crosses his arms. His biceps tense and strain against his T-shirt, so she looks down. But then she is faced with his thighs, which are pleasantly thick. So she looks away, out of the window.

'Why? Does that bother you?' he asks gently.

'It doesn't, obviously.' When she eventually looks at him, he seems incredibly smug, which is why she says, 'Truly, it was just a question.'

He nods. 'Okay. I believe you.'

She continues to look through the canvases, though she doesn't focus on any of the art. She is thinking about how to bring the conversation back to safer ground. Then she stumbles upon a portrait of Henry and lets out a sound between a tut and a laugh of derision. Henry's eyes are big, his lopsided face magnified. Kian has given his face likeability somehow, added something extra that gives the piece warmth. If Shirin didn't dislike her friend's boyfriend, she might be able to appreciate it.

'I think this is your best piece yet,' she says, rolling her eyes.

He pushes her with his shoulder. 'He asked for a portrait to be done of him. It was quite hard to say no, and I thought it'd be good practice.' Kian looks like he is resisting smiling.

She continues her perusal of his space, to give herself a break from feeling so stupidly excited. She hasn't felt this way around a man in a very long time, and it feels in many ways treacherous to have such a reaction now. She is always saying that men are disappointing, but when she says it, she realises, she never means men like Kian.

Atop his desk is a sketchbook that looks familiar. She is thinking: *Surely not*; and without asking, she reaches for it and flips it open. And there she sees some of his older work from the very beginning; his sketches that were scrappy but beautiful all the same. As she flicks through, she stops when she sees herself reflected on the page. Shirin at fifteen. Her fingertips lightly touch the paper. 'You kept this?'

The familiar steps of Kian's Converse can be heard against the linoleum floor, his nervous laugh audible, too. 'Yeah. I keep all my sketches.'

She turns to face him. His face is pink, embarrassed, but he keeps his head up to attempt to mask this.

'Really? All of them?'

He scratches his neck, a vein visible on the back of his hand as he does so. 'Only the ones that are special to me.'

She doesn't allow herself to venture into what this means. It is something she will tuck away to dissect later, when she is alone in her bed and needs something to keep her up at night. 'So what you're saying,' she begins, jokily, 'is that I was special to you?' She is smiling, thinking he will laugh and make a dig.

Instead he says, 'Yeah, you were, actually.'

She is dumbfounded by this admission. Of course she is. Who says that? Even if they mean it? Especially if they mean it? So she clears her throat and says, 'I best go soon, I've got an early-morning meeting with an author tomorrow.'

He nods, the tops of his ears pink now, matching his cheeks, and if it were not for that, she might think him not bothered at all by the abrupt end to their night. 'Of course,' he says. 'It's getting late.'

Skipping School

Then

Cars whizzed past them. It was three weeks after the cross-country run. Skipping class was Shirin's idea. She had told Kian that it was only PE that she skipped, because it was 'pointless' and 'teachers get a power trip from making us do things we don't want to do'. She ended her rant by saying it was 'sadistic, really', and he scoffed and asked her if she even knew what that meant. She glared at him. PE was Kian's favourite subject. He was naturally athletic, so it didn't feel like class to him. He told her this and then it was her turn to scoff.

Shirin was looking ahead now, her eyes squinting, as though she was focusing on something in the distance. Though, when Kian followed her gaze, he couldn't see anything worth staring at. Her cheekbones were a sharp contrast to her soft eyes. She looked at him and he looked away from her, ahead, like he had only been looking at her very briefly. He wanted to study her face, to imprint it into his memory to dissect later. He thought she was attractive, but not in an overwhelming way. As he walked with her now, he considered her again and concluded that she was quietly

113

beautiful, which was maybe more special than if she were overtly beautiful.

They turned down a side street, and he kicked a rogue Dr Pepper bottle out of his way. It bounced twice before rolling under a car.

'You don't have to answer this if you don't want to, but why did your brother go to prison?' Shirin asked.

He chewed on the inside of his mouth. No one at North Oak had asked him this. He thought no one even knew he had a brother. He didn't realise until now how much he wanted people to talk about him – even if it was to ask the question that kept him up at night.

His brother hadn't always been the kind of person to get into trouble. He had loved all the same things Kian had loved: comic books, *South Park* and WWE. The change had happened when Mehdi had gone to upper school. Kian was still in primary school during that time, though he remembered Mehdi returning home each day and going directly to his bedroom and staying there until their mum forced him out for dinner. Afterwards he would go right back upstairs. This only lasted a few months, and it was such a brief period that Kian sometimes forgot it. Though there was one particular moment that, looking back, he thought was the cusp of his brother's change. Perhaps, if he'd known then what he knew now – if he'd told someone, done something – maybe he could have changed the course of his whole family's life.

His brother had just returned from school, and Kian wanted to ask him something – it was so inconsequential that months later he forgot what it was – and approached Mehdi's door. As he advanced, he noticed the door was ajar. He was about to make a joke, shout 'Boo' or something to scare him, when he caught sight of Mehdi's bare back. It was bruised: a large discoloration that took up most of his top-right shoulder. Mehdi was inspecting himself in his mirror, using a hand-held mirror to see his back in the reflection. He was facing away from Kian, so he did not know that he was watching.

When Kian asked his brother what had happened, Mehdi turned quickly and the look he gave him seared into Kian's memory. It was a cross between a scowl and absolute loathing. He told Kian to not tell Mum and Dad about what he'd seen, before slamming the door in Kian's face. It wasn't spoken about ever again. But looking back now, Kian thought it must have meant something, must have been instrumental to the moment his brother changed.

He couldn't bear to say any of this now to Shirin, or tell her the actual reason Mehdi was sent to prison – couldn't even think about that, really. He barely knew Shirin, but he already knew that she likely wouldn't judge him. Even so, he didn't want her to see him the way he saw himself. He wanted her to like him. So he settled for a half-truth.

'He was in a fight with some racist pricks,' he said. 'He always got into fights, always got into trouble with the police. If he hadn't had prior offences, he would probably have got off, but this was one too many, I guess.'

They rounded the corner and made their descent up a steep hill leading to a vast field. He opened the wooden gate for Shirin to enter before him, which she did, and he made sure to close it properly after him. Deeper into the field, horses stood in clusters, each looking off into the distance, unfazed by their arrival. The grass beneath them was yellow and sad. It was unseasonably warm for October, so he left his coat in his locker and rolled up his jumper sleeves. Shirin edged away from the horses. She would later comment that while she would never eat an animal, that didn't mean she wasn't scared of them.

She nodded now, like she understood, but he thought she couldn't really – not the full extent of it. 'I saw them stop him once. I was driving past in the car with my dad, and they were searching him. The police, I mean,' she said.

They walked deeper into the field, past the windmill, which he thought made the area look twee, until they found a good patch of grass to sit on. They sat cross-legged in front of each other, their bags laid between them.

'They did that a lot. Even before they had a reason to search his car. I think that's why he got into so much trouble.'

'What do you mean?' she asked, leaning towards him to open the side compartment of her bag. She took out a little jar of Vaseline, which she proceeded to rub across her lips with her forefinger. She did all this while looking at him, not breaking her concentration, though Kian was momentarily distracted by her glossy lips, feeling a stirring within him that he hadn't expected. He shook his head. He didn't even know why he was telling her all this. There was something so open about her. It made him think he could tell her everything. Almost everything.

'The police, his teachers, every adult, got this impression of Mehdi as a troublemaker, as the kind of person who would be part of a gang, who was good for nothing. And I don't know, but once you get that stereotype, it's hard to shake it. And when people in his class started to bother him ... I think he just did what was expected of him.'

'That's really sad. I'm sorry,' she said. 'Do people look at you that way?'

Kian shrugged, laughed a little, though it wasn't funny, so he didn't know why he was laughing. 'Not as bad as him, but sometimes, yeah. He was a lot bigger than me, a lot stronger, had – has – muscles, and he's taller than most of his teachers, so they treated him as if he was an adult like them. By comparison, I feel like Mr Rodgers is almost too nice to me. It's weird; like, because I'm foreign, I need special attention. Do you know what I mean?'

The first week Kian started at North Oak, Mr Rodgers had called him into his office to see how he was getting on. For a headmaster, he seemed alright. He'd said if Kian ever needed anything, his door was open. He'd told Kian he found Iranian culture fascinating and that Iran was on his bucket list of places to visit. In the same breath he'd said he'd just returned from India, actually, and had pushed the collar of his shirt aside to show a brown beaded necklace. He'd mentioned Shirin then, had asked if they were related, and when Kian had said they weren't, he'd laughed, backtracked that of course they weren't.

'He does that to me too,' Shirin said now. 'Always talks about Iraq or India, like any country beginning with I is the same ...'

They both let out a laugh. Kian's was shaky, a mixture of nervousness and relief from expelling half-held truths.

'Do you remember his speech in assembly last week?' Kian asked. The headmaster had given a long-winded talk about people needing to be more tolerant towards ethnic minorities because he had first-hand experience of being an outsider when he'd visited India, and it not feeling 'nice'. Afterwards, Rob had shot his hand up to ask, if foreigners didn't like it here, why didn't they go back to their country, like Mr Rodgers had eventually done? To this, Mr Rodgers had said it was because these people might come from war-torn countries and not be able to. When he'd said this he'd looked at Kian. Kian's parents were not migrants and his country was not war-torn.

'You'll get used to it.' Shirin shrugged. There was a short silence, before she asked, 'Can you speak Farsi then?'

'Ye kam,' he said. 'I can understand it more than speak it. My dad wants me to do a class after school to learn it properly, but I'm crap at languages.'

'Yeah, but it's different when it's *your* language, Kian.'

His stomach felt all weird when she said his name and he diverted his gaze down to the straw-like grass. He plucked a strand of it, rolled it around in his fingers, in a bid to both distract himself and look more nonchalant than he felt.

'I take it you can speak it then?' he asked.

'Baleh,' she said. *Yes.* She said something else, but he didn't know what it meant. He didn't want her to know that, so he smiled and swiftly changed the subject.

'So do you have a watering can next to your toilet?' he asked.

She laughed. 'Yeah. It's pink. Do you?'

He nodded. 'Mine's green. I've never met someone in Hull who had one too.'

'I'm glad we can bond over this,' she said jokingly, before moving her bag behind her and lying onto her back, using her backpack as a pillow. Kian did the same. The sky was clear, with a perfect-looking cloud just above them. He watched it slowly move across the sky, and everything was so still and peaceful that he didn't want the moment to end.

Dulwich

Now

The wellness café they meet in was Abigail's choice. She told Shirin it was her local café, where she goes sometimes to write. The café has dark wooden furniture and the walls and floor are pastel pink. Plants line the window sills, peace lilies and ctenanthes, some of their leaves decorated with pink lines. In the middle of the café is a large table, and creatives share the space with their laptops and flat whites. Shirin thinks this is the life she aspires to have – to work for herself on her laptop in aesthetic coffee shops. It is a source of wonder for her how people achieve this lifestyle – how they evade the nine-to-five grind with enriching, creative jobs that still cover their rent.

In her weekly catch-up with Lilian, progression was discussed – and by discussed, Shirin tacked it on in the remaining five minutes of their meeting, after putting off broaching it for the hour. Her manager said she wanted to see Shirin acquire a book with big commercial potential, to prove herself as an editor. Shirin mentioned that she's friends with Abigail, who has been on the *Sunday Times* bestseller list for the four weeks since her launch party. Now, everyone wants to publish her next book. When Shirin suggested a collection of essays by Abigail, exploring some of the themes in her novel, Lilian jumped at the idea. She said if Shirin could pull it off, it would help her case for a promotion. So here she is.

She feels herself clinging to this – that she needs it now, more than wants it. That with it she might finally live the life she has always longed for. That maybe it is the fact that she is an assistant editor that is continuing to make her so unhappy.

Abigail is seated at a corner table. As Shirin approaches, she shuts her orange Moleskin notebook and tucks her pen inside simultaneously. She is wearing red lipstick and no eye make-up, her cheeks slightly flushed. On the table is a carafe of water and two small cloudy glasses.

Shirin waves hello, and Abigail stands. They hug lightly; with people she does not know well, Shirin struggles to decline an embrace. After they greet each other and order coffees, Shirin sits straight, attempting a professional front. 'Thanks for meeting me,' she says.

'No, thank *you*,' Abigail says. It is formal, and awkward, and Shirin cannot unsee Abigail at parties off her face, or them singing 'Anaconda', shaking their bodies at their graduation party.

'So, as I mentioned, we'd love to work with you on a collection of essays,' Shirin says.

She hasn't mentioned any of this to Hana, because she knows exactly what her response will be. Only if this goes through, she decides, will she bring it up with Hana.

'I've had a few publishers say they're interested in another book, to be honest with you,' Abigail says. She leans forward, her elbows planted firmly on the table, lifting her cappuccino to her lips. She holds it there, looks up in thought. 'But I'd like to work with you on it. I think it'd be fun.' She finally takes a sip of her drink, and Shirin realises she has been holding her breath. It is embarrassing to need someone this much, especially someone who is her peer. They were in the same classes at university, went to the same parties, and now it is Shirin who needs to impress Abigail to get ahead. It is a strange, unenjoyable dynamic.

'It'll be great,' Shirin says. 'The whole team is so excited by this idea.'

Abigail leans back in her chair. Shirin notices a small hole in Abigail's black wool rollneck, just at the shoulder. It is an odd place for a hole, and she idly wonders if it is from moths. This imperfection makes Abigail less intimidating – like she has moth problems, exactly like the rest of us.

'My only concern,' Abigail says, 'or rather question, is about Hoffman. The publisher of *My Corner Shop* is an indie, and I really like their ethics – we stand for the same things. So what is Hoffman really like?'

Shirin's head moves back reflectively; she has not expected this question and cannot think of a rehearsed answer. 'It's really great,' she says, knowing that sounds empty. In this moment she is unsure how she works with words for a living.

'You don't find it too corporate then?'

She shakes her head. 'No, it's really fun and innovative.' As the words roll out, she realises this is a lie. She does not know why, or how, it came out so effortlessly.

Abigail raises an eyebrow, though her shoulders soften. 'Really?'

'Honestly,' Shirin continues. 'It's amazing. Hoffman – they're amazing. It's a really innovative publisher.'

'You already said that,' Abigail says. 'Okay. You don't have to convince me any more, Shirin. I'm really excited about this – and working with you.'

Shirin smiles and takes an unsteady sip of her water. Her hands are shaking slightly and she is not sure if Abigail notices, though she doesn't say anything about it.

'I'm talking as a friend here, though. Are you happy there?'

'Of course,' Shirin says, though she is also not sure if this is the truth any more.

When she returns to the office, Lilian calls Shirin into a meeting room for a quick chat. Her heart beats uncomfortably at the words 'a quick chat' and she imagines all the possible reasons she might be being fired, from half-heartedly completing an admin task for a book, to bitching about the company to Mariam. They go to a tiny meeting room that people go to for private phone calls. Lilian leans against the table, so Shirin stands opposite her, hands clasped together.

'Just a quick one,' Lilian says. 'How'd it go with Abigail?'

'Good,' Shirin says. 'She said she'd like to do it.'

Lilian smiles and it doesn't touch her eyes; it rarely does. 'Brilliant. I was hoping you'd say that. I think you should pitch the project in our acquisitions meeting next week. I also wanted to quickly let you know that Florence will be working with you on this, so you'll present together.'

Shirin's eyebrows furrow ever so slightly. It is not like she is being paired with someone more senior to guide her, or more junior to assist her. It makes little sense for them to work together, because Shirin and Florence are at the same level, both in competition for a promotion. That and the fact she thoroughly dislikes Florence and spends most of her time avoiding her stares. 'Oh?'

'I think it'd be good for you to have someone to help you with it. It'll make it less work for you, as I know you've got a lot on.'

Shirin nods and they leave the meeting room. Her steps are slow to her desk. It doesn't feel right to her that she came up with an idea for a book and used her connections to secure the author, to then have to share it with Florence. How will this show her as being ready for the next stage? Won't it show she can't do it alone? And won't it benefit Florence too?

She sits back at her desk, looking at her screen, but isn't processing any of her emails. Her mind is whirling. It is a strange feeling. She has never been the type of person to demand credit for her work, but she sees the way editors around her are praised for their ideas and is confused about why she can't get the same treatment. Why Florence is brought into exciting projects, whereas Shirin is only really brought into conversations about diversity and inclusion. There is, she is realising, an imbalance between what Shirin and Mariam are expected to do, compared to their white counterparts. She thinks she must have known this, but it has never been quite so discernible before. Or maybe she wasn't paying attention.

In the afternoon, once Florence has been briefed that she will be working with Shirin on the project, Shirin begins to see what is happening more clearly. Without discussing it with her,

Florence uses Shirin's original pitch email that she sent to their editorial team and sends it to the wider company, saying she would love to discuss this exciting exclusive proposal in their acquisitions meeting next week. She mentions Shirin in passing in one line, deeper into the email, and signs off with her own name.

Colleagues from the wider team – ones Shirin has never had the chance to be seen by before – reply to the email, saying it's incredible they've secured Abigail exclusively, that this will be such a big acquisition for them.

The email from the MD, Allegra, is what really tips Shirin over the edge: *Brilliant work, Florence. Looking forward to discussing.*

She is left sweaty and angry and, beyond all, speechless at her desk. She looks through the gap between their monitors and catches Florence's eye. Florence smiles; it is an excited, team-player smile, like she is unaware. And Shirin might think she really is, but then she remembers the industry they're in, and how attention to detail is literally their job. Florence is not oblivious, and neither is Lilian – it is Shirin who is the fool.

That evening, Shirin jiggles the key into the front-door lock – it consistently jams and she has to lift it up as she rotates it at just the right angle for it to open. Once inside, she goes to her bedroom, removes her backpack and jacket and heads straight to the bathroom, where she takes a long, hot shower. The temperature is a touch too hot, but she likes the feeling of the water being uncomfortable, like dull needles jabbing against her skin. It gives her a renewed alertness when she steps out of the shower, her skin pink afterwards. She gets into her pyjamas and bounds down the stairs to make pasta. None of her housemates are home yet, though her movements are reflexively quick to avoid bumping into anyone.

She boils more pasta than she thinks she should, and when it is finished she drains it, and adds half a can of baked beans and cheese to a pan. As she heats the ingredients together on the stove, the cheese melts pleasantly into the sweet tomato sauce, turning it a soft orange colour. Her cheesy-bean pasta is a dish reserved for comfort; when she consumes it, it's akin to being hugged – albeit with the caveat that it is by someone she wants to be hugged by. She adds a sprinkling of ground black pepper, like that might make the meal more sophisticated.

She has been looking forward to this moment all day.

With her steaming bowl in hand, she trudges up the stairs to her room. She shuts her door, opens her laptop, puts a Netflix show on and gets into bed with her meal. She chooses a TV show she is not invested in, for background noise. Her life would be much more depressing, she thinks, if she did not have that noise. Silence is too much of a reminder of what we are, that we will all die, that she is alone in this big city with not many people who care much about her. She is not sure if such thoughts are entirely true, but they creep into her mind more and more lately. Perhaps because, since the author party, she has been more sporadic in taking her antidepressants. She thinks maybe allowing these thoughts in is better for her, rather than blocking them, leaving her feeling nothing at all.

Or maybe that's not quite true – it's not nothing, that heaviness in her heart that she cannot explain.

Ten minutes later, once she has finished her food, she puts the empty bowl on her bedside table and nestles her head into her pillow, her hair still damp from the shower. She stares at her laptop screen, at the characters and their lives, with all of their friends and relationships. The laughter prompts annoy her, because it is not that funny a show. She lies like this for an hour before reaching for her phone. She texts Hana.

What are you doing at the weekend?

Hana replies almost immediately.

Hana: *Having a quiet one I think*
Shirin: *Wanna do something?*
Hana: *I can't I have no money* ☹
Shirin: *We can do something free?*

She sees Hana typing, for what feels like too long. It is long enough for Shirin to feel embarrassed that she is almost begging her friend to see her. It never used to be like this. When they lived together, it would be Hana who arranged things for them to do.

Hana: *Yeah maybe*
Hana: *God Abi is relentless with her book. She won't stop going on about it on her Insta stories, I've had to mute her lol*

Shirin has not told Hana about her meeting with Abigail. Of course she hasn't. Hana would only call Shirin a traitor and give her a hard time about it. She puts her phone down and looks up to the ceiling.

Her phone pings again. She lifts it up to see. When she sees who it is from, she drops her iPhone directly onto her face. It hurts. She curses, scrambling to retrieve her phone and bring it to eye level once more.

@KianRahimi: Hey

She clicks on the notification to open the message. Three dots indicate Kian is typing, so she waits. This goes on for a while, until the dots disappear, and he doesn't say anything else.

@ShirinInTheCity: Hello

She has the urge to lock her phone, but only because she finds this thrilling and over-stimulating for her small brain, so she does not know what to do with herself.

@KianRahimi: Thanks again for the book. I hope I didn't seem weird or anything yesterday
@ShirinInTheCity: You didn't seem weird. Why would you say that?

She knows exactly why he would say that, but she types quickly, so as not to let herself overthink this. She realises she wants him to say something like he did the night before, even though it makes her uncomfortable.

@KianRahimi: Ok good. It dm. Did your meeting go ok?

@ShirinInTheCity: It did actually. I mean, I kinda felt set up by my manager. I did all the work on this project only for it to be given to someone else for them to get the credit lol

She is of course not laughing or smiling as she writes this.

@KianRahimi: Damn. That's rough.

@ShirinInTheCity: Sorry, it's boring work chat

@KianRahimi: It's not boring at all. You can talk to me about this stuff.

@ShirinInTheCity: I just always thought life would be different once I got my dream job, but it doesn't really make a difference, does it?

She almost deletes the message, but there is something cathartic about pouring your heart out to someone over DM and not being able to see their facial expressions, their pity or lack thereof. She clings to her phone, sees the three dots flashing as he types.

@KianRahimi: I'm so sorry Shirin

@ShirinInTheCity: You've not done anything lol

@KianRahimi: But it sounds shit. I was really hoping you'd be happy. You deserve to be.

Something about that last message renders her teary-eyed. It takes her by surprise. And yet there is a familiar discomfort within her of being seen and laid bare, of being pitied. She can't take any more, so she likes his message and puts her phone on Do Not Disturb mode. Pulls her Kindle out from her bedside drawer, to begin some reading for work. She reads the same sentence numerous times, but she is too pent up. She is about to slide further into bed and turn her light off, despite it still being early. Her polyester-blend sheets are scratchy against her skin, and she writhes around, trying to get comfortable. Inevitably she checks her phone. Kian hasn't said anything else.

She lets out a held breath. Then she looks at her mailbox. Her mum has finally replied to one of her emails, a week later. She tells Shirin not to get her hopes up about a promotion, that she always gets ahead of herself. The email is cordial, bordering on blunt – with no exclamation marks or emojis, like Shirin's – and ends with her asking Shirin if she can get birth control under her name to send to her cousin in Iran, who can't get it, due to Iran's sanctions. Shirin locks her phone. They've never had a close relationship, though it worsened when Shirin moved out of Hull. The small moments that showed her mother cared for her didn't translate well in a long-distance relationship, especially since her mother moved to Tehran. Now it is almost like she forgets she has a daughter at all.

From her bedside table Shirin retrieves her packet of sertraline. She has one week's worth left. She can feel herself spiralling, and yet there is this urge to stop taking them. It is like someone has their hands over her mouth, and because she is quiet, it is assumed she is okay. That is what her drugs are like. They muffle the pain. They make it quiet but it's still inside her. She is still struggling. She weighs the blister pack in her hand. She thinks if it lands in the bin she will stop taking them, and if it misses she will continue to do so. It is such a stupid thing to do and yet she is committed to it now. She thinks she is leaving it in God's hands, even though she knows that isn't how it works.

She shoots and, against the odds, she scores.

In exchange, she reaches into the drawer for one of many packets of Night Nurse. She pops two tablets out of the packet, holds them in the middle of her palm. For a moment she gazes at the two large capsules. Each one is two-toned, white and blue. She puts them both in her mouth and takes a long sip of water, swallowing them down.

She turns the light off and waits for sleep to take her.

Waiting.

Waiting.

Waiting.

And eventually, when she is asleep, it is not Kian she dreams of, but Rob Grayson. He has broken into her house in Hull, and she is there alone. When she hears the front door click shut, she knows it is him, as you often do in dreams. He follows her into the living room and she runs through the side door into the kitchen, her feet slipping on the laminate flooring in the process. He is far enough away from her that she thinks she can get away, but his voice is in her ears.

Paki.

Disgusting.

Slag.

I will tell everyone what you are.

She thought she had forgotten how thick his Yorkshire accent was, but here it is: loud and with a drawl, just like he jokes in his comedy sketches. He reaches for her, and she feels herself being pulled from side to side theatrically, like a rag doll. He then throws her against the countertop but she manages to take hold of it, rather than let her body slam into it. On the table is a kitchen knife with a green handle and she grabs it quickly, raises it in the air to protect herself, but when she turns to Rob she is too late. In his hand is a rolling pin and it is about to hammer down directly onto her skull.

She jolts awake, her body damp with sweat. The moon shines in from the crack in her curtains and she has to turn her lamp on to calm her wildly beating heart.

Her face is wet. She has been crying.

Peckham

In September, when summer draws to a close, Shirin sees Kian again. She's spent the last month assuming she would see him at every social event, only for him not to be there. They message occasionally – small talk – though the subject of them meeting again does not arise. It is ironic, therefore, that she sees him just when she has assumed she never will again.

They're at Millie's twenty-seventh birthday drinks at a bar in Peckham. A large outdoor table has been reserved, and Kian is across from Shirin, talking to a dark-haired woman with strong eyebrows and full lips. They lean in close to speak, and in their closeness Shirin feels embarrassed. Embarrassed to be here, to be glancing over at them, like it is obvious to everyone that she is looking at him.

She sits in the only empty space, next to Henry and a girl she does not know, who has her back to Shirin, in conversation with someone else. She leans past Henry, over to Millie.

'Hana told me to say sorry again that she couldn't make it,' Shirin says.

Millie waves her hand in the air. 'She's always unreliable, it's fine.'

'It's a hard time for her right now,' Shirin says, gently, so as not to seem defensive.

'It's always a hard time for her,' Henry says, a speck of spit landing on the back of her hand when he says this. Shirin can feel it there, sitting on her skin, and she hasn't got it in her to embarrass him enough to openly wipe it off. She waits a few seconds before scratching the back of her hand against the table. 'Like, how hasn't she got a job since uni? What does she do with her time?'

'Fashion is hard to get into . . .'

'We don't live in fucking la-la land,' Henry continues. 'She should get a shit job like the rest of us.'

'Speak for yourself,' Millie says. 'Shirin and I have jobs we love.'

Henry's jaw tightens and they begin a dull bicker that Shirin interrupts to ask Millie what she wants to drink. Millie points to the table; there are three full drinks there – she is fine for now.

Shirin climbs out of the bench and makes her way towards the bar. It is situated under the railway arches, the walls curved, the floor grey and unfinished. On one side are five or six long tables and benches, and they are filled with people who look just like Shirin and Millie – young people in Dr Martens and Reeboks, wearing gold hoops or cord shirts. A stark reminder that none of them are original, that they are a product of being millennials in London.

In the queue, she texts Hana.

Shirin: *Wish you were here*
Shirin: *Kian is here with a girl*

Shirin: 💀

Hana: *Damn, and you're jealous?*

Shirin: *No. It's just weird to see*

Hana: *Well, have a Ginger Bonfire for me to get through it*

A Ginger Bonfire is a cocktail that consists of gin, Cointreau, elderflower and ginger beer. Hana gets drunk off two and makes terrible decisions thereafter.

'Hey.' Shirin hears a familiar voice next to her.

She turns and it is, of course, Kian. He is wearing a dark green T-shirt, which complements his skintone well, and clear-framed glasses. He looks good.

'Hi,' she says. 'How's it going?'

'Alright,' he says. 'I'll get this one. What you having?'

She shakes her head and says it's okay, but he insists. When she tells him her cocktail choice, Shirin notices his eyebrows rise marginally. She knows what he's thinking, so she says, 'They weren't working for me.' The antidepressants.

'They weren't?'

'Maybe they were. I don't know. I can't be bothered any more.'

He nods. 'I get that.'

They reach the front of the bar, and he orders for them. She leans against the bar; it is damp from some unknown liquid and gets onto her sheer blouse.

By the bar the voices are louder, echoing around the space, and she has to lean into Kian to hear what he is saying properly. He asks her something about work, to which she waves her hand and says, 'Work is what it is.' He smiles again, though when he looks down at her she can tell he wants to press it further.

So she leans over to the bartender and asks for two Jägerbombs as well. Kian looks initially surprised and then laughs. When they arrive, Shirin puts her hand on top of his at the bar and says they must down them.

She picks up the weighty tumbler glass, with the shot glass inside. They lock eyes before they drink the shot and Red Bull in one quick motion. The effect is a sugary burning down her throat and a warming in her belly. It is pleasant and she licks her lips afterwards, relishing the bitter and sweet taste of it.

They take their drinks away from the bar, though they do not go outside, back to the rest of the group. Instead they stand to the side of the bar.

'Who's she?' Shirin asks, nodding her head towards the dark-haired girl outside. Or just in the general direction of outside. Either way, Kian knows what she means.

A sliver of a smile traces his lips, which he touches with his thumb, his eyes following her gaze. 'Salma. She's on my course.'

'Are you guys dating? You'd make a cute couple, if you are.' The words come out so easily that she thinks if they were not her own and she were to hear them, she would believe them. They are also incredibly familiar, though she cannot tell why. It is not jealousy, she thinks, but something indescribable. Kian is a figment of her past, someone she thought she'd never see again. She shouldn't be seeing him around unannounced now, or the women he's dating. It is like seeing Christmas decorations in spring. It isn't right.

He raises both eyebrows. 'I wouldn't say dating.'

An image of them having sex flashes before her eyes and that's even worse.

'Cool,' she says, biting the side of her mouth lightly, repeatedly, to divert her attention elsewhere. She picks up her cocktail from the bar and takes a long sip. It is sweet and juice-like. That's why Hana likes it; it's so tasty you forget the alcohol content.

'Cool?' he repeats. His eyes have a glassy look and he is smiling, which makes her smile – and that is how she knows she is already on her way to intoxication.

'Well, she's beautiful and you're very good-looking, so yes, I'm happy for you, whatever you're doing.'

'You think I'm good-looking? That's news to me.' He sips his beer, and when he puts his drink down, his lips are glossy.

'I mean,' she says, 'I think you know you are. Look at the glasses you're wearing. Very few people can pull them off naturally, without looking like they're trying too hard.'

The tops of Kian's ears are pink and this gives her satisfaction – like, Yes, let's both be embarrassed.

He rolls his eyes. 'So what you're saying is: you don't like my glasses? Thank you for humbling me.'

'No, I do like them. They suit you. You look good.'

Neither of them says anything for a moment. They just look at each other. Until Henry bounds over and puts his arms around their shoulders, jolting them both into reality.

'What are you both talking about?' he asks, his beer-breath entering Shirin's space.

'Fashion,' Kian says at the same time as Shirin says, 'Nothing.'

They all go back to Millie's house. It's getting darker earlier, which is jarring in comparison with summer's long evenings, but she is pissed, so barely notices.

Millie puts 'Wrecking Ball' by Miley Cyrus on her Bluetooth speakers, and Henry groans that he wants proper music on, but the women in the group insist that no, this is important. The living room is a haze of cigarette smoke, and flashing lights from the mini disco-ball Millie whipped out from the storage cupboard (at whose appearance they all yelled in jubilation).

She is conscious of Kian and Salma. Of the way Salma leant into him at the bar when they returned to their seats. Of the way, when they walked back to Millie's, they hung back together, to walk separately. And of the way they are now outside in the garden together, while she is singing along badly to the music with Millie – enjoying herself, but a small part of her is outside, with them both. Like most times in life, Shirin cannot be fully present in the moment; there is always something niggling away in her mind.

It is at the end of the fourth Miley song that Henry interjects, putting on Travis Scott. Shirin rolls her eyes, staggering to the sofa and plopping herself down onto it. It is only when she is sitting down that she realises how drunk she is. Sitting still, everything around her is moving. She closes her eyes, but she can still sense that everything is moving, and that just makes it worse. She liked the way it felt to drink, that with drunkenness anything she felt towards her work, her life, faded away. But now she is left with regret.

She staggers towards the downstairs toilet and, once inside, sits on the floor, head between her legs. It is enjoyable, sitting on the floor. Until there is a tap on the door. Then she scrambles up, washes her hands and leaves. The girl Jasper is seeing stands before her, and she gives Shirin a polite nod before going into the bathroom.

Back in the living room, it is only Henry, Millie, Jasper and Kian left. Shirin is not sure how long she has been in the bathroom for, but the party is decidedly drawing to a close. She cannot see Salma. Then she looks back at Kian, who is looking at her too, and rather than look away, he continues to gaze at her. She makes her way to the kitchen to get herself a glass of water, and Millie laughs when Shirin stumbles.

She fills a glass with water, and the tap water runs between the glass and her hand. It is soothing against her skin. She closes her eyes and leans her body against the countertop. In the near distance, she hears Kian asking if she's okay.

'I'm fine,' she says, the tap still running, the drink overflowing.

Kian reaches across to turn it off, and it's the closest she's been to him. She lets herself lean into him, be supported by him. In the process she inhales his scent too. It's more than pleasant.

'Do you wanna get some fresh air?' he asks.

'Okay,' she slurs.

Sara Jafari

He places his hand lightly on her waist and guides her out of the room, through the sliding doors and out into the garden. He pulls up a chair, which she sits on. The plastic is cool against her legs. He has brought the glass with him and lifts it to her lips for her to drink. Shirin wants to make a joke that she's not an invalid, but as she struggles to sit up straight, she concedes that she probably does need some assistance.

After she takes a sip, he pulls a chair to sit opposite her, clutching the glass in his hands. 'Just focus on breathing,' he says.

'This is embarrassing. I didn't even drink that much.'

'It's probably because you haven't drunk for a while. It happens to the best of us – don't worry.' He strokes her back briefly and it is calming. It is exactly what she needs and when he stops, she wants to tell him to continue.

'Where did Salma go?' she asks.

'Home,' he says.

'Why didn't you go with her?'

Her vision is hazy, but she can hear Kian chuckle. 'Because I wanted to stay.'

'The party is pretty much over now, anyways.'

He puts the glass of water down on the floor and leans forward, his hands on his knees. 'Well, we're still here.'

'I have a lot of regret, you know,' she says, words coming out thick and fast. 'The past ten years I've thought about you a lot. I even wrote you a message a few years ago, to say I miss you and I'm sorry, but I never sent it. I was too scared you'd tell me to fuck off – or, worse, that you'd say nothing.'

'Shirin,' Kian says softly. 'You don't have to—'

'But I want to,' she interrupts. 'You said I was special to you. Did you mean it?'

He breathes out deeply. 'You're drunk. Let's not talk about this, not now.'

'I want to though.' She sits straighter and leans forward. 'It feels important.'

'Important how?' he says, his eyes dark, though the sides of his mouth are perked up. He has such a defined Cupid bow and Shirin finds herself staring at it now, until she realises he's asked her a question.

She shrugs, intending the movement to be casual, but she overdoes it. 'I just want you to know, you were special to me too.'

'Shirin ...'

They lock eyes, and she notices his flicker briefly down to her own lips, before looking back up to her eyes.

'If I asked you to kiss me right now,' she begins quietly, 'would you?'

Kian chuckles again, clears his throat and looks away. 'You're drunk. You don't mean any of this.'

'But what if I did?'

'If you weren't drunk, then yeah, I would,' he says.

Her heart is beating quickly now, and her mouth is dry. Hearing these words, knowing for certain what she had suspected, and it being exactly what she wants right now, makes her say, 'I want you to kiss me, Kian.'

They lean in slowly, inch by inch, at the same time, their faces so close to each other that their breaths mingle together.

'When you're not drunk,' he breathes.

She shakes her head. 'But if I'm not drunk I won't let myself have this.'

He moves his head back then, eyebrows cast together in a frown. 'What do you mean?'

Millie comes out to the garden, half whispering, half shouting that they need to leave before her housemate, the live-in landlady, comes home in ten minutes.

The boldness and closeness that Shirin felt in that moment slips away, a heaviness instantly settling in her heart. Their conversation is not resumed.

Wetherby Prison

Wetherby Young Offender Institution was an hour away. For the car ride, Kian's mum brought a flask of chai, with three porcelain cups that clanked against each other in a plastic bag. When she asked if he wanted any, a packet of ginger biscuits also in hand, Kian shook his head. The thought of consuming anything right then was unpleasant and unfathomable. His stomach was in knots. It was the first time he had been to visit his brother since he had been sent away.

He hadn't been yet on purpose. When his parents had asked why he didn't want to come, he'd given them feeble excuses, like that he had already planned to play football with his friends Koyer, Ahmed and Teddy. That, without him, they wouldn't be able to play against another team. Or that he'd forgotten he had homework to do that would take him all day. They'd never pushed, but he'd seen the confusion in the furrow of their brows. They couldn't understand why Kian didn't want to see his best friend – the person who'd defended him and been sent down because of it.

Breathe.

When they pulled into the car park outside the prison he wasn't sure what he'd expected, but it wasn't what stood before

145

him. The building was more depressing in its mundanity than he'd thought it would be, not helped by the grey cloud-filled sky looming over it. The tall barbed-wired fences were a grim reminder of the purpose of the place they were walking towards.

'They'll do a search,' his mum said, clutching her bag to her front, looking ahead as they walked towards the entrance. 'Just let them do it. Your dad tried to argue with them one time and it didn't go well.' Kian's father was walking ahead and turned round at this. He was sure his dad had more grey hair at his temples now, contrasting with his black hair. His dad frowned and opened his mouth to argue his point. 'They wanted me to take my trousers off – I didn't see them do that to anyone else!'

Kian looked from his mum to his dad, at first mildly amused, but then with a sense of dread that they could do that to him, too.

'Payam, not now,' his mum said, both gentle and firm. She turned to Kian with a softened expression. 'It'll be fine, don't worry, azizam.'

She ran her fingers through his hair and he moved away from her, muttering, 'Stop it.'

When they arrived at the reception they signed in and gave their passports to the receptionist to check. They put their belongings in a nearby locker. The guards were a mixture of races, which surprised Kian, because from the TV shows his mum watched, like *Bad Girls*, they were always white and mean-looking.

Kian and his parents were escorted to another room, where they were searched. They lightly patted his mum, but asked Kian and his dad to take off their jackets and shoes, and then their bodies were tapped with a roughness. It was like going through airport security. Whenever they went away, Kian, his dad and his brother were always asked to move to the side for a deeper search. It was because they were Middle Eastern. He would watch white families passing them by, not being violated by airport security, not being treated like criminals because of their race.

After they were searched, they were taken into a room with other visitors and sat in their assigned seats at the back. The visitor room was akin to a hospital waiting room. The seats they sat on were faux leather, grey and bulky, curved at the back, with no armrest. His mum sat in the middle, between Kian and his dad. There was a scuffed, orange coffee table in front of them, and on the other side of the table was a similar chair to the ones they were sitting on but this one was orange. There was no decoration, and he wondered whether this was to make the experience more depressing or whether it was so that the prisoners couldn't use something as a weapon.

Looking around, Kian saw a blonde woman in her thirties with a young child on her lap to one side of him, and two Asian men who must have been in their early twenties to the other side. Directly across from them was an elderly couple. Despite their differences, he could see in all their faces a desperate kind of hope. It was the kind of expression that made him sad – like they were trying to be positive in the midst of a miserable situation. He saw so much of himself in it, and hadn't realised that that was what he looked like, until he saw how obvious it was in others.

After a few minutes the prisoners flooded into the room. Kian shifted in his seat, before looking at his parents. His mum had her hands clasped tightly together, the tops of her fingers pink. His dad looked blankly ahead. He wanted them to say something, break the ice, make the moment less tense, but instead it dragged on.

Mehdi arrived in a blur. He was escorted by a police officer. At first Kian didn't recognise his brother. It hadn't been that long – just over a month – but Mehdi had the beginnings of a beard now and was visibly slimmer. He wore a baggy grey cotton sweatshirt and jogging bottoms, the same as all the other inmates who'd come out for their visits. He had shaved a slash in his left eyebrow, which was the first thing Kian noticed as Mehdi drew closer. His brother broke into a smile on seeing Kian, and he couldn't help his own grin in return.

'K,' Mehdi said.

Kian half rose, but his mum put her hand on his thigh to push him back down. He remembered one of the rules was that they should remain seated, that they couldn't hug. He plopped himself back down.

There was small talk, as his mum and dad asked Mehdi how he was doing, whether there was anything he needed, whether he had received the books and clothing he had requested. Mehdi barely read, so Kian was surprised when he'd asked his mum on the phone if she could get him Malcolm X's biography. His mum had said he was taking Islam more seriously in prison. It wasn't that Mehdi hadn't been religious before. The whole family were Muslim, though they didn't really practise it. The only time Kian had seen Mehdi pray was at their uncle's funeral, when everyone had their heads bowed down as he was lowered into the coffin. Some of the people Mehdi had hung out with in the outside world had said things like 'Inshallah' and 'Mashallah', but Kian was pretty sure a few were drug dealers, which seemed at odds with their religion.

Kian struggled to look his brother in the eye. Their dad and mum asked them what they wanted from the vending machine, and Mehdi requested a KitKat and a Twix almost immediately. Kian shook his head and said he wasn't hungry. He knew his parents were leaving them both alone because they thought it would be what they wanted. But it wasn't what Kian wanted. He felt his heart quickening, his body clammy and cold. He wanted to get out of there.

'You're quiet,' Mehdi said.

Kian looked up then, into his brother's eyes, finally. There was a softness in them, a reminder that this was Mehdi, the boy he'd grown up playing *Teenage Mutant Ninja Turtles* with, and who he loved. Whose life Kian had aided in fucking up.

Breathe.

'What's it like in here?' Kian asked.

Mehdi shrugged. 'It is what it is.' Smiled, but it didn't show in his eyes. Sadness permeated there and it was a devastating sight. Like Kian's worst fears were confirmed: that his brother was miserable because of him.

Their parents returned. His dad slid the chocolate bars over to Mehdi, who received them hungrily.

'You've been learning how to pray, haven't you?' his mum said, to bring the dead conversation to life.

Kian struggled to focus on the people around him, his eyes downcast, looking at the shiny navy fabric of his trackie bottoms.

'Yeah, I've been given time to think. There's an iman who comes here every week. It's pretty chill,' Mehdi said in a muffled voice, his mouth half full.

The knot in Kian's stomach had travelled up to his throat.

'You've lost weight,' Mum said to Mehdi, frowning.

'Do they not feed you in there or something?' Dad said, looking like he was ready to complain.

Mehdi laughed, waved his hand in the air. 'I told you before, man, the food here is shit. They won't get us halal meat, so we just eat veg and mash.'

'But you always ate non-halal food at home,' Kian blurted out. He didn't understand. It hadn't been that long. He could remember, not long ago, Mehdi devouring Big Macs, never once uttering the word 'halal'.

'Yeah, but that was before. I'm changed now.'

Kian leant back in his chair and let his mum lead the conversation. Mehdi was changed now. There was so much about him Kian no longer knew – and, sitting across from him, it felt like their connection was gone. He used to always know what his brother was thinking, but now it was different. While Mehdi spoke to their mum, Kian searched his face. He wanted to see if Mehdi blamed him, like he blamed himself for all this mess. How could he not?

Near the end of their visit, a boy at the other end of the room laughed a bit too hard and was told to quieten down.

He told the officer to 'shut the fuck up' and things turned sour. He was handcuffed and taken out, shouting to his visitor that the officers were 'pussies' and that he wasn't scared of them.

Mehdi leant in. 'That guy killed his mum. He's fucked up.'

Kian's mouth opened involuntarily. 'What? Seriously?'

Mehdi nodded. 'Not okay up here,' and he pointed to his head.

'And he's in here with you? Aren't you scared?'

Mehdi's expression was sharp and they locked eyes. 'No, obviously not. I don't get scared, K. I could take him.'

'Enough of that,' Dad interjected. 'You don't need to "take" anyone. Don't say that.'

Mehdi continued to hold Kian's eyes. It was like he was telling him something. That Dad knew nothing, that he *did* need to take people on. That was his life now.

Because of me. Fuck.

Spinning in Kian's mind was the realisation that he had hoped, on seeing his brother, he would gather evidence that juvie wasn't so bad, that his brother was doing okay. But instead his worst fear had been confirmed. Mehdi was in there with murderers. Mehdi had to fight people in there to survive. Mehdi had changed now. And it was all because of Kian. If he had handled himself differently, Mehdi would never have stepped in and made things so much worse.

Kian wasn't sure if he could ever make things good again – or if he could ever forgive himself.

White Tears

Now

The Hoffman non-fiction team is seated in the largest meeting room, a space that is overbearingly corporate and rarely used. In the corner is a Nespresso machine that very few people know how to work, with assortments of individually wrapped biscuits that have gathered dust. Shirin thinks back to her younger self and wonders what she would think if she could see herself now. She might be proud – that is, if she could only see her future, and not hear the conversation going on around her right now.

It is not discussions about diversity and inclusion that Shirin has developed an aversion to, it is how often they are spoken about with little follow-through. It is the assumption that the few people of colour in a team should speak up about a company's issues – and provide solutions – even though they are rarely listened to, because they are all assistants. It is the phrase *We need to do better*, which people have adopted to cop out of actually doing better. It is the repeated conversations about the senior team being painfully middle-class and white, and then the company repeatedly hiring more white middle-class staff in senior positions (and, in turn, not promoting junior staff of colour).

Perhaps she might not have let herself get wound up by all of this if it wasn't for the fact that Florence is now the lead on Shirin's project with Abigail Underwood. At the acquisitions meeting for Abigail's book, Florence, with her gratingly posh voice, dominated the meeting. It didn't help that at the start of it, the MD – Allegra – forgot Shirin's name. She said, 'Welcome, Florence,' paused for three beats, looked down at her piece of paper, and then said, 'and Shirin.' Shirin and Florence are now working together to put in an offer to Abigail's agent, though Shirin does most of the work, while Florence is congratulated by their managers.

There are twenty people sitting around the table now. Shirin is next to Mariam, and they exchange glances as Allegra speaks. She tells the team that the results of their employee and consumer survey suggest that Hoffman is not a diverse or inclusive publisher.

As Allegra speaks she has a grim look on her face, as though the fact that the non-fiction team has not published a book by a non-white author for more than two years now is news to her; as though their attempts to fix the issue by asking white authors to write about Black British history is not part of the problem. It is strange to Shirin how senior team members act as though they are not aware of the issues in their company, when it is their literal job to oversee everything.

'Does anyone have any suggestions about what we could be doing better? Remember, this is a safe space,' Allegra says.

Covertly, eyes are cast towards Shirin and Mariam. They are the only people of colour seated at the table. It is funny how their input is so much less valuable when talking about a potential acquisition, which is what they are paid to offer input on, rather than about issues of diversity and inclusion in the workplace.

Silence.

Shirin taps her leg with her forefinger.

One.

Two.

Three.

Four.

Five.

Her gaze remains on the grey table, at a stray hair there. It is blonde and mid-length, with a slight curl in the middle. It could belong to any one of her colleagues really.

Six.

Seven.

Eight.

Nine.

Ten.

'Our author base could be more diverse,' an editor named Cassie says. 'We definitely don't have enough LGBTQ authors.'

'Or people from working-class backgrounds,' one Northern marketer adds.

'And we are doing our best trying to acquire BAME authors, they're just hard to find. But for representation, we should show different types of people, different col—' Cassie stumbles on her words, smiles as though she is trying very hard.

Everyone gives her patient, encouraging smiles back. Shirin keeps her gaze on the table.

'Different races, ethnicities, I mean – BAME people. Or people of colour.'

Shirin brings her eyes up and sees Cassie's face is pink now. The conversation swiftly moves away from her faux pas and on to another one.

'We're meant to be following trends and we're missing such a big one,' a publicity director named Jessica says. 'We need to move quicker with our D&I goals to get ahead of other publishers.'

Trends.

Shirin feels her heart quickening and grips her hands together. The conversation swiftly moves along, and she cannot help but wonder how no one in that room, apart from Mariam, whose jaw is also tight throughout the conversation, sees that calling their lived experiences a trend is desperately insulting.

She looks to Florence, who is watching with an impassive look on her face, and it is infuriating, because she *can* be impassive, whereas Shirin is rendered deeply uncomfortable – like she wants to escape her own body – in her attempts to be detached from the conversation. The conversation about people like her.

'But,' Lilian begins, 'we still need to remember our target audience and retailers, and who is actually buying our books. It's difficult to get the balance right.' The more senior members of staff make murmurs of agreement.

It takes Shirin a moment to piece together the implications of such a statement – that it is only white people who read, who deserve to see themselves in books.

'I would like to say something,' Mariam says next to Shirin, her voice so clear and sharp that it startles her. 'If this is a safe space to speak.'

Allegra nods, an unnaturally encouraging smile plastered onto her face.

'Well, I couldn't help but notice diversity has been referred to as a trend. I've heard other people say this before, too. I think this messaging is a bit of an issue, if I'm allowed to be honest here. We're talking about people, when we speak about diversity and inclusion. About including everyone and being representative of the society we live in. None of this is a trend that can come and go. We've always been here – and will continue to be here.' Mariam is putting on her closest attempt at a posh accent. She often does this in large meetings. Shirin does too. 'Also, to say people of colour are not readers is a bit ... it feels a bit off to me. I'm obviously a massive reader – and yeah, I'm Palestinian, so it's not like I can speak for every brown or Black person, but it just seems like too broad a statement, which I think could be damaging.'

Jessica in particular looks appalled, though at herself or at Mariam is not clear. Her blue eyes suddenly fill. She tucks her hair behind her ears quickly, before responding.

'I'm sorry, Mariam, I didn't mean to offend anyone. God, that was awful of me, wasn't it? I don't really know what to say ...' Jessica falters, her eyes fully filling now with tears that threaten to spill at a moment's notice.

The woman next to Jessica taps her on the shoulder. 'It's okay,' she says softly. 'We're all learning.'

Shirin looks to Mariam, whose eyes are also red, but sympathetic eyes are on Jessica, so no one but Shirin notices. 'You okay?' Shirin mouths to her.

Mariam shakes her head, as though to say, *Leave it*, not wanting attention.

Shirin does not know what to do. She is debating saying something, and being seen to pile onto Jessica, or not saying anything, and thereby not supporting Mariam, when she is the only person with sense in the room. She feels a rush of adrenaline, and simultaneously her throat tightening, and she knows it is ridiculous to be so afraid of being heard, but she is terrified.

She finally opens her mouth to speak just as Allegra says, 'Indeed, we are all learning. Thank you, Mariam, for being honest with us. I think we don't quite mean it in the way you've interpreted. But I do apologise if something that has been said today has offended you. It can be difficult to get these things right, and mistakes will be made, but of course you know all our intentions here are good, and this is a safe space to explore ways to be better.'

Shirin sees that Mariam's gaze is now down at the table, presumably at the stray blonde hair. The conversation ticks along elsewhere. The moment to speak up passes her by and Shirin is left spent, feeling both cowardly and pathetic.

'I should have backed you up,' Shirin says later. They are in the stationery cupboard.

Mariam is deflated, like a shrivelled balloon. Shirin knows her own expression is akin to Mariam's, though mingled with remorse.

'Nah,' Mariam says. She picks up one of the red pens from a multipack cardboard box. As she speaks, she clicks the pen on and off repeatedly. 'It shouldn't have to be us versus them. I just feel stupid, thinking they'd listen.'

Shirin considers this, but even so, she feels she should have said something. She would have liked to have made Mariam feel less alone, to take a stand for something she believes in too. There is something dirty that comes with being a bystander.

'I'm sorry anyway,' she says.

'Shirin, you have nothing to apologise for.'

'You did really well, you know. Like, it's not easy to speak up in a group that big, and you said what needed to be said. That's brave.'

Mariam's lips curl up in a very small smile. She shrugs, but they both know that in a corporate job what she did was really big. Speaking up for yourself – for people like yourself – is big. Shirin wonders at the emotional labour of her job. It is a strange industry, publishing, in which you bare your soul because you care so much for your readers, for the power of words, but the lines become blurred between what should and should not be acceptable in a job. How much you care about things that are not life or death, but are treated as such.

Back at her desk, she is still deflated and unseasonably sweaty. She never used to be like this. She remembers at university overcoming her inwardness, with the help of Hana, and being confident, finally feeling as though what she had to say mattered. Now, though, she has returned to her shell and finds herself still struggling to speak in large meetings, like she is fearful of being heard, of people looking at her. Like she's back at school and, to get by, it's best to be invisible. Often what she wants to say becomes stuck in her throat, her heart beating rapidly at all the potential outcomes.

She looks at her phone, at the message Kian sent her days ago, asking her how she was feeling after Millie's drinks last week. She hasn't opened the message until now, fearful of the things she said to him, how candid she was. She almost replies, but stops herself; her mind is too busy and she cannot allow herself to go there right now.

Instead she continues with her work, and goes through her endless emails. She has one from two minutes ago, with no subject, from a colleague. She opens it: *You spoke so brilliantly and eloquently earlier. I just wanted to let you know x*

Shirin furrows her brows and does not respond, does not move for a moment. She is thinking: Surely not, *surely* ...

Another message comes in almost instantly: *Sorry, I just realised I emailed the wrong person. Ignore this!*

Mariam looks nothing like her, is five-foot-ten, Palestinian, and wears a hijab. Shirin is five-foot-three, Iranian, and her hair is bleached blonde.

Shirin promptly forwards the email to Mariam.

Mariam replies: *LOL.*

Shirin shrugs it off as being one of those things, but for the rest of the day she cannot stop thinking about how, to some people, if you're not white you're all the same.

A Charitable Comedian

It is two days later and Shirin is on the Central line with Mariam. They have just had dinner at a pancake restaurant in Soho. The decor was minimal and chic, with hiked-up prices. And as with most gimmick restaurants, the food was mediocre, though they both said in the restaurant that they enjoyed it. They went, in part, to soothe their wounds after what happened in the Diversity and Inclusion meeting.

Shirin had attempted to recount the events of the meeting to Hana, an outsider in publishing. Though what had happened had sounded so inconsequential out loud. 'They gaslit us,' she had said to Hana, in a high-pitched tone, to get her point across. She had found herself wanting to exaggerate, to really hammer home how it had affected her.

'Wow, that sounds rough,' Hana had said.

'Like, Mariam was nearly in tears,' Shirin had continued. The words aloud had sounded dramatic, like Mariam and Shirin were being childish, and though Hana hadn't said so, Shirin could tell the gravity of the moment was not being fully registered. She'd realised then that it's only through experiencing the specific publishing micro-aggressions that one can truly understand them and their capacity to wound.

The windows between the carriages are open, and the Tube shrieks as it moves, getting increasingly intolerable. They are unable to talk due to the noise, so Mariam shuts her eyes, her hands rested on her lap, like she is about to sleep.

Shirin looks across from her and sees someone holding open a newspaper. There is a picture of Rob Grayson. Atop the picture is the headline:

ROB GRAYSON DONATES ALL PROCEEDS FROM UPCOMING SHOW TO HOMELESS CHARITY

She stares at the page, the words in the article too small to read, though she squints to try and make them out anyway. When the person across from her gets off, he leaves the newspaper behind. She reaches for it, even though she knows it will only anger her.

The piece goes into great detail about Rob's charitable acts, mainly tackling homelessness and poverty. He is called an 'inspiration' and his upbringing as a working-class boy from Hull, who knows what it's like to struggle financially, is mentioned, as it always is. The charitable work he is doing is good and worthy, but that doesn't make him a good person, not like the article would want the reader to believe.

The piece quotes Rob saying, 'Britain needs to help their own people. The government have failed so many rough sleepers and families living in poverty, and I urge everyone to donate and do their bit.' There is no mention of his comments online about England letting in too many refugees, or of his sketch that laughed at migrants dying in waters as they attempted to flee their countries. Of course not.

Shirin nudges Mariam, who jolts into alertness and looks down at the paper in her hands. 'Does this sound racist to you?' Shirin shouts over the screeching train tracks. She angles the newspaper so Mariam can better see what she is referring to.

It takes her a moment to read the piece, and then Mariam says, 'Maybe? I mean, he is racist, so he probably does mean "own people" to mean white people, so yeah. Are we surprised?' She takes the newspaper from Shirin's hand, folds it and places it on the empty seat next to her. 'I love how he's being lorded as a man of the people. He's rich – he gets paid for one show what we'd only dream to get in a year.'

Shirin thinks: If only Mariam knew everything. If she's outraged as an onlooker at Rob's fandom despite the vitriol he spews, imagine if she knew what he did to Shirin and Kian all those years ago. She always thought the bullies and racists from school would grow up to be unsuccessful and pathetic – like Jordan, who's now in prison – not celebrities who continue their hate speech on a public scale, who have adoring fans and an abundance of wealth. It's like with every passing day he's becoming bigger and bigger, and she is forced to just accept that she will see his face around – and thereby forever be confronted with a time, a moment, she wants so desperately to forget. But she can't. That is, unfortunately, not how life works. So she finally replies to Kian's message.

*

If you'd told Shirin a year ago that Kian Rahimi would be sitting in her damp living room drinking a cup of tea from her *Kiki's Delivery Service* mug, she would not have believed it. But here he is. She apologises that the room is ugly, and cold, and he says it's neither, and not to be silly.

They only have one sofa. It is a strange maroon colour and faux-leather. When Shirin first moved in she attempted to make it cosier by adding a cream fleece blanket on the seat cushions. Her brain is whizzing between different things, because she is not sure how it got to this – how Kian ended up at her flat at 9 p.m. on a Thursday.

He removes the beanie atop his head and shrugs out of his borg jacket, which he folds and places on the arm of the chair. There is something so satisfying in how well he dresses now. She is superficial in this way.

'I'm sorry if I seemed dramatic in my text,' she says to him.

His lips curve marginally at the sides. 'You didn't seem dramatic.' He puts the mug down by his feet, without drinking it. He turns to her and leans a little closer. 'I was surprised you texted me though. You've been ghosting me since Millie's birthday.'

Shirin lets out a little light-hearted gasp at this. 'I wouldn't say ghosting ...'

'Okay, you didn't reply to my message. Is that better?'

'I just said things I shouldn't have. I was drunk.'

'I gathered that,' he says. 'It's okay. I get it.'

'You do?'

He nods. 'I think we always suited being friends.'

'Really?' The conversation is not going in the direction she hoped it would, but she has only herself to blame. 'And that's why you came round then, when I said I was upset about Rob – because we're friends?'

She notices the way his eyes go doe-like and less focused, how he bites his bottom lip. She notices this and so she isn't expecting him to say, 'Yeah, exactly that. I was heading east anyway when you messaged, so popping round was no bother.'

'You were?'

'Yeah, Salma lives round here.'

'Oh,' she says. 'You're still seeing each other then?'

'We're exclusive now, yeah.'

She nods. It has only been a week. Of course their relationship escalated that quickly. 'I bet you have loads in common,' she says. 'Lots of art chat.'

He leans back, scratches his forehead and lets out a long breath. Like he is relieved he has told her. Like he thought she'd be upset or something. 'I forgot how much you deflect sometimes,' he muses.

She looks at him like he has shoved her. 'I don't deflect.'

'You do – you're allowed to be upset about Rob. It's shit. But come on, you don't care about Salma. It's obvious you don't like her.'

'I like Salma.'

'She said you were giving her bitchy looks at Millie's,' Kian says, though he is smiling, while she is aghast.

'I definitely wasn't. It's just my face.' He does not look convinced. 'I have resting bitch face. You know this.'

'I mean, I did tell her that.'

'Good. And why aren't you annoyed about Rob? You're so chill about it all the time. I don't get it.'

'I love how you said we can't talk about school any more, and yet here we are again.'

'I created the rule, I can break it,' she retorts.

He sighs. 'Well, I'm *not* chill about it, Shirin. I fucking hate him.' He lets out a short, sombre laugh. 'You know, a few years ago after a night out in Manchester I saw his face on a poster. Then I turned the corner and there were at least twenty of them, all in a row, advertising one of his shite shows. I ripped them off, one by one. I'm pissed off too, but sadly terrible people will continue to be successful and we have to make our peace with it.'

Shirin's phone buzzes and she sees it is her dad. She rejects the call. He rings again, this time requesting to FaceTime. He only calls when he wants something. When he wants a chat about his mental health. Or how he misses her mum. Or when he wants her to order something for him online. There is something building within her. It happens often, like she is a glass and each issue in her life fills her up, and now she is at risk of overflowing. Though she's not sure why she feels this way. She knows she needs to get over seeing Rob everywhere. But it's not just that – it's that nothing about life in her twenties is how she imagined it would be. She is unhappy and does not know how to make herself happy. All she does is make herself feel worse.

'It's my dad,' she explains.

'He's still being useless?' Kian says, even though she hasn't told him about her dad recently. He remembers from when they were younger and she would complain about her parents. Though Shirin and Kian's dynamic has changed now. When she was younger she had so much energy, would give him advice with such confidence, and now it is like the life in her has gone.

'Nothing new,' she says, though she feels her eyes tearing up; even as she tries to laugh it off, it comes out shaky and strange.

Kian is looking down at her intently, trying to catch her eye. 'Do you speak to your mum much?'

She doesn't answer because she doesn't want to cry. She doesn't want to be tipped over the edge, though she hasn't realised until now that the topic of her family has the ability to do so. Instead of replying she looks up at him, pushes her lips downwards in a *what do you think?* expression.

Her dad tries to call her again, and she mutters something like *fuck off*, before throwing her phone across the room. The outburst is unexpected, but she is shaking and has the urge to scream and break something.

Kian's arms are around her now, tight and warm. Her face is pressed against his chest and she is paralysed, stock-still. His jumper is scratchy against her face, but she does not move. 'It's okay,' he whispers, and her face is wet. She is crying and she isn't sure when or how that happened. 'You don't need to be strong all the time,' he says, still holding her. 'Let it out.'

But Shirin's thinking, That's the whole problem. She is not strong enough. She is not enough.

MSN

Then

It began with an MSN message.

Shirin had been skiving off the occasional class with Kian for a month now. Sometimes they would talk about deep things, like their family, and sometimes they wouldn't say much at all. They listened to songs on their phones, with the volume as high as they could get it, and they would sit either in the fields near school or in the woods by Kian's house. One time Kian had brought a joint with him, which after much deliberation they'd smoked. They hadn't felt any effects for ages and Kian had told her to wait, that it was meant to take time to kick in. After an hour Shirin had asked him where he'd got it from, and he'd said he'd found it in his brother's drawer, underneath some textbooks. It was probably years old, off by now, she'd told him, half scolding, half laughing. He'd been embarrassed, his cheeks pink at the top, and that had made it harder not to properly belly-laugh.

It was a drizzly autumn evening when Rob Grayson messaged her. She did a double-take when his name popped up on her screen, convinced it must be a mistake. While Rob was not overt in his harassing of Shirin, unlike Jordan, he was not a measly bystander like Tom. He laughed at Jordan's insults and egged him on. He was known around the school for being a joker, so while Jordan wasn't particularly well liked, Rob was.

At the start of the year, in German, Jordan and Rob had both sniggered loudly, over at the table next to her. She'd thought she was being irrational, big-headed even, to think whatever they were laughing at was related to her. That was until she'd heard them say 'hairy' and had seen they were pointing to her fingers. They were slight, fine hairs, though dark. It grew quickly, the hair dark and thick against her light skin – perhaps the worst combination for a self-conscious hairy person. Following the incident she'd shaved the hair off using one of her dad's multipack razors. It had grown back days later into stubborn stubble, much worse than before.

Rob_93: hey – do you know if we have any german homework?

She replied that they did and told him they needed to revise for a test next week, expecting the conversation to end swiftly there.

Rob_93: what you doing?
Shirin_x_x: nothing
Shirin_x_x: why?
Rob_93: I feel bad about what Jordan said to you today. It was out of order.

Jordan had shouted 'paki' at her when she'd walked past him to go to her class. There had been crowds of students in the corridor, so she hadn't seen him say it, but she knew his voice. It obviously hadn't been the first time, though she'd still had a little cry on the walk home from school when she was alone. She had almost forgotten about it, though there had been an emptiness inside her for the rest of the evening, like she was now hollow. It was often like that after someone had called her a name. She wanted to brush it off, so she pretended to do so, but when she was alone, inadequacy engulfed her. She felt so painfully like she wasn't worth anything, unlike her friends; unlike Phoebe, whom everyone liked and who didn't have hairy fingers that people laughed at.

Shirin_x_x: why does he hate me so much?
Rob_93: idk
Rob_93: don't tell anyone I said this but he's having a hard time atm. His parents are divorcing and he's just pissed off at everyone tbh

She didn't reply. It was hard to have sympathy for someone who made your life a misery, especially when their reason was as feeble as his. Her parents were constantly fighting. She sometimes wondered not only if they loved each other but if they loved her. None of that meant she'd ever go out and intentionally hurt someone.

Rob_93: are you going out with Kian?
Shirin_x_x: no

Shirin_x_x: why would you even ask that?
Rob_93: i saw you both skiving off one time so jw
Shirin_x_x: well no, we aren't
Rob_93: good ;)
Shirin_x_x: good?
Rob_93: yeh, cos i think ur alright

It was the most bizarre message she had ever received. And she had been in many a strange MSN group chat with Phoebe and boys from around the world.

She didn't tell anyone what Rob had said because she didn't want to embarrass him. Like someone saying they thought she was 'alright' was something to be embarrassed about. They continued messaging sporadically for the rest of the month. What she didn't know about Rob was how passionate he was about performing arts. He went to Stagecoach every summer. She knew he did drama because they were in the same drama class, but she hadn't realised that he wanted to be a performer. It made sense though; he always made everyone laugh, even when the script they were reciting wasn't that funny. He just had a way about him.

Eventually he told her about his family, how his dad had left them when he was eleven and he hadn't seen him since. He called sometimes, he said, from Tenerife – where he lived now – but it wasn't the same. She never told him about her own family. Her gut knew there was something off, and she only partly listened to it. She wished she'd trusted herself more and had ended it in that moment. But she had misunderstood the feeling in her gut for her aversion to new things – and change – such as being desired and talking to boys. She really thought she was uncomfortable in a good way.

The next weekend Phoebe had invited Shirin and their friend Carmen to her house for tea. Their house was a semi-detached, down a wholesome cul-de-sac, different from Shirin's house, which was bigger, though on a main road with cars speeding past day and night. Phoebe had parents who seemed happy to be together, which was a strange sight to see. They gave each other pecks on the cheek when they said goodbye, and Shirin couldn't remember a time when her parents had done that. She imagined being part of Phoebe's family must be nice: less anxiety-inducing and more comforting.

Carmen was more Phoebe's friend than Shirin's, though they had known each other for years. They sometimes did things without Phoebe, but that was rare; Phoebe held them together. Carmen was much more focused on boys than Shirin and had a way about her that made Shirin feel bad about herself. She casually bragged about things Shirin didn't care about, but she did it in such a way that made Shirin start to care about them. She compared herself to Carmen in these moments. Carmen was desired by the boys in their school – and the opposite sex in general. Whenever they went to town on the weekend and wandered the shopping centres, boys – and grown men – would stop and ask for her number. If this ever happened to Shirin or Phoebe, they would stutter and say they had to go. But Carmen was so used to it that she weighed the boys up, would have conversations with them before deciding if she wanted to hand over her number. She wasn't necessarily street-smart, though, and they would have to drag her away from men who were too old for her, who might not realise she was only fifteen – or maybe they did know and that was even worse.

Everyone fancied Carmen, and that was fine, but she was not gracious about it, and Shirin hated that she thought such things, that she thought Carmen even needed to be gracious, because would she herself be, if she got that much attention?

In front of them now, in Phoebe's front room, was an extra-large Margherita pizza, noodles, soggy chips and spring rolls. Phoebe's mum was known to be anally clean, and it had spread to Phoebe, who insisted they used a coaster when putting their drinks down on the coffee table – and who always washed her teaspoon straight after making a cup of tea. Their sink never had dishes in it, and always gleamed. Shirin was very careful when eating her slice of pizza on the sofa now, sitting on the edge of her seat so that if she dropped anything, it would go on the laminate flooring and not on the new corner sofa.

'Do you fancy anyone at the moment, Shirin?' Carmen asked between bites of pizza.

Shirin looked to Carmen, then to Phoebe. Phoebe's gaze remained on the TV, as a pop group performed under Simon Cowell's steely stare. This was not a wholly unusual question for Carmen to ask, because she liked talking about boys, but Shirin's answer was always the same, so by now it seemed a pointless ask.

'Not really, no,' she said.

Phoebe turned then, narrowed her eyes slightly, and said, 'What about Kian?'

Shirin's cheeks coloured at the directness of the question, and at the two pairs of eyes on her now. 'We're just friends,' she said.

Phoebe rolled her eyes. 'You always say that, but you hang out alone a lot ...'

'Is he Muslim like you? Would your parents be okay if you went out with him?' Carmen asked.

This was another reason why she didn't like Carmen. She didn't listen to Shirin when she spoke. She didn't compute that it wasn't a case of Shirin dating a Muslim man that would be okay – it was that Muslim people shouldn't be romantically involved with anyone, period, before marriage. But no, Shirin didn't need to have an arranged marriage either. She had explained this on countless occasions to Carmen, who seemed to forget time and time again, likely because she had her own fixed idea of what coming from a Muslim family meant.

Shirin opened her mouth to explain all this again when Phoebe interjected, 'No, she can't date anyone, remember? But you'd like to – wouldn't you, Shirin?'

'Well, yeah, if my dream guy came along, I wouldn't say no.'

'So you don't think Kian is your dream guy?' Phoebe said. 'He is quite fit.'

'Agreed,' Carmen said. 'So you're *sure* you don't like him?'

Shirin felt her heart quickening. Did she? She didn't really know. It wasn't like he'd shown any interest in her, not in that way anyway. She'd only ever regarded him as a friend, though with these prompts, she began to wonder. 'I don't think of him like that,' she finally said.

Carmen curled her feet under her, and then ran her fingers through her blonde hair. Shirin thought it was quite a gross thing to do since her fingers were greasy from the pizza, but because Carmen had this air about her, it looked more nonchalant than anything else. 'Right, I'm glad, because I *really* fancy him.'

'Fancy who?'

'Kian,' Carmen said. She was smiling without her teeth, a sort of shy but smug smile.

Phoebe turned to her, her attention fully on the conversation now, eyes widening.

'You *do*?' she said. 'Have you spoken to him?'

Carmen explained how she sat next to Kian in Maths and how they often messed about. She said she hadn't initially thought he was fit, but he'd taken his jumper off and his polo top had been stuck to it, so she'd seen his chest. She'd realised, then and there, that he was actually very fit.

Phoebe was lapping all this up, saying Carmen needed to go out with him, that they'd be such a cute couple, and Shirin had a stilted smile on her face.

She considered telling them about Rob, to have something to say to make her feelings less embarrassing. She knew, though, that he wouldn't want her to tell people, that if it got back to him, he might be angry with her. When Carmen asked if Shirin could put in a good word for her with Kian, she said, 'Of course.'

She was not sure how to actually broach this with Kian in a casual way, as Carmen had stressed to her it had to be. 'Make sure it flows with the conversation,' she had briefed. 'Don't make it sound like I'm in love with him or anything.'

The temperature had definitely dropped, so instead of sitting in the fields they went to a greasy spoon two blocks away from their school, which didn't care that they were there in their school uniform in the middle of the day. Shirin had an excuse on the edge of her tongue, that it was lunchtime, even though it was 1 p.m. and lunch finished at 12.55 p.m. No one asked though.

They both got hot chocolates and sat in a corner booth.

Shirin leant her elbows on the table and examined Kian in a way she hadn't before. He was good-looking. His features, she thought, were quite beautiful when you looked at him properly. His eyes were big, his lashes long and dark. His lips plump and pink. It was a sad realisation. At the very same time she imagined his lips on hers, and she was so embarrassed at herself that she took her elbows away from the table and sat back.

'What do you think—' she began at the same time as he said, 'Did you see—'

They both stopped, laughed, and indicated for the other to go first. 'No, you go,' he said. 'I wasn't going to say anything important.'

'Mine isn't anything big either really. Just wanted to know what you thought of Carmen.'

'Carmen Thompson?'

'Yeah ... She might like you, basically.'

His brows furrowed together, and he didn't speak for a minute. 'Right.'

She hadn't expected this reaction, like he was annoyed at her. Everyone fancied Carmen, so his response was especially strange. 'I mean,' she began, not knowing where she was going with this, 'it doesn't matter if you're not interested – I know you've got a lot on. I just wanted to float it out there.'

'But you think I should talk to her?'

She picked up the teaspoon on the table next to her drink and lifted the skin out of the hot chocolate and onto a piece of tissue. She began to stir the drink like she was thinking about his question, when really she was thinking: No, I don't think you should; but she couldn't justify saying that. Carmen was her friend, even if Shirin didn't like her that much.

'I think you'd be cute together,' she said, echoing Phoebe. The words sounded awkward and not convincing coming out of her mouth.

'Interesting,' he said. He leant back. He still hadn't touched his drink.

She felt him slipping away from her, like she had done something wrong, though she wasn't entirely sure what. So she blurted, 'Rob randomly messaged me on MSN the other day, you know.'

That got his attention. Kian cocked his head to the side. 'Seriously? What did he say?'

'Just asked about homework and was weirdly nice.'

Kian made a ticking sound, like he was frustrated. 'He's a dick, you shouldn't talk to him.'

'I dunno ...'

'He's horrible to you, Shirin. You've said so yourself.'

It was strange how quickly she'd forgotten this, how quickly she'd forgiven. She thought from speaking to Rob, hearing the way he viewed things, that maybe he didn't mean to encourage Jordan. Maybe he felt pressured into it – a bit like Kian's brother. Maybe he didn't want to be like that any more, maybe he wanted to change.

When she didn't say anything in response, Kian said, 'You don't fancy him, do you?'

'No,' she said quickly. 'I literally don't fancy anyone. I wish people would stop asking me that question.'

He pretended to be taken aback, a slight smile on his face, hands raised in the air. 'Alright, I was only asking.' He picked up his mug and took a sip, despite the skin on top. And, in Kian's smile, she felt that order was somewhat restored.

The Bookseller

5 November 2018

WODEHOUSE TERMINATES CONTRACT WITH ROB GRAYSON

Libreria & Co. division Wodehouse Publications have cancelled their seven-figure book deal with Rob Grayson following an onslaught of controversial comments made by the comedian online.

Grayson's memoir, *How to Be Funny*, was scheduled to be published next September as Wodehouse's super-lead non-fiction title.

Wodehouse confirmed that their contract with Grayson had been terminated. Libreria & Co.'s MD Jonathan Webb said: 'We can confirm that we will no longer be publishing Rob Grayson's memoir. His most recent comments were deeply concerning and go against our values as an inclusive publisher.'

36,454 people signed the viral petition for Grayson's memoir to be cancelled, following his increasingly concerning comments on Twitter about who 'deserves' to be in this country, and against migrants and Islam on the whole.

When asked for a comment, Grayson said: 'I am sad that it's come to this. The woke brigade are attacking freedom of speech. My publisher knew my views when they offered me my book deal, so it's clear they're only trying to appease the overly sensitive by cancelling my book, and in turn are partaking in dangerous censorship.'

His agent, Laurie Rees from John Ryan Agency, said: 'It is troubling times when publishers make rash decisions based on pressure through social media. We are going to continue to look for a home for Rob's brilliant book, which focuses on his upbringing, being raised by a single parent from a working-class background. It is funny, heart-warming and very real, and any comments Rob may have made should not detract from the quality of the memoir he has written.'

The incident has sparked a lively debate online about who deserves to be published, and whether freedom of speech is being impacted by publishers' decisions to publish only books that sit with their values. Many of Grayson's fans have been outraged at the cancellation and are calling on other publishers to pick up his hotly anticipated memoir.

Journalist and activist Zahra Chandran was embroiled in a Twitter spat with Rob Grayson, and when asked for a comment said: 'Rob Grayson is a disgrace. How he got a book deal when he was always making racist and Islamophobic remarks is beyond me. I'm glad it has been cancelled because we don't need any more hate in the world, but it begs the question: why was he given a platform – and a book deal – to begin with?'

Hot Takes

Now

The noise is deafening.

On Twitter people who don't know Rob create threads, some against him, others making him into a victim.

Colleagues around Shirin speak at her desk about 'the whole Rob Grayson debate', saying he is an embarrassment.

Florence and Lilian talk in the kitchen as they make their cups of tea. 'It's all gone a bit too far,' they say in hushed tones. 'We should be able to separate the author from the writing.' Shirin is mute as she dunks her teabag into boiling water, using a spoon to press it into the side of the mug. She is stone-faced, though breaking inside, thinking: No, it's a fucking memoir, you idiots.

She is desperately empty – and lonely. She recognises all of this and her routine takes over. She gets up every morning, goes to work, gets through the day, returns home, makes dinner, sits on her bed, eats, watching TV, until it is acceptable for her to sleep. She lies there for hours, eyes closed, mind whirling. Soon, even food is unappealing. So much so that she resorts to soup for dinner, which always grows cold as she scrolls through Netflix for a show to watch.

In a last-ditch effort to pull herself out of the hole she is in, she asks Hana if she wants to do something. Hana replies that she is busy over the weekend, with the new friends she has made. They are going to a nightclub in Chelsea. Brunch in Knightsbridge. Things Shirin knows Hana can't afford. She knows she shouldn't blame Hana for not being there. She hasn't confided in her. But she blames her anyway. It is easier to have someone to blame.

And so, for the next month, she continues. Work, dinner, TV, sleep.

Rumours

Then

Shirin was wrong. About many things. Kian and Carmen met up twice and it quickly fizzled out. Shirin pretended she wasn't burning inside the entire time. While this was happening, Rob continued to message her. He was a distraction. Kian might be seeing her friend, but she was talking to a boy, which made her feel less pathetic, though no one even knew they were talking. At school Rob acted like they never spoke, unless it was only them in a corridor, in which case he would smile at her. He would message her afterwards saying she looked pretty, or that he liked her hair tied up.

When Kian and Carmen were no longer a thing, she was surprised that she continued to look forward to logging on to MSN after school to talk to Rob. He was sensitive, and much softer than he appeared. He told her he enjoyed studying *Romeo and Juliet*, that he liked Shakespeare in general, which surprised her. She had always assumed he didn't like literature – likely because she was in the same class as Jordan, and he always mucked about in English Literature. Now she was slowly untangling Jordan from Rob and seeing them as two separate people.

They talked for almost two months, and it was over the Christmas break that things began to escalate.

Rob_93: can you send me a pic?
Shirin_x_x: of what?
Rob_93: a sexy pic, you know what i mean
Shirin_x_x: no lol
Rob_93: oh come on, why not?? I promise i wont show anyone

She logged off, discomfort coursing through her. When she logged back in, a few hours later, she saw a string of messages:

Rob_93: hello?
Rob_93: ur such a tease – are you really not gonna send any?
Rob_93: we've been talking for months
Rob_93: ur ugly anyway bitch
Rob_93: i was only talking to u cause i felt sorry for you
Rob_93: u probs only suck paki cock
Rob_93: slag

Initially she was stunned, her hands trembling as her eyes scanned the words over and over. Then surprised that she was even surprised by this. She removed him as a friend from MSN. The rest of the Christmas break was spent wondering if she was ugly, looking in the mirror and critiquing the features on her face that she'd once thought were attractive.

She thought that was the end of it. But when she returned to school in January, at lunch Phoebe took her aside and said, 'There's some rumours going around about you ...' They were just outside the canteen, down one of the corridors, and no one except for the occasional student passed them to go inside.

'What do you mean?'

Phoebe's face was pinched. 'I heard in Maths you'd given Rob ...'

'A what?'

'A blowjob,' Phoebe mock-whispered.

The colour had gone from Shirin's face. 'What? That's obviously not true.'

'I know, I said that. I mean, you've not even kissed a boy before, right?'

'Okay, you don't need to shout that, Phoebe. What the hell – who has he said this to?'

'Everyone was talking about it. He said you'd begun messaging him on MSN and asked if you could come round. Then he said he'd stopped talking to you after.' Judging from Phoebe's expression, Shirin knew there was more to the story.

'What else did he say?' she asked. Phoebe shook her head, so Shirin pushed again. 'Phoebe, please.'

'He said some other gross things, like you're easy, that it wasn't good, and that you begged to see him again, so he blocked you.'

They were interrupted by Jordan, Rob and Tom walking out of the canteen, past them. Rob had his head down, like he was a victim in all of this, while Jordan and Tom laughed loudly when they saw Shirin, making gestures with their hands and choking sounds.

As they passed Jordan muttered, 'Paki slut.'

Now, as an adult, Shirin can see clearly the power that certain white men have. That they can rise through the ranks, no matter their views, that they can stand there and say freedom of speech is more important than treating people fairly and with respect. That what Rob did to Shirin was merely the start of what he would do to her – and to people in general. The rumours Rob made up about her are something she has buried within the recesses of her mind. She had intended to keep them there, but she accidentally told Hana in their second year of university. They were high in the smoking area of a club, and it just came out. Hana was horrified, hugged her tightly, and said, 'I bet he has a shit-sad little life now.' And when she said it, Shirin thought he probably did. She saw herself living in London, working her dream job, as karmic retribution. It had been something, subconsciously, that she had held on to, when she thought back to school. It was fine because she was doing well, and the people who had bothered her back then weren't. The tables turned on her when she began to see Rob's gigs being shared on Facebook and Instagram. A profile of up-and-coming comedian Rob Grayson in the *Guardian*. His shows being reviewed by *Time Out*.

He caused so much embarrassment, so much pain, and with no consequence. His book deal being cancelled is nothing. He should never have been given one – let alone a million-pound one – in the first place. In fact he is only getting more attention because of the cancellation. None of it is fair. Because that wasn't even the worst thing he did to Shirin.

The worst thing he did was stop Shirin and Kian speaking.

Tehran

Now

December. Her planned visit to Tehran is a much-needed escape. No one cares about Rob Grayson there. The whole UK publishing industry means nothing there either.

While Shirin would not say she has a strong connection to Iran – having lived in England all her life – it is her Maman Bozorg that she associates with the country. There is nothing Shirin relishes more than sitting next to her grandmother while she speaks about the universe and Allah's love, imparting calm wisdom and grounding guidance. Iran is special to Shirin solely because it is where her Maman Bozorg is.

She takes a direct flight from Heathrow Airport to Tehran, via Iran Air. At the airport she takes a picture of her ticket and passport and posts it as an Instagram story with the caption 'Goodbye 👋'. When she is in Itsu getting a pre-flight snack, Kian replies to it:

@KianRahimi: Sick – I didn't know you were going. I hope you have a great trip ☺

She has no right to be jealous that he is seeing someone, but she is. They have not spoken much since the night at hers.

They sometimes message, though she is cautious not to entertain the conversation for too long. He asks her how she is and Shirin always says she is great, even though she is tearful most of the time and is constantly thinking: I want to die. Though she does not actually want to die, she doesn't think. She just wants things to be different.

She Hearts his message, though she would like to reply. It's simpler this way.

The plane is loud, with Iranians shouting across their seats to each other, some laughing, others arguing. There is always a buzz on planes to Iran; it is unlike any other flight she has been on. The familiarity of the language they are speaking, combined with quite how fussy her people are, makes it both a stressful and humorous experience.

Two women, one next to her and the other in the row behind, get into an argument because the lady in front leant her chair back, and the one behind asked her to pull it back up. Shirin cannot help but think if they were English they would be more passive-aggressive in their response. Perhaps the person next to her would do as asked, but grumble about it.

But instead the woman says, 'No, I don't want to.'

The woman behind says, 'Fine,' before turning to the person next to her and saying loudly, 'Some people are so selfish. I'm not going to be able to sleep a wink for the next seven hours because of this khar.' *Donkey*.

Shirin is not sure what happens next as she puts her headphones in and cranks the volume up. Each time she shuts her eyes, though, she's taken back to Hull, to North Oak. It wasn't like this before she saw Kian back in the summer; he's awoken a time she'd buried in her mind. She lets her thoughts wander to what would have happened if she had never met Rob, if he'd gone to another school. Kian wouldn't have been suspended and forced to go to a different college. They wouldn't have been forbidden to speak to each other. She wouldn't have said the things she said to Kian – ugly, untrue words that she wishes now she could take back, but alas. Their lives would be different.

Six hours later they are informed that the plane is about to land. The women who do not already have their hijabs on get theirs out of their bags and begin to put them on themselves and their young daughters. Shirin gets hers out of her backpack. It is a navy cotton-polyester blend. She has patterned ones in her suitcase, but made the decision to be subtle when going through security. Her mother always warned her, before flying to Tehran, that it's not good to stand out in airport security. That if they saw her British passport they might take it away, as they don't believe in dual citizenship, leaving her stranded in Iran.

Passing security, however, is smoother than she's built it up to be. She is not even asked why she is visiting. She only shows her Iranian passport, keeping her British one safely tucked away in her backpack's inside compartment.

Once she retrieves her suitcase, Shirin scans the people waiting at Arrivals. She sees a group with red roses, even balloons, waving towards her. Her heart skitters, she looks down, briefly embarrassed, until she realises she does not recognise any of them and that they are waving at the woman behind her. She shoves her hands into her coat pockets, gazing ahead, trying to find her mother's face. She cannot see her. After five minutes of waiting she perches on a nearby bench and attempts, unsuccessfully, to log onto the airport's Wi-Fi. She keeps trying, even though it is clearly not going to happen. She went to the toilet on the aeroplane because she cannot bear to use an Iranian squat toilet – especially a public one. But because she knows she cannot use any nearby toilet, she now feels as though she needs to go. She crosses her legs and gives a heavy, prolonged sigh.

Twenty minutes later her mother arrives, tapping Shirin on her shoulder from behind, jolting her into awareness. She gives a string of half-hearted apologies, blaming everything from traffic, to parking, to Shirin being early (she wasn't), to the airport being too big and getting lost.

'Don't worry,' Shirin says, hugging her mum. It is only when she is next to her mother that she realises how petite she is. From a distance she has a real presence about her, which makes her appear much taller than she is.

Her mother wears her hijab loose on her head, the top of her hair marginally showing. This is not her mother bending the rules, as many in Iran do, but likely because it is the dead of night and her mother has rushed over to the airport. She wears a long monto that falls above her ankles, and she can just about see the black leggings she is wearing underneath. Her mother is slender; she is habitually on a diet, which she habitually breaks, continuing a cycle of cheat days and restriction. Her face, though, looks a lot more relaxed, compared to the last time Shirin saw her in person.

Shirin is led to the car, a white Fiat that has seen better days. The inside is clean, however, with brightly coloured cushions on each seat. Her mother puts the heater on, and initially it blows out only cold air.

'It just needs a minute to warm up,' her mother says, pulling out of the parking spot. 'Did you have a good flight? No one bother you?'

'It went smoothly, thanks.'

Silence drags between them. She loves her mother, but she has nothing to say to her. Shirin has always been hyper-aware of what people want from her; what kinds of conversations she should have with the different people in her life. There is nothing she dreads more than being considered boring or uninteresting. So, knowing that any life update she gives her mum will not pique her interest, she assumes silence is better.

'Thanks for collecting me,' she eventually says.

'Of course. Remember, though, no one but your Maman Bozorg and aunt know about the divorce, so if anyone asks, *he* couldn't take time off work for it.' Her mum sighs heavily. It is like the sigh pushes her mother's worries onto Shirin. She can feel them heavy inside her now, and instead of telling her mother how she is feeling – her own struggles – she stacks her mother's troubles atop her own.

'Yeah, yeah, I know.' A pause. 'When do you think you're going to tell people?'

They slip onto the motorway, her mum's car audibly straining in its attempts to go more than 65 kph. Shirin looks to her mother, sees the way her lips are pursed, the curves of her eyebrows.

'I don't know. I'm just trying to get through one day at a time. There's a lot going on here, you know. I'm glad I'm here to help Maman Bozorg. I think now that's all that matters.' Her words are cagey, alluding to something. This is something her mother often does. She knows Shirin will prod. How can she not?

'What do you mean? What's going on?' Her mind jumps to the worst-case scenarios: cancer. Dying. Death.

'Your grandma's carer.' She shakes her head before indicating to change lanes. Even so late at night the highway is busy, with cars cramming together, not following the three lanes, but creating five, sometimes six. Driving in Tehran lacks rules – you need to be comfortable with constant near-misses and the occasional bump to your car. 'We fired her.'

'Why?'

Maman Bozorg always has issues with her different live-in carers. She says they are unkind to her, and to begin with her complaints were taken seriously, but after a while the family concluded that Maman Bozorg craved attention, due to her loneliness. It is through complaining about her carers that her many children surround her and give her what she needs. She has had five carers in a year, and with each new carer her complaints about them become wilder and wilder. She says they swear at her, they starve her, they do a whole manner of shocking things. The last Shirin heard was that they got a nanny-cam installed in the flat, which the current carer is unaware of, which links to Maman Bozorg's children's phones.

'It's horrible, Shirin. Dayi Saman saw the carer bring a man to the house and they began ... in the living room.' She mutters what sounds like *Disgusting* under her breath.

'What? Were you both in the house?'

Her mother nods sadly. 'She was in the next room, asleep. I was away.'

Shirin's mouth opens involuntarily, but she can think of no words to speak.

'Saman called us all, rushed over, phoned the police and kicked them both out. Maman says she thinks she was drugged; she remembered feeling so drowsy just before, and said she saw figures standing over her – checking if she was asleep.' Her mum shudders. 'I've not been a good daughter. I was out in Shiraz with my friends, travelling. I should have been at home with my maman. I'm never where I need to be,' she says.

Shirin agrees with her mum's last statement. She never is. Even now. Shirin is aware her thoughts are selfish, but it doesn't make what she feels any less true.

'Is Maman Bozorg okay? What happened to the carer?'

'Yes, she's fine. We dropped the charges in the end. The carer had separated from her husband but hadn't yet divorced, and the punishment for what she did with that man would be too much.'

'Death penalty?'

Her mum nods. 'It's ridiculous. They should be punished, but *death* is extreme. It means they're going to be let free because of our goodwill. It's not fair.'

Shirin is silent.

'Maman Bozorg's looking forward to seeing you, though. She says you're her favourite grandchild, even in front of her other grandchildren,' her mum continues, smiling now.

They are now in the city. They pass grand murals of important figures, elaborate graffiti proclaiming 'Death to America', with the American flag bleeding. Shirin's head strains to get a good look at them as they speed on by.

She checks her phone. No messages. It is always difficult to get Wi-Fi when she visits. Eventually they make it to the only street in Tehran that Shirin knows like the back of her hand: Maman Bozorg's street. It is narrow, with grand mismatched gates, each one a different style, some tall and black metal, others low, white and wooden, with gold accents. Her mother parks over the pedestrian path, close to the front door.

Maman Bozorg lives in a large house that's been converted into flats. Once they get past the electric gate they walk up the smooth white steps, and two flights of stairs. Next to every flat's front door are shoes, an insight into the people who live in each apartment.

They quietly enter the apartment, but it is unnecessary, for Maman Bozorg is awake. She is a short but large woman. She unsteadily pads over to Shirin, grabs her in a very powerful headlock-hug, and kisses her head.

'Shirin, I've missed you so much, my love,' Maman Bozorg exclaims. They speak in Farsi.

'Hello, Maman Bozorg,' Shirin says.

'Do you want tea or something to eat? I got some fresh pastries from the bakery.'

'It's bedtime, Maman,' her mum says, her hand lightly placed on Maman Bozorg's back. 'We can have all of this in the morning.'

Shirin retrieves from her suitcase the various diabetes medications she has brought with her from England, because they struggle to get them, due to the sanctions against Iran, and places them on the side table for her grandmother. The apartment has tiled floors running through each room, Persian carpets laid on top of each other in the living areas. Maman Bozorg insists that Shirin sleep in her bed and she sleep on the futon on the floor of Shirin's mother's bedroom. They argue about this for a long while, Maman Bozorg's taarofing getting more and more extravagant, in which she insists that she prefers the futon to the bed, as her bed hurts her back. Shirin lies, saying she prefers the futon because she feels closer to the earth that way. She has never, in her life, considered that she would prefer to be closer to the earth when she sleeps.

In the end, Shirin wins and Maman Bozorg relents. The futon is not so bad. Her mother's night-time habits, however, are not conducive to easy sleep. She's forgotten how her mum listens to an Iranian psychologist's YouTube channel every night to sleep. Even though her mum puts her headphones in to listen to him, Shirin can still hear his voice and cannot sleep from the light coming from the phone, the brightness on maximum. Then, just a few hours later, she is woken once more by her mum getting up to pray.

'I'm speaking to Allah, Shirin,' her mum retorts to her groans.

'Well, yeah, but could you *not* turn the light on to do it?' she snaps.

After she says this, she is certain she will be going to hell when she dies.

Maman Bozorg

Under the careful instruction of Maman Bozorg, Shirin's mother lays out an assortment of food, some especially bought for Shirin's arrival. Various shirini are spread out, many with crushed pistachios sprinkled on the top. Shirin's favourite of these is ghotab – an almond-and-walnut-filled crescent coated with powdered sugar. The outer shell is hard and the inner nutty and soft. Also brought out is freshly baked barbari with honey, tart jam, butter and boiled eggs. It is a welcome sight.

Her grandmother lives more traditionally than Shirin's other relatives. And so for each meal they lay down a sofreh, and sit cross-legged around it to eat. Maman Bozorg asks Shirin to sit down next to her. 'I've missed you,' she says. She often speaks a mixture of Farsi and Turkish, which gives her voice a shrill quality that is home to Shirin. It makes her instantly smile.

'What's new?' Shirin asks.

Maman Bozorg shakes her head. 'Not a lot.' Shirin raises her eyebrow. 'Your mother told you then,' she says, waving her hand, before giving Shirin's mum daggers. 'It's ... it's okay, it's life, these things happen. I'm tough. Pass me some honey, joonam?'

Shirin hands her grandma the jar and a spoon. Her grandmother drizzles the honey over her bread, before breaking off a piece and placing it in her mouth. She sits with her back rested against a poshti, one leg tucked under her, the other out in front of her. Maman Bozorg has arthritis and diabetes, which is why she needs a carer, though her mind is the sharpest of anyone Shirin knows; it's just her body that needs a little help. In fact it's a running joke in the family that Maman Bozorg is psychic. She often senses things before they happen, correctly guessing the sex of her children's babies before they were born, even predicting that her own daughter would marry a man who looked like Tom Selleck – whom Shirin's dad in his younger years uncannily resembled.

The flat has no Wi-Fi, and Shirin is bereft at not having checked her messages since she was in Heathrow, a day ago now. That said, this break in her routine – in her constant doom-scrolling – is refreshing, even if it's hard. She already feels differently from how she did in London.

The telephone rings, and Shirin's mother goes to answer it. She leaves the room with the wireless headset. Shirin is about to question who it is when her Maman Bozorg puts her hand lightly onto her leg. 'Azizam, when are you going to get married?' she asks, because she is an Iranian grandmother with a single granddaughter in her twenties – how can she not?

Shirin rolls her eyes, takes a ghotab and plays with it in her hand. 'I'll marry when I'm ready. It's not all about marriage.'

'I know,' she says. 'But you look a bit different on this trip – more tired, excited. What are you excited about, joonam?'

Shirin's heart jumps at the questioning she was not expecting. It is too early for this, especially in combination with her jet lag and the difficulties of sleeping in the same bedroom as her mother.

'I'm not excited about anything,' she replies slowly. She takes a tentative bite of the ghotab. This is more delicately than she would normally eat it; if she were not being accosted, she would pop the entire thing in her mouth.

Her grandma smiles, her bright blue eyes crinkle. Her skin is so pale now, a result of staying in most days, which only makes the colour of her eyes even more pronounced. Her hair is cut short into a bob and she has let it remain grey, a recent change. Now she says there is no shame in grey hair, that ageing is no bad thing, it is something to be celebrated instead.

'Tell the truth,' she says. 'I won't tell your mother.' Her smile is genuine, cheeky even. Shirin's mouth is open, though she does not say anything. 'As long as he makes you happy,' Maman Bozorg continues. 'That's all we want.'

Shirin nods in acknowledgement, but she wants to say that that isn't what everyone wants. There is so much focus on marriage – romantic relationships overall – and how that will fix a person. No one notices how lost she is in herself, and how a partner can't solve that problem. She *is* tired. Both physically and mentally. But her Maman Bozorg isn't right about her being excited about someone – because if she were, it would be Kian, and he is unattainable, thus filling her with the opposite of excitement.

When her mother returns, she says it was Zahreh – Shirin's aunt – and that she is coming to visit later. Maman Bozorg is distracted by this news, thrilled at further visitors. The topic of Shirin's love life is not returned to.

The next day Shirin stays at home with Maman Bozorg while her mother is grocery shopping. She is waiting for the samovar to boil. There are patterns imprinted into the antique copper frame, and making chai this way requires more effort, but the tea is smoother, crisper, thus worth the additional time. When the water is hot enough, Shirin pours tea into two clear glasses.

Making her way into the living room, she sets the two black teas in front of her grandmother. She sits on the armchair next to Maman Bozorg, leaning against the hard chair. It is uncomfortable, though her grandmother says it's good for her back.

'Merci, Shirin jan,' Maman Bozorg says, taking a glass of chai with one hand and using her other to pop a sugar cube in her mouth. She takes a sip, sucking on the sugar cube as she drinks. 'There's sweets in the top cupboard. Why don't you get them for us to eat with our chai?'

'Your diabetes . . .' Shirin begins.

Maman Bozorg waves her hand in the air dismissively. 'We're all going to die anyway, why not enjoy ourselves while we're still here?'

This is where Shirin gets her lack of restraint when it comes to food. She is usually of the same opinion as her grandmother, that there is often so little joy in life that it is hard to restrict food that gives such instant pleasure. Her appetite is slowly returning since being here. She retrieves the box of pastries and sets it in front of Maman Bozorg. While her grandmother is making her selection, Shirin gets out her diabetes tablets and leaves them on the coffee table for her to take afterwards.

'You look after me,' Maman Bozorg coos before taking a bite out of a piece of zaban. 'I'm glad you're here.'

'Me too,' she says.

'Do you remember, Shirin jan, when you were very little and it was just me, you and your Baba Bozorg?'

'A little. Less memories, but more how I felt.' She, too, picks up a zaban. It's been so long since she's had one. It is a puff pastry that is sweet and crunchy on the outside, but soft on the inside. She is not sure she loves the taste, but it reminds her of being young and hopeful.

'How did you feel then?' Maman Bozorg asks.

'Loved.'

Her grandmother smiles at this. 'We were happy, weren't we?' There is sadness in her eyes that Shirin hasn't noticed before.

'I really am sorry about what happened to you, with the carer.'

She frowns. 'No one believed me,' she says, her voice suddenly forlorn. Maman Bozorg's moods change so drastically – you often know exactly how she's feeling when looking at her, when hearing her speak. It is something Shirin once thought would be a curse, but she now thinks must be nice. There is no pretending.

'We're all stupid. We should have. Everyone will believe you now.' Shirin puts her hand over her Maman Bozorg's – the one that isn't holding her tea. Shirin's hand is small in comparison, but she hopes it has the strength to comfort her, like her grandmother has comforted her all her life.

It is like Maman Bozorg can read her mind because she turns to her and says, 'Why are you upset, azizam?'

'I'm sad that you're sad,' she says, a part-truth.

'Tell the truth. What's going on?'

'Well … I feel unhappy, even though I've got the life I always wanted,' she begins, testing the words out loud. 'I'm not sure I want this life, any more. And it's hard to explain, but I feel like the things I've been trying to forget about my past – bad things that happened – are coming back to haunt me. Like I can't escape them any more, and it's only making me more miserable.'

'Oh, Shirin, your maman should be there for you, instead of hiding here.' There is derision in her voice. 'Always hiding, leaving her only daughter in England all alone.'

'I have my dad,' Shirin lies.

'I know that man, he's as useless as her.' Shirin laughs at this. 'I'm sorry, my azizam. If there's one thing I've learnt, though, it's that you shouldn't dwell on your past if you want to be happy in this life. Each hardship moulds us into who we are today; each thing that happens to us was meant to be, Allah willed it. Look forward instead, to what you want your life to look like *now*, not what you wanted it to look like. You're young, you have time to do anything you want.'

Shirin knows the words are wise and true but she struggles to internalise them. It is so much easier said than done. She thinks her grandmother knows she is thinking this, for she continues.

'I am so proud of my granddaughter.' She places her hand on top of Shirin's. 'I know you will find your way.' She points to a patterned box on the mantelpiece and asks Shirin to bring it over. Next to it are school pictures of Shirin, when she had thick dark hair, with the tops of her ears poking out and an awkward half-smile on her face. When Shirin returns with the box, she gives it to Maman Bozorg, who opens it carefully. Inside are various pieces of gold jewellery: earrings, necklaces and bangles. She digs inside, takes out a small scarlet cloth case, and gives it to Shirin.

Shirin pulls the drawstring apart and feels inside. Within is a delicate gold oval locket. The front is striped, in a croissant pattern, with white gold and yellow gold, the back shiny and smooth.

'Open it,' she says.

When she does as her Maman Bozorg asks, Shirin sees inside the locket are two mini photographs. On the left side is a picture of Maman Bozorg and Shirin when she was a baby. She is wearing a sailor's outfit and is seated on her grandmother's lap. Her grandmother is much younger in the picture, her face freer of wrinkles, her blue eyes bright as always. On the other side is Baba Bozorg when he was in the army – his stoic face unsmiling, though proud.

Her Baba Bozorg was in the army in his younger years, but in his older age he worked as a cleric. He continued to wear a freshly pressed suit, and everything he did was controlled, neat. He was so different from Maman Bozorg, who slept in most days, rushed cooking dinner because she was distracted by the soaps she was watching or hot gossip she had heard from her neighbours. This difference, unlike for Shirin's mum and dad, complemented their relationship, gave it a depth and texture they needed in order to be married over forty years and not want to leave each other. They bickered, of course, but not for a moment would they consider a life without each other. Neither of them had relished the thought, as Shirin's parents had. She was twelve when Baba Bozorg died. She took a week off school to go to Tehran with her mum and dad. The trip is a blur to her now, but she distinctly remembers her mother's wails in the graveyard, the women around them dressed in black chadors, which makes the scene even more distorted in her memories.

'This is beautiful,' Shirin says now.

'It's yours, azizam. I want you to keep this, and whenever you feel lonely or uncertain of yourself, remember I'm here for you, no matter how far away I am. And Baba Bozorg. He's looking down on you. He loved you so much, Shirin. We all do. Your maman and baba too, but they're stupid, not as wise as you and I.'

Shirin feels her eyes filling up, but laughs at Maman Bozorg's final dig. 'Thank you,' she says.

Her grandmother puts her hand over Shirin's again now. Her hand is large and covers Shirin's easily. The weight and warmth of it is comforting, like Shirin is no longer expected to carry the burden any more, like everything in England is so small when she is around so much love.

'Don't ever let anyone bother you. We're Iranian, Shirin jan, we don't let people bother us,' Maman Bozorg says.

'I didn't say anyone was,' Shirin says slowly.

'I know these things. I know what you're feeling. You need to stand up for yourself. I'm not there to do it for you in England, so you have to promise me that you'll stand up for yourself?'

She rolls her eyes light-heartedly, but Maman Bozorg tells her to promise, and Shirin finally relents – because she thinks: Actually, yes, I'd like to make this promise. She wants to stand up for herself, to no longer cower away from things that bother her. Because her Maman Bozorg is right: if Shirin doesn't back herself, no one will.

And even though she didn't say exactly what was bothering her, or the intricacies of it all, she feels supported by Maman Bozorg. Supported in an unconditional way, when before it felt like all the love around her was only conditional. It is the respite she didn't know she urgently needed.

She spends the rest of the day sitting next to Maman Bozorg watching Iranian soaps, listening to her grandmother's commentary, eating shirini and drinking chai. There is no urge to check her work emails or Twitter, where publishing news and hot takes are so often rampant and overwhelming. She is content and present. This is the love she has desperately needed.

Humber Bridge

Then

They had agreed to meet by the entrance of the Humber Bridge Country Park. It was the first time Shirin and Kian had hung out during a weekend. She'd told him that her dad had gone to Iran without her mum, so it would be easier for them to meet. He didn't need it explained to him that her parents wouldn't want them to see each other. His parents were fairly liberal, as were Shirin's, but there were limitations to their liberalism.

Locals went to the country park to walk their dogs. Kian used to have picnics on the table benches there, when family from Iran came to visit. His mum would pack egg-mayonnaise sandwiches, and salad olivieh, with tough, delicious Iranian bread. It was Hull's most picturesque area. If you looked at the bridge in a certain light you might have thought you were in San Francisco. Emphasis on *might*. Now Kian went with his friends and willed time to speed on as they rode their bikes through the woody marshes, and ended their trip watching the sunset while throwing pebbles across the river. The water was grey and dirty-looking most of the time because the sky was grey most of the time. Sometimes they saw people wading into the water, their trousers rolled up, mudlarking, and they would come out with random objects like a quarter of a teacup, with a look of absolute triumph on their faces. His friends from Foxview, Koyer and Teddy, would make fun of them, say it was *sad*, and Kian would laugh along, but not really mean it. If it made them happy, what did it really matter?

Today, the sky was a baby blue, the air crisp. As Shirin walked towards him, he realised he had never seen her in clothes other than her school uniform. She was wearing black leggings with ankle boots, an oversized cream jumper, and the same puffer jacket she wore to school. He noticed her eyelids were lighter, glistening with glitter. It made her eyes look bigger, and he thought that if she wore make-up at school she would definitely get more attention from boys.

He shoved both his hands in his pockets, straining the fabric as he pushed inwards. 'What time do you call this?' he said, his tone light compared to his heavy heart.

A glimmer of a smile traced her eyes and lips, but as she drew near, he could see a hollowness within her. He had never seen her look so deflated. It took him aback. 'Well, it was a trek to get here,' she said in a wry tone.

Together, they made their way up the steps to the country park, which Kian had long ago counted to be 105 steps exactly. Halfway up he could hear Shirin muttering something like *Jesus Christ*. He stifled a laugh, which he was sure she heard because she turned to give him daggers, which only made it harder not to laugh out loud.

Once up the steps, they walked along the woodland bank. Trees lined each side, the floor stuck with dried mud, broken tree trunks and fallen branches. An older man was walking a dog ahead of them. The dog was carrying a large branch, almost bigger than the animal itself, and the owner was trying to wrestle it out of its mouth. Shirin and Kian walked around this tug-of-war. He gave Shirin a quick glance and saw she was trying not to laugh, the heaviness in her expression lightened somewhat now. But he knew something was up. He knew her now, could sense when something wasn't right with her.

'Is everything okay with you?' he asked.

'Did you not hear or are you pretending not to know?' she said, not looking him in the eye.

He frowned at this. 'What?'

She revealed what Rob had told everyone, though because Kian was on the outskirts of the groups at North Oak he hadn't heard the rumours that were being spread. When she spoke he noticed her eyes fill, ever so slightly, with each word, each sentence. She was trying to hold it together, and he wanted her to know she didn't have to do that around him. Unadulterated anger swirled within him, rendering him momentarily speechless when she had finished.

He swore under his breath, before taking hold of her hand. She seemed surprised by this but didn't pull away. He was surprised by his instinct to hold her too, but squeezed her hand. It was soft within his, small and warm. 'He's a worthless prick. I'm sorry, Shirin.'

She looked at him briefly and looked away towards the bridge, a lone tear trickling down her face, which she speedily wiped away.

'I'll talk to him,' Kian said, his voice strong.

She turned back to him, mouth ajar before she snapped it shut. 'No, you won't,' she said. 'It's dying down. I don't want to make it worse.'

'But Rob can't just go around lying about you because you weren't interested in him – that's fucked up.'

'I know, but we've only got six months left of school and I just want it to go by as painlessly as possible,' she said. They were nearing the river now. The Humber Bridge stood before them; the sky a striking blue behind it, the river mirroring the blue so that it looked refreshing, as though to set foot in the river would be an enjoyable experience, rather than absolutely rank. 'I'm glad you see that it's messed up though. Phoebe keeps telling me I should see the funny side.'

'What?' He hadn't had many interactions with Phoebe but, from what he'd seen of her, she'd seemed like a rational, sane human being, but now he questioned his initial assessment.

Shirin shrugged and let out a deep sigh. 'I think people feel I'm someone to be laughed at and not taken seriously, you know?'

'I don't think that,' he said.

'I know,' she said. 'It's one of the things I like about you.'

When they were close to the river, Kian bent to collect a selection of pebbles, which he kept in his left hand. With his right hand he threw them, one by one, into the river, watching how many times he could make them bounce on the surface of the water. His personal best was four, though it had been months since he'd last done it.

Shirin sat on the ground and gazed up at the sky. 'You've had a lot going on yourself, I can tell,' she said.

He turned briefly and said, 'You can?' He then threw a pebble. It bounced twice over the water at an impressive distance.

Truth be told, Kian had been spiralling. Sometimes it was okay and he could handle the guilt about his brother going to prison, he could pretend he was fine. But it came in waves. Mehdi's birthday had just passed. They'd visited him that week and had bought him way too many chocolate bars from the vending machine. Everyone had been teary-eyed, trying to pretend this was normal, that this was not devastating and depressing. It was probably the reason Kian hadn't noticed the rumours going around about Shirin. Guilt about his brother encircled him and he wanted so badly to tell the only person he thought might get it, but it was fear that was holding him back. He liked Shirin so much; he didn't ever want her not to like him back, to think badly of him, to think the same things he thought about himself.

'Even from the way you're standing, I can tell something is up,' she said. He could hear her approaching, the pebbles knocking against each other as she made her way to his side. She reached out and took one of the pebbles from his open hand, and in the process her fingers brushed against his wrist. It was such a normal, simple touch, and yet he felt his heart pounding in response.

She didn't throw the pebble, but balanced it in her palm reflectively. 'It's about your brother?'

'I feel guilty,' he said. It was the first time he had said the words aloud. She didn't say anything, merely gave him a look, an invitation to continue. 'That he's locked up while the rest of us are living life.' His throat caught. He cleared it quietly and wanted to crawl into a hole. He thought Shirin would look at him differently, but in her eyes he saw that she understood, even if she didn't, not really. He hadn't told her the full extent of *why* he felt guilty, and he still couldn't, but he had shared a bit of himself with her and it was liberating.

'Your brother made a choice,' she said. 'You can't beat yourself up for what other people do.'

He wasn't sure what he thought about that. It was true that his brother had chosen to intervene, but Kian couldn't help but think he hadn't been man enough to handle the situation himself. If he had been, he wouldn't have taken it as far as Mehdi and no one would be in prison now.

He mumbled that he guessed so and turned to face her. They were close to each other, so close that he felt if he shut his eyes he would still be able to feel her presence. He tested this theory and he was right. He could feel her drawing closer, and her hand slowly make its way onto his shoulder.

'I care about you, you know,' Shirin was saying, but he could barely hear her. 'I feel like I've known you ages.' He knew he fancied her, of course he did. He valued her friendship, but more and more lately he imagined her lips on his. She had given no indication that she felt the same way, and he was about to tell himself to get a fucking grip, when he opened his eyes and saw a look in hers that made him think she was thinking the same thing.

'I care about you too,' he said. 'Obviously.'

Her lips turned up. 'Obviously?' He thought they might kiss, but then she turned away from him, looked out onto the murky water and said, 'I'm glad.'

The pebbles trickled from his hand, clattering to the ground one after the other, as they gazed out onto the water.

New Year's Eve

Now

Shirin had planned to spend New Year's Eve as she always did – in London, not Hull. Though when she arrived at her dad's house on Christmas Eve and mentioned that she would be returning to London on the twenty-seventh, he was aghast. He said lately she only visited once a year, and when she replied that they were not even Christian, he said that that had never stopped her from asking for Christmas presents when she was younger.

His words evoked memories of her taking her parents to Asda, picking out what she thought to be traditional Christmas food – even though she didn't like it – because she wanted to be like her friends, to have those picturesque Christmas spreads. The reality was badly seasoned, undercooked vegetables, rice that her mum insisted they needed on the table, and a chicken she hated the sight of (this was before she turned vegetarian).

They would sit at the table and she would try and lighten the mood, but her mum and dad would never bite. Instead, they would argue. Every day they argued. She remembers her mum making fun of her dad one Christmas, and him being so embarrassed he pushed the tree over in a fit of rage, threw the mince pies Shirin had bought on the floor, stood on them in his slippers, and said, 'We aren't fucking English, so can we stop pretending?' He left the house and didn't come back until very late. Her mum said he was probably with one of his whores, if he could still get one, 'the bastard'. Shirin was eleven, so didn't fully comprehend how dysfunctional this behaviour was. It is convenient that, in older age, her dad has forgotten all this.

So in addition to spending a long, uncomfortable Christmas Day with her dad, Karen and her children, Shirin stayed for the limbo period between Christmas and New Year's Eve too. This time was spent in her old bedroom on her laptop, bingeing on different TV shows, regressing to her teenage years. She thought she'd be able to see Phoebe more, but as she is actually English, her diary was packed with plans to see various family members.

It is Phoebe's house that she is at now. The plan is to pre-drink before going to the nightclub they frequented in their youth to celebrate New Year's Eve. She assumes they are doing this ironically, though this has not been verbally acknowledged.

What she doesn't expect is Kian to be the one to open the front door. She pretends to clear her throat, to cover her intake of breath. 'Hey,' she says.

'Hi,' he says. He, too, is surprised to see her standing there.

She is wearing wide-leg trousers with a corset top, intended to make her waist look small, with her cleavage almost showing, which feels more suggestive than if it were fully visible. She sees his gaze on her chest. Kian notices her noticing him noticing her and he quickly looks away.

'You look nice,' he says in a husky voice, which he promptly clears.

She laughs, even though nothing he has said is particularly funny. 'Thanks, you look nice yourself.' He is wearing a thick cream T-shirt and his hair is longer now, to his ears, his locks curly and glossy.

'I didn't think you'd be here,' he says.

Her eyes widen in mock-annoyance, though her heart is thudding painfully in her chest. 'Oh, I see how it is.'

He laughs as she enters the house. 'No, I didn't mean that, I just didn't know. I'm surprised is all.'

Up this close she can smell his aftershave, and it brings her back to when he was at hers, when she cried into his chest and Kian held her.

He doesn't move away from her in the narrow hallway, and they are now inches from each other, for a moment or so, then he steps aside to let her in. She can hear the chatter coming from the living room and she thinks she would rather stay here, pretending that she is just hanging out with Kian, that this is something they do. He places his hand on her cheek. For a split second she looks surprised, before standing very still, letting it lie there.

'You're so cold,' he says, like this is the most normal thing to say and do. She cannot think of words, so says nothing. He clears his throat and removes his hand. 'How was your trip to Iran?'

'It was good,' she says. 'The restorative I definitely needed before spending Christmas with my dad, Karen *and* her children.'

'Ouch!'

'How was yours?' she asks.

'Good, I guess. I mean, I'm very keen to go back to London now.' He laughs. 'Anyway, come on in. Everyone's in the living room.'

She nods, following his lead out of Phoebe's hallway and to their friends.

'Why is Kian here?' she asks Phoebe in the small kitchen.

Phoebe is mixing various liquors in a large jug to create her 'special cocktail'. Shirin watches as she haphazardly throws in unmeasured amounts of vodka, gin, cranberry juice and lemonade. She is concentrating on her creation and does not look up at Shirin when she speaks.

'Um, sorry, I was going to text you about it, but things got a bit manic here. He's mates with George's friend Connor who's round, so he came along.'

Shirin leans against the counter. The house is stuffy and smells like wet dog, though it is well decorated. She wishes Phoebe would turn round and take the situation seriously. It's obvious, though, that she is distracted, that this is granular compared to her own concerns. Then Shirin has a thought and is not sure how to ask, or whether she should be asking. 'How are things anyway, with George?' she asks in a hushed tone.

Phoebe puts a bottle of Tesco's own vodka down, sighs, her shoulders slumping, and looks Shirin in the eye for the first time that night.

'How's the baby-making going, you mean?'

Shirin does not say anything, though grimaces, which says it all.

'I don't know if it'll happen for me,' Phoebe continues. 'Trust me not to be able to.'

'It's meant to take a while,' Shirin soothes. 'They just always make it sound easy when you're a teenager, but it's normal for it to take time. You've only been trying a few months—'

Phoebe waves her hands in the air. 'It's fine. I'm having a night off being good. I've been eating so healthy. I even lost a stone, because I read being overweight makes it harder.'

Shirin raises an eyebrow. 'Phoebe, you've never been overweight.'

'According to my BMI—'

'Which is a load of shit, remember?'

Shirin puts her hand on her friend's arm and massages it, because she doesn't know what else to say, because this problem is so adult and she still, pathetically, doesn't feel adult enough to handle it. Her present concern is that the man she likes is unexpectedly in the next room, whereas her friend is having fertility issues. She is not sure how their lives split off in such disparate directions. How different they are now. The things that bother Shirin on a daily basis – the way she is treated at work, and how it's not like she once dreamt – feel alien and minuscule when she is not in London. And while she wanted this distance when she was in Iran, back in England now she wants her concerns to be recognised as real. She cannot imagine speaking to Phoebe about racism or representation, or any of the things she and Mariam would effortlessly rant about in the canteen. It is like there are two completely different worlds and versions of herself – and it is only now that she can see that this is damaging to her sense of self. Because how can Shirin ever be, and accept, herself if she does not present the real her to the people she's closest to?

In the end, ten people come to pre-drinks before they go to the club. A mixture of boys and girls Shirin vaguely knows from school, but who she did not stay in contact with, including Carmen, who is there with her fiancé, a hench man who works in IT. For the first half-hour she watches as Kian, George and another man chat animatedly at the dining table, a little way away from where she is sitting on the sofa. At certain points, though, she can see Kian glancing over at her, from the corner of her eye, and each time she finds herself holding her breath, not knowing what to do with her body. She is suddenly conscious that she has hands, and that there is really no natural place for them to go when she is sitting down listening to people speak. She rearranges them multiple times in a minute, from clasping them together, to twirling the hairband around her wrist, to laying them limply on her thighs. No position feels right. It is only when she cannot take this awkwardness any more that she tells Phoebe she's going into the kitchen for another drink and stays there on her phone, franticly texting Hana, who likely does not care about the situation.

When Shirin asked Hana what she was doing for New Year's Eve she was cagey and said she might have plans with people Shirin has not met before. They have names like Valentia and

Hamilton. Hana said she met them on a night out in Chelsea, and that one of their dads is a multimillionaire, that she visited their house and it was so big she didn't have a phone signal in certain areas. She said all this like it was a good thing, a clear glint in her eye over FaceTime. Fairly quickly she mentioned, too, that one of them had connections in fashion, which would help her get a foot in the door. It's hard for Hana, so Shirin understands her need to build this connection. But it still stings that she will be spending New Year's Eve with them, people she barely knows, instead of with her best friend.

Hana texts her back with a picture of a glass of champagne in her manicured hand, raised in front of a window. It looks like a hotel room and she is about to type her reply when she notices something very significant in the window behind the glass of champagne.

Shirin: *Is that the Eiffel Tower?? You're in Paris?*
Hana: *It's MAD. I'll tell you about it when I'm back xxx*

Shirin hears the kitchen door swing open, the quick *whoosh* breaking her from her reverie. Her head whips up and it is Kian. He makes his way towards her, his face earnest until it breaks into a small smile.

'You hiding in here?' he says.

'No,' she replies quickly, before realising he was joking. 'I was just getting a drink.' She indicates her short glass with the clear liquid inside. There are bits of mint floating in it and she is not entirely sure what this cocktail is, but she can smell the gin from a distance.

He goes over to the countertop where she is standing, and leans over to pour himself a drink too. He takes a sip and purses his lips afterwards. 'Well, that's strong.' She takes a sip, too, and pulls the same face.

'Wow,' she says. She can feel her insides getting ever so slightly warm and there is a sudden lightness within her. She has been so tightly wound, and it is only now she is a tad loosened that she realises it. She takes another long sip. 'I thought you'd be in London.'

He straightens his back, and looks down at her, into her eyes, as he speaks. He seems to have no problem maintaining eye contact, but she needs to look away every so often as she finds his gaze too intense, even though she doubts that is his intention.

'Yeah, that was the plan, but Connor mentioned a night out to Welly and it felt too nostalgic to say no, to be honest.'

In the recesses of her mind Shirin remembers Connor from school. He was an anomaly back then; he floated between various groups, teetering between popular and middling, though he was never unkind to the less popular kids. Because he was inoffensive, she has no particular opinion of him.

'He's here?'

Kian nods and says he's wearing the striped top, and Shirin is surprised by how much some people have changed in the past ten years, so much so that they are unrecognisable. Despite this, though, she doesn't think she and Kian have changed all that much. Phoebe certainly has; her hair colour has changed from mousy blonde at school to an auburn now that some would mistake for natural. Back then, too, she was very thin, and now she has filled out in a way that is healthier, less restrictive than in her younger years.

'How long are you here for then?' Shirin asks.

'Until the second. I had actually planned to message you tomorrow,' he says, his voice the sound of complete ease.

She runs her finger over the edge of her glass. Not in a particularly sexy way, but because she has noticed the rim is stained red from her lipstick, and she needs a distraction from what Kian has just said. When she looks up, she sees he is chewing the bottom of his lip, resting his hip against the countertop, arms folded. The tops of his arms strain against his T-shirt, making the fabric ride up, and she notices that he has a tattoo running up his arm. She can only see part of it because it's cut off by his top. It is vertical, rather than horizontal, and looks like it's words written in Farsi, the ink delicate and subtle against his tanned skin.

'You were?' she says. 'You'd planned to message me?'

He smiles, a little embarrassed now. 'Yeah. I wanted to see if you'd be up for meeting in London. I definitely didn't think you'd be spending New Year's Eve here.'

'Why?'

He shrugs. 'You never did before.' He continues, 'I mean … I'm glad you are here.' He steps closer to her, and there is about a foot between them.

'You are?'

He nods and they edge closer to each other.

'Did Salma go home, too, for New Year's Eve?' Shirin doesn't particularly want to know but is testing something.

'Her family lives in London, so she stayed there.'

'Right. Cool,' she says.

'We broke up, by the way.'

'Oh?'

'Yeah. It just didn't make sense to start something new now.'

She nods, looks up to his lips, then to his eyes, and they are even closer now. It is so at odds with their conversation, and so unlike Shirin. She is not sure what he means, but either way she is not taking it in. All she knows is that Kian is single – the reasons why are irrelevant. Even if he was unavailable, she thinks the normal rules wouldn't apply, not with Kian. It is dangerous. She can feel his breath on her face. His fresh, citrus aftershave. She feels this longing within her to lean even closer into it. She thinks they are for sure going to kiss – of course they are – when Phoebe calls from the other room that the taxis are here, and for everyone to down their drinks.

New Year's Day

Shirin and Phoebe are seated at Ethel's, a café often frequented by young mothers and which serves various specialist teas and all-day breakfasts. On the table between them are eggs, pancakes and hash browns. Phoebe wanted a bit of everything and ordered various plates to pick from.

At 8 a.m. Phoebe texted Shirin to see if they were still on for brunch and if anything had happened between her and Kian. Shirin replied *Yes*, and that she would tell her in person.

Sitting opposite her now, it's clear that Phoebe is either very skilled at acting or maybe she does not recognise that they had an argument. 'Did you guys ... then?' Phoebe asks between bites of crispy hash brown. 'Doesn't he have a girlfriend?'

Shirin is wearing the same outfit from last night, with a black jumper that Kian lent her. It is a struggle to look her friend in the eye.

The night before, Kian took Shirin aside from the dance floor at about 1 a.m. and said he was going home. She wanted to go home too, though she was staying with Phoebe, a person who by this point she resolutely did not want to go home with. Just beforehand, she had been in the smoking area with Phoebe. And it was in the smoking area that Shirin first saw him: Tom. One of Rob and Jordan's friends from their schooldays. He was among a crowd of people smoking their cigarettes jubilantly after the countdown. If she had kept her head down half a minute longer, perhaps not looked in his direction at that moment, she might not have known he was there too. But she had.

'Is that who I think it is?' Shirin asked Phoebe. 'Tom Possitt?'

'Oh, yeah, it is,' Phoebe replied. She was hammered by this point, seated on one of the benches, her head resting against a wooden support beam. 'He's alright now, you know.'

'*Alright?*' Shirin repeated, her voice unexpectedly sharp. 'He's a huge racist. That doesn't go away with age.'

'I don't remember that.'

'He was awful. How don't you remember?'

'It was years ago now, anyways,' Phoebe slurred, waving her hand in the air to mean *Leave it*.

Shirin knew Phoebe didn't really get the hard parts of her school experience, but this was different. Phoebe was reimagining their school experience, whitewashing it as though Phoebe's own experience was in some way akin to Shirin's. Like she could ever understand how it was for Shirin.

'How can you say that?' Shirin asked, trying to keep her voice neutral but failing. 'He and the others terrorised me. What the fuck?'

And just when she thought Phoebe would get the memo, would apologise, like a normal human being, she did the exact opposite and waved Tom down. Tom caught Phoebe's signals and made his way towards them – and Shirin was so surprised by this that she simply stood there. Then Tom was next to her, his shoulder almost touching hers as he greeted Phoebe.

'You're alright now, aren't you, Tom?' Phoebe said, patting his back.

Tom's face was fatter now, compared to back then. His teeth a pale yellow. His eyes a bright green. He laughed at Phoebe, like it was all a joke. Turned to Shirin and said hello, said she looked great now, that he had seen she was working down in London. He asked her how it was, and she said nothing, looking between her close friend and her enemy like this was a terrible dream.

She considered leaving wordlessly, had her shoulder poised to turn, but then thought of her Maman Bozorg. About how she needed to defend herself, even if it frightened her, even if it was easier to run.

'Don't talk to me, you racist prick,' she said through gritted teeth, jabbing her finger in Tom's face. Then she turned to Phoebe. 'And you – you should know better.' She pushed her way out of the crowd of people and made her way to the dance floor, where she bumped into Kian, who had just retrieved his coat to leave.

And this was why Shirin did not want to crash at Phoebe's, as originally planned. Her dad thought she was going to Phoebe's house to spend New Year's Eve, so she couldn't return home. She explained this to Kian.

'Jesus. You can crash at mine, if you like,' he said. And so she went back to his.

She had never been to his house before, though she had walked past it many times back in the day. He lived in Kirk Ella, the posh part of Hull, much further away from the club than her own family house. When the taxi dropped them off, she asked if his parents would be home. Kian told her they were at a party in Leeds and they had booked a hotel for the night there.

As she entered the house, she noticed the way the floor was tiled, the hallway large and open. She left her heels by the door, walking barefoot into the house, though there were slippers for visitors in a box next to the shoe rack. It was much neater than Shirin's mother's past method of frantically searching the bathroom and garden for plastic slippers, when Iranian visitors arrived.

He turned on the lights as he walked deeper into the house and they walked up two flights of stairs to his bedroom. His room was a large loft space, with its own en-suite. Most of his belongings looked like they were from his teen years, with tickets from bands that he'd seen live collaged over one wall. He had pictures of himself as a teenager, with people she recognised and some she didn't.

She sat on the end of his bed, folding one foot underneath herself, while he went to the bathroom. She heard his electric toothbrush's vibrations. It wasn't clear in what capacity she was there. During the taxi ride they'd sat close to each other, his hand on the top of her thigh, though he'd looked absent-minded as he'd done this. Whereas she'd been acutely conscious of his hand there.

When Kian came out of the bathroom and sat down next to her, the first thing she could smell was his minty breath. She liked it very much.

'Do you need anything?' he asked. She shook her head. 'I'm sorry about how the night ended.'

'Let's not talk,' she whispered.

His hand caressed her face then. She removed his top, and he attempted to unlace her corset. The front laces were decorative, and she reached over to her side to unzip it. His hands were on her chest, her stomach, her cheek. Her nerves were hypersensitive to his touch. They kissed slowly, tenderly. It felt both like she had finally sighed, after holding her breath for so long, and like it wasn't enough, that she needed more. His grasp on her tightened and she shifted even closer to him. He kissed her sides, and she focused on her breathing, trying to steady it, and failing. He hovered over her, the weight of his body on his biceps. He asked her if she was sure she wanted this, and she said yes, thinking there was nothing she wanted more than this with Kian.

Afterwards, they lay in bed together. His hand lightly on her stomach, the other arm around her shoulders. He nuzzled her neck, planting a soft, supple kiss there.

She played with his hands, and he took her thin hair-bobble from around her wrist and put it around his. Even his wrist was handsome, so she let him keep it there.

'I like you,' she said.

'I like you too,' he replied, smiling.

'No, I mean, it's quite rare that I like someone.'

'I mean, I've always liked you, Shirin.'

Now, with Phoebe, in the cold light of day, her stomach turns at the sight of the café food; she's definitely not ready to eat. She places both hands on the table and spreads them out, thinking over her words, before blurting out, 'Are we not going to talk about last night then?'

Phoebe's chewing slows and she swallows audibly. 'What is there to say?'

'I feel like you gaslit me with Tom. I can't believe you called him over to us after everything he did. That you're even friends with him—'

Phoebe frowns, then her whole face crumples. 'Gaslit?'

'You know, made out something didn't happen when it did.'

'But, Shirin, you're annoyed at Tom for something that happened so long ago. It's not healthy to hold on to it all. People change. And the way you spoke to him was so rude. You should really apologise. You're an adult now.' She speaks with authority, her face the picture of composure again. Her words shock Shirin into almost giving in. But she needs to do this. She regrets not backing up Mariam all those weeks ago. It's impossible to change the past, but she can do things differently now.

'No, I don't believe any of that. He and his friends were awful to me. Don't you remember? *They* never apologised to me – why the hell should I apologise to them?'

'They were mean to everyone then, weren't they? It was school, we were kids then; it's different now, Shirin.' Phoebe has moved on to the pancakes, eating a stray blueberry on the side of the plate, while Shirin's heart is hammering in her chest.

There are only a few other people in the café. It's relatively quiet for a bank holiday, though that doesn't stop Shirin leaning forward to Phoebe, speaking in hushed tones so they don't hear. 'They got Kian and me suspended – don't you remember that? How can all of that not be something you're bothered about?'

Phoebe gives Shirin a sharp look, like she is seeing her for the first time and it is an ugly sight. 'I thought we'd have a nice brunch, and that, I don't know, you'd maybe comfort me about everything I told you yesterday. I thought maybe you'd ask how things were between me and George, seeing as you snapped at me while you were drunk and left without saying goodbye. It's always about you, Shirin. I'm sorry I tried to patch things up between you and Tom, but it's in the past now. I have real-life problems *right now* and you don't give a shit.'

What few people there are at the other tables are now looking over at them.

'I do give a shit.' Shirin's voice wobbles. 'I just wanted you to know how you made me feel is all.'

'Yeah, but that's the problem – you have major main-character syndrome. You act like you're this big deal living in London, that your feelings are the only thing that matter. Whenever you call me, you bang on about work, when your job sounds cushty to me – or it's about Kian and how you're obsessed with him. You only ask about me as an afterthought.'

'That's not true—'

'It is, Shirin.'

Shirin looks down at the food, focuses on it because it's the only thing that seems real and makes sense right now. The conversation is not going how she envisaged at all. She thought Phoebe might defend herself, but would eventually apologise. While the things she's saying don't make sense, they're also things Shirin has thought about herself. That she is a shit friend, that she uses people to offload her own anxieties, that she's sad for clinging on to the past so tightly.

'Well, I'm sorry if I've been doing that,' Shirin eventually says.

'Okay, let's forget about it. Alright?'

Shirin nods, not wanting to argue any more, though she knows it's not alright. It never has been.

Pillow Talk

When Shirin shuts her eyes, memories of the night before creep into the recesses of her mind. She remembers how she and Kian struggled to sleep. They lay in bed, under the duvet, the sheets smooth and crisp against her bare legs, her arms, which were outside the covers, cool from the winter chill. Kian lay with his arms behind his head. His biceps looked good, and she considered how different he had looked at school, how slender he was then, compared to now. She ran her finger along the tattoo on his arm, and he shifted it so she could see it better.

'It's a Hafiz quote,' he said. She pulled a face, about to lightly rip into him, but he raised a finger to stop her. 'Before you say anything – I was eighteen and drunk.'

'Who gets a Hafiz quote when drunk?' she exclaimed. 'That's even worse than if you got it earnestly.' He pushed her playfully, and she bounced back up to read it properly. 'What does it say?'

'"The sun never says to the sky, 'You owe me.' Look what happens with a love like that, it lights up the whole sky."'

'That's beautiful.'

He was almost bashful and shrugged, putting both his hands back behind his head. 'I was young.'

'But it means something to you, doesn't it?'

'Not really, I was just being pretentious,' he said. Shirin didn't believe him, but didn't push it. 'How are things at work now? Last time we spoke you said you were struggling.'

She finds it hard to articulate why the things that bother her at Hoffman increasingly get to her so much. Aloud, they sound small, insignificant, like she is making a big deal out of nothing. But the little things build up inside her. It damages her soul and she is tired of it.

So she told him everything. She told him about Florence – about how she is in competition with Shirin, but already has a head start. That she took Shirin's project from her, though it was her manager's suggestion. She told him that she is often expected to be a Diversity and Inclusion officer, even though the only 'experience' she has in the role is that she is Iranian, as though her simply not being white means she can speak for every ethnic minority, every LGBTQ+ person, every working-class person, every disabled person – even people who encompass all of these categories. 'It's too much pressure,' she told him. 'My chest feels so tight sometimes. It's only really been during Christmas, going back to Tehran and seeing my Maman Bozorg, that I've been able to breathe again, to wake up and not feel this dread.'

He stroked her back, a look of concern on his face. 'You should leave,' he said.

'I can't.'

He looked confused, his dark brows downward. 'Why not?'

'It's my dream,' she said.

'Well, dreams can change. Is it still your dream?'

'I don't know. It isn't always this bad. I used to really enjoy it – like, I'd get up excited to go to work at the beginning. I love editing and brainstorming book ideas and speaking to authors. It's the other things, like the micro-aggressions and structural issues, that taint it all for me.'

Her job is like a relationship that she knows she should leave, but can't. Every time she considers quitting and moving back home or finding a job in a new field, she cannot help but think how ungrateful she is. How there are thousands of people who want her job – that she was one of them, as a new graduate.

'I don't know if it's because I'm depressed, you know. Like maybe that's the reason nothing in my life is what I want it to be. I have everything I once wanted, and it's not making me happy.'

'I mean, it could be. But it could also be that what you wanted isn't what you want any more,' he offered.

'That feels even scarier. Because then I have no idea what I want at all.' She thought Kian saw the sadness within her, though also her reluctance to discuss it further. 'It's fine, honestly.'

'I got the Hafiz quote to feel something. I was acting out because of my brother,' Kian said suddenly. 'I wasn't even drunk. That was a lie.'

She looked up at him and frowned. 'What do you mean?'

He sighed, opened his mouth to speak, but then shut it again. He shifted his position on the bed, so that he was sitting straighter and was able to look at her directly.

'You knew about my brother back then,' he began.

She nodded.

'I didn't tell you the truth about it all at the time.'

She noticed a familiar look in his eyes. He was deciding whether to tell her the whole truth or a more palatable version of it. She knew this because she also presents different versions of herself, depending on who she is talking to.

'You didn't?' she said.

'No, but now I want to.'

Talking Big

Then

The incident that led to Mehdi's imprisonment happened when Kian was walking home from school with Teddy, Koyer and Ahmed.

Teddy was telling a story about a girl he was seeing. He was red-faced and excited as he relayed how far he had got with her, leaning into the group to emphasise his point. They all knew he was exaggerating. Kian imagined that if any of it was really true, Teddy would be cooler about it, less excited, more satisfied.

For late May, it was more muggy than sunny. They had their jackets off, shoved in their backpacks, and had undone their ties so they hung looser around their necks. There wasn't long left until the summer holidays and life was good.

As Teddy continued, going into more graphic detail because he wasn't getting the reactions he wanted, Ahmed said, 'Shut up, man.' It was said in a jokey way, but Kian could sense he wasn't really joking. Of the four of them, Ahmed was the quietest. He was also the most religious; though he didn't mind most of the shit they did, he drew the line in particular places.

Teddy's face grew an even darker shade of scarlet. Kian felt a bit bad for him. He laughed to enforce the fact that Ahmed was obviously joking, and Koyer joined in, slapping Teddy on his back. The air was a bit tense after that, as though foretelling what was to come.

Teddy and Koyer walked ahead, while Ahmed and Kian hung back. 'Why do we hang out with him again?' Ahmed asked, his dark eyebrows furrowed. His lips were curled into an almost-smile though. His face was oval-shaped and thin, and he had a wisp of a moustache that he had let grow. It was the most impressive facial hair of anyone in their class.

'You know he's alright,' Kian said. 'He can just be annoying sometimes.'

It had always been Kian, Koyer and Ahmed since primary school. Though when they'd moved into high school, Teddy had joined the group. He fitted in for the most part, though maybe Kian only thought that because he liked him. Ahmed shrugged, defeated.

A red car driving past them slowed down to honk its horn three times, before the passenger leant out of the car window to shout 'Wankers!' at them. Ahmed and Kian shook their heads and laughed. Koyer, however, stepped forward, onto the kerb, turned to the car and shouted, 'Fucking dickheads!' He stuck his middle fingers up at them, waving them in the air, before adding, 'Don't run away next time, pussies!'

Teddy laughed, loud and raucous. The smile on his face soon dissipated, however, when the vehicle suddenly stopped in the middle of the road to reverse at speed towards them. Kian and Ahmed continued to walk, pretending they couldn't see what was happening, but Teddy and Koyer did not get the memo and squared up to the people in the car.

'What did you say?' the passenger said. He was a chubby lad, older than them, at least eighteen, with short strawberry-blond hair and a scowl imprinted on his pink face.

'I said,' Koyer began, elongating each word, '"Fuck off."'

The passenger spat out of the window.

'You think you're a big man, do you? Get out the car then and let's talk,' Teddy said. He didn't think they would actually leave their vehicle, which, of course, they did.

'Fuck's sake,' Ahmed muttered. 'We have to help them now.'

The driver got out of the car, a hench skinhead with tattoos on his neck. The passenger, who they had been arguing with, was smaller, fatter and less intimidating, though he looked like he could pack a punch.

'Who do you think you're talking to?' the driver said to Teddy.

'You – you started it,' Teddy said, his voice wavering now, less confident.

'I'm out now, let's talk,' the passenger said, clenching his fists. Kian was sure everyone had clocked his clenched fist, which made it obvious he didn't mean actually talk.

'Go on then,' Koyer said, fists raised. Koyer was so angry, so ready to fight all the time. There really would be no calming him down now.

'Fucking paki, go on then,' the driver said.

What happened next went by in a blur. The passenger went for Teddy and the driver for Koyer. Kian pulled the skinhead off Koyer before he could punch him, yanking him away with all his might. The driver, in return, elbowed Kian out of the way and winded him, knocking him to the ground. Other people from their school had gathered around to watch the fight. The skinhead punched Koyer square in the face and he, too, fell to the ground. The skinhead turned to Kian, laughing, picking him up by his shirt.

'You shit-faced prick touched *me*?' he said.

Kian's heart was beating out of his chest. He knew it was a clichéd phrase, but it truly felt like it was going to jump out it hurt so much, even more than his ribs where he'd been elbowed. He was scared – and so ashamed of how scared he was. The skinhead had his arm raised, drawn back, ready to hit Kian when, from behind, he heard a familiar voice say, 'What's going on here?'

Mehdi. He felt such relief. He was promptly let go. The skinhead said, 'Mehdi, mate, how's it going?' his voice softer, more jokey, with a touch of fear.

Kian straightened up his clothes, realising his shirt was ripped down the front. His first thought was: How was he going to explain this to his mum?

Looking around him, he saw his friends in similar disarray. Their clothes ripped. Koyer's nose bleeding. Ahmed with a black eye. Teddy gripping his mouth in pain. He had got off lightly by comparison.

While he was relieved to see his brother, this quickly turned to dread because Mehdi wouldn't let this go; he wouldn't defuse a situation, of course he wouldn't.

'That's my brother,' Mehdi said, pointing to Kian. He was with his friend Marshall, who was just as big as him, muscled and tall. Together they towered over the boys from the car, even though they were probably younger than them.

'It was a misunderstanding, mate,' the passenger said, stuttering.

'I don't think it was,' Mehdi said. 'You touch my brother and his friends and think you can get away with it. No, no, no.'

Unlike the previous scrapping, uneven punches, pulling of bodies – a mess of a fight really – what happened next was clean and terrifying. Mehdi punched the skinhead squarely in the face, so hard that he fell to the ground instantly. Marshall grabbed the passenger by his coat, because he was about to run away, and slammed his face into the back of the car. They then proceeded to kick them both on the ground, despite their whimpering, despite the many witnesses around them, despite Kian shouting at them to stop.

'Go home,' Mehdi told Kian after it all. 'And don't tell Mum or Dad.'

Kian realised then that he had been frozen to the spot as he'd watched it happen. When he and his friends walked back home, their legs heavy with each step, they said nothing, not even Teddy. Spinning around in his head was the thought that maybe if he had defended himself properly, instead of being so weak, his brother wouldn't have had to step in.

Maybe, if it hadn't been for Kian, Mehdi wouldn't have been sent to prison after all.

Old Wounds

Now

Kian's body is shaking as he tells the full story to Shirin, though he pretends it isn't. He has imagined her turning on him, seeing him so differently, but she only wipes tears that he didn't even know were streaming down his face and says, 'It wasn't your fault.' He says he knows it wasn't, though that is only partly true. It doesn't matter how many people tell him that, he knows the only way he can believe it is if Mehdi says it – and he hasn't. He still hasn't spoken to Mehdi about it at all since he was released, ten years ago now.

His brother now lives in Manchester with his wife and two children. He works as a substance-misuse support worker, but his road to this life was not easy. When Mehdi left juvenile prison, it was bittersweet. He returned agitated, impatient for life to resume as he'd hoped it would. He struggled to secure a job because of his criminal record. He had done poorly in the GCSEs he'd taken and, as a result, couldn't get into college. He was lost – considering different career moves every week – limiting himself to the ones that allowed a criminal record, even though they didn't suit his skillset. Meanwhile, Kian completed college, then moved to Glasgow to study Art at university. In the end, their parents were so overjoyed that one of them was going to university that they didn't fight Kian half as much as he'd expected when he told them he was going to study Art.

It was only when Mehdi dedicated himself to Islam, and began going to the local mosque, that he found some semblance of peace and calm. He met other reformed men who mentored him, related to him on a level no one else had. He completed an access course to go to university to study Psychology, and his life took a different path. Despite this, though, Kian cannot help but feel responsible for the path Mehdi could have taken. The subject of his imprisonment is glossed over. As if that year – and how it affected Mehdi's future – never happened at all. Though Kian's part in it, his guilt, sits heavy in his chest. It is a burden he'll carry for ever.

A Perfect Subject

Then

Shirin was one of the few things that kept Kian afloat. Even if he never quite acknowledged it, each day when he woke up he looked forward to seeing her in school, even if it was only in passing, even if they didn't have a chance to speak. And if they had planned to skip class together, he would think of all the things he wanted to say to her. Like had she listened to The xx before? Yes, she loved them. Did she like Kings of Leon? No, 'Sex on Fire' was a song that made her cringe (they then had a ten-minute debate in which he tried to convince her that she was wrong). Or sometimes they could tell that the other had something on their mind. Like when his brother got into a fight in prison, and his parents said he might not be let out after a year, which made Kian feel physically sick for days. Or when, later, they agreed just to give him a warning, because it wasn't that severe. Back then, the world didn't openly talk about anxiety. So Kian didn't know the sick feeling he had was anxiety. That his thinking sometimes, over and over and over, *I wish I didn't exist* was an intrusive thought. It wasn't true, because he had no intention of acting on the wish, but the sentence still pervaded his thoughts.

He had never had a friend like Shirin. He had friends he saw after school and weekends, but talking about their feelings wasn't something they did. With Shirin he discovered that it was something he needed to do, and she was there for him. Without her he felt he would drown completely.

Decisions needed to be made. While his brother's life was paused, his was moving on. His parents made passing comments about university, about their friend Tahereh's son and how he was studying Engineering at Oxford, or about Pouran's daughter, who was doing Law at UCL. In the air was expectation, though Kian preferred it to the perpetual stench of disappointment and anguish.

On a dry spring day Shirin asked, 'What subjects are you going to study in sixth form?'

She had brought a polka-dot fleece blanket with her, which they sat on, looking ahead of them at the Humber Bridge, which had become a regular spot they met at. He often wondered who she told her parents she was seeing. Her mum had even dropped her off today, though Shirin had told Kian to pretend he didn't know her until her mum had driven off. On the blanket between them now was a half-eaten Easter egg that they had got on clearance. They broke off pieces to eat.

He was wearing a hoodie, shorts and Converse. It wasn't really hot enough to justify the shorts, but between the travelling clouds the sun would shine down on them, warming his legs up. Shirin wore dark jeans and a black jumper, her eyes smoky. Everything with Rob had died down, and Shirin said she was over it, but Kian knew she wasn't completely.

He paused as though he had not thought about what he was planning to study, though he had. 'History, Politics, English and Geography.'

Shirin's hand landed on Kian's shoulder. 'Hold up. Not Art?'

He shrugged, though he didn't mind her hand there. She removed it and clasped both her hands behind her back, like she was stretching. 'I want to do Politics at uni, so it doesn't make sense to do Art,' he said.

'But you only need three A-levels to get into a good uni – can't Art be your fun fourth one? That's what I'm doing with Drama.'

'Yeah, I don't know. My parents are having a hard time right now. I don't want to cause any arguments or anything. And I get where they're coming from – they just want to make sure I can get into a good uni.' Kian felt weak saying these words aloud. It wasn't him, he didn't think, to be like this. But his mum was always sad now, his dad always quiet, though snappy when he needed to be.

'I mean, do you even want to do Politics at uni? I thought you were really into art.' She took a bite out of an uneven piece of Easter egg.

He gulped, though his throat was dry and, rather than look ahead, as he had been doing, he turned to glance at Shirin. He could feel the almost helpless look on his face as he said, 'I dunno.'

Her face softened and she looked down for a moment before looking back up at him, this time her face more confident, less sympathetic. 'I think you know what that means.'

Sara Jafari

'You don't get it,' he said. 'Your parents are quite relaxed with you.' She gave him a look. 'Obviously not with boys and stuff, but you can tell them you're doing Drama and they will simply accept it. Mine are so stressed about my brother, and me turning out like him, they won't let me do anything that strays from the path they want for me.'

'It's your life though,' she said slowly, as though testing out his reaction to this hard truth.

He shrugged. 'I mean, what job prospects would I have if I did Art at uni? I'm not gonna be an artist or anything. How many artists from Hull do you know?'

'Isn't David Hockney from Bridlington?'

'I said Hull.'

'Well, there probably are, but I'm not the one into art, so I dunno.' Her tone was joking, and his lips curved up into a small smile.

'It stresses me out sometimes, always having to be the good child,' he confessed.

'I bet,' she said. 'But you need to live your own life. Your brother will be out of prison soon, and it's not fair for you to do things you don't want to do – which can affect your whole life – just so they'll feel a bit less bad about the situation. They'll get over it if you do Art, trust me on this.'

'Maybe,' he said, not believing it.

She paused for a moment before saying, 'I can't wait till I can move out of here and start again.'

'Where would you want to go?'

'Maybe London or Manchester – somewhere big and different.'

'Is that because you want to get away from Rob and that lot?' It came out of his mouth before he'd processed what he was asking.

Shirin visibly gulped and looked away. 'No, it's not only that, or them.' In the past, she had told him about her parents. How they argued and she was often caught in the middle. Once she'd told him that she thought she was an inconvenience in their lives, and Kian had told her that couldn't be true. She'd replied that he didn't know them like she did. He had noticed, though, that her parents hadn't come to parents' evening. When he'd asked her about it, she'd said they hadn't wanted to go, and that the only family member who really cared about her was her grandmother, who lived in Iran.

'I just want to start afresh, reinvent myself and work at one of the big publishing houses as an editor and read books all day. That'd be the dream,' she continued.

He didn't think he had seen Shirin with such a dream-like expression on her face before.

'Well, I like you as you are, so I don't think you need to reinvent yourself,' he eventually said.

Her eyes were soft as they locked with his, until hers moved towards his open backpack, to the sketchbook that was barely visible. Then he felt himself go still, all funny, like he had been doing something wrong – or maybe that was a reflex from hiding his drawings from his parents for so long.

Sometimes he'd sit here alone with his sketchbook, before Shirin arrived, and he would attempt to draw the bridge, or the greenery, with mixed results. He was getting better, but his shading needed work. It was embarrassing doing it when there were people his age there, so he'd only really do it if he could be bothered to come early in the morning. He had done some light sketching before he'd met Shirin here. He was venturing into drawing portraits of people now. It had begun as cartoons that he would doodle at the back of his workbook, and now he'd moved on to more realist sketches.

'Can I look at it?' she asked.

He hesitated, wasn't sure if he could say no, so he said, 'Er, okay.' He handed the sketchbook to her slowly, wondering if somehow he could not show it to her, but she took it from him readily and began flicking through. The majority of the drawings were of the Humber Bridge, or greenery; a few of Mehdi that he thought were a bit shit, and he told her this.

He had attempted to draw Mehdi just after he'd been sent away, but it was hard to imagine him exactly as he was. Kian had found the most recent school picture of him and had copied that, but it was missing something. The smile was stilted, fake. It was so alien from what he knew his brother looked like smiling. The way his eyes crinkled, his lopsided, broad smile; not this close-lipped, barely there, can-this-be-over smile. Though even this version of Mehdi was long gone now.

'They're really good – what you on about?' Shirin had the most recent sketch of Mehdi open, and her fingers lightly traced over it. 'So beautiful,' she whispered.

He felt his face getting hot, began to give a step-by-step critique of his work and what could be better about it.

'You need to learn how to take a compliment, mate,' she said. The *mate* made him laugh, and then she began to laugh too. 'You know, if you ever want to draw *me*, I'd very happily be a model.'

'Seriously?' he said.

'Hell yes.'

'Right now?'

'Why not?' She smiled, adjusted herself so that she was sitting cross-legged in front of him, and raised her chin dramatically high. 'Go on then.'

He took the sketchbook from her and retrieved a pencil from his backpack. He sat so that his knees were raised to support the sketchbook as he began. They sat there for the next two hours, talking about not much, but also everything. She asked if she could keep the drawing when he was done, and he said she could. He thought it'd be weird if he said he'd like to keep it, which he would have. In the end, though, she forgot to ask him for it, and he didn't remind her. It was the best sketch he had done, though he wasn't sure if the sole reason for that was because Shirin Bayat was his subject.

A Portrait

Now

At midday on 4 January, Shirin arrives at Kian's flat. He opens the front door with his hair dishevelled, wearing a grey hoodie and Adidas shorts, his feet bare. The way the hoodie hugs his shoulders is attractive, in the way Shirin thinks men's bodies often are in athletic wear. He steps out of the way for her to enter and she removes her boots by the door. Without her platform shoes she feels especially small next to him, her eyes level with his chest now. She wonders if his heart is beating as quickly as hers, if being this close to each other for the first time since New Year brings back all the memories of their night together for him, too.

He asks her if she wants a cup of tea and Shirin nods, even though she doesn't. He leads the way to the kitchen and it looks different from when she was here last, for his house-warming party. It appears bigger now it's empty of people, the winter sun shining through the windows. The kitchen is at the back of the house, with ugly wooden cabinets from the nineties. And it is this that makes her feel a little less on edge somehow, this ugliness.

As Kian fills the kettle with water he asks her how her train journey was, back down to London, and she murmurs something like, *Okay – long*. With his back to her, she thinks he looks tense, not at all relaxed, and again this calms her, like it's not just her; all this spinning isn't only in her head.

There is this thing between them now and it makes them awkward, the conversation mundane. They don't look into each other's eyes, until Kian flicks the power on the kettle and turns, leaning against a cabinet. It is only then that their eyes lock. And even this makes Shirin go funny inside, reviving a stirring within her. It is embarrassing, how much she wants him. How on the Tube over here, each time her mind wandered she imagined his hands on her body, his lips on hers. She hasn't felt this strongly about someone in a long time. It is almost reminiscent of the way she felt with her first serious boyfriend, but she was clouded by first love, not yet hardened by failed relationships and situationships. So while she wants to indulge in this feeling, she knows leaning into it wouldn't be wise, that it has never been easy for them, so why would that change now?

Kian bites his bottom lip, unconsciously, and her eyes flicker down and then back up again, meeting his gaze. The hiss of the kettle grows louder in the background. Before the kettle clicks, there is a sudden urgency between them. She is not sure who steps forward first, but his hands are around her waist, pulling her towards him, against him. She feels as though she needs him – needs his lips on her again, needs all of him.

They kiss and his hands move up to her face, his palms cupping her cheeks as they do so, while his hardness is pressed against her. And it's this that makes her bite his lip a little too hard, but he shakes his head, says, 'It's alright, it's alright,' a glazed, concentrated expression on his face that is very attractive.

When they make their way to his bedroom, she vaguely notices that it is neat, like he has just tidied it. They undress each other, at first slowly and then more quickly. The bed sheets are cool against their bare skin. There is the Kian she knew, growing up – the boy who was both sensitive and angry; the man she has been speaking to the past few months, who is confident, well adjusted to adulthood; and then there is this Kian, who she is seeing with fresh eyes. He is tender in the way he handles her, in the way his hands skim over her abdomen, in the way he touches her in exactly the right places, like he knows her body, like he has been with her many times before.

She can finally let out a breath when he begins stroking her, and it is like she has been holding it since they were last together, like she needs him to breathe now. She wants him so badly it feels like she might burst. When he enters her, he kisses the side of her neck and she thinks they fit together so perfectly, which makes her lift herself higher and wrap her legs tighter around his waist, wanting all of him – all of this – right now. He groans in her ear, his breath warm, her own sounds quiet and uncontrollable. She hates how right this feels, how she thinks that only in this moment does she feel most herself, unclothed with Kian atop her. It feels like such an unfeminist, un-Shirin thought, but it's truthful.

'I've missed you,' she breathes, and she isn't even sure what she is referring to, whether she is saying she has missed him in the three days they've been apart, or during the ten years they weren't speaking.

'Shirin,' he says, moving slowly. 'I've not stopped thinking about you.' His eyes bore into hers. She feels a bubbling within her, and the urge to say something that she thinks can't be true, so she presses her lips against his to stop it from coming out.

After, they lie on his bed, her head against his chest. He smells of aftershave and sweat, his sheets of washing detergent.

'That was nice,' he says.

'Very nice,' she agrees. 'When are your housemates back?'

'Tomorrow. Will you stay over tonight?'

'I could do, yeah,' she says, having already brought her toothbrush, contact lenses and three-step skincare routine with her.

He smiles, a genuine smile, like this greatly pleases him. She feels high – it is an unfamiliar feeling, this kind of happiness. But unlike when they were having sex, Shirin can see their situation more clearly: that while she does feel herself when she's with Kian, there is still the thing they've not spoken about hanging between them. The incident. The words that were spoken after, especially given what he told her about his brother, about the guilt he still carries. It is this thought that makes her pull away from him and reach across for her slip-dress. Without her tights or cardigan it looks more like lingerie. She puts it on and turns to see Kian lying there, frowning. His abs are tight – and she thinks how, even now, can she be such a pervert, how can her brain fixate on how hot he is?

'Something wrong?' he says.

She shakes her head, says no, and that she needs to pee.

It is just past 3 p.m. when they go back downstairs for food. Kian rummages in his fridge and retrieves grapes, olives, hummus and crusty bread. Shirin jokes that these are very middle-class snacks, and he tells her to do one. She wonders whether this food they're eating now is something he's bought especially for her, because when he transfers the food from the packets into bowls and plates, she notices they haven't been opened yet.

He asks if he can paint her, properly this time. He says he has always wanted to, and as he says this the tops of his ears go a wonderful pink, and her pathetic heart goes *pitter-patter*, which prompts her to say, 'Okay, why not?'

On their way to the summerhouse he grabs her hand between his, lifts it to his lips and kisses it. A ginger cat is walking along the wooden fence that separates the gardens from each other, and Kian tells her the cat often comes into their house, and she is nodding but can barely concentrate, even his hand on hers distracts her.

The summerhouse is more homely now. The boxes are no longer there, and neither is the record player. He tells her it's in the sitting room now, and in its place are a pair of black Bluetooth speakers on his desk. He unfolds a chair that has been leaning against the wall and indicates for her to sit on it.

Shirin watches as he sets up his easel and paints, a look of concentration on his face. She finds it enticing, seeing a person focusing on something they are talented at. 'You don't have to stay in the exact spot or anything,' he says. 'But try not to move too much.'

The easel is now holding up a medium-sized canvas, and in his hand is a wooden palette, with various blobs of paint on it, ranging from creams to pinks and reds. He smiles to himself, his face half hidden by the canvas in front of him. The last of the daylight shines into the room, creating the patterns of the windowpanes on Shirin's face as she poses.

'That seems like a contradiction, but okay.' She debates how to sit, never quite liking photographs of herself sitting down. She crosses her legs and leans to one side, looking off out of the window.

'No,' Kian says. 'Look at me.'

'I like my profile,' she says. Her mum would always ask her to look down or away for pictures – something about her eyes being a bit too wild, not soft enough.

'I want to see you, properly. It's important for me to see your eyes.'

'They are the window to the soul,' she says with an eye-roll, though taking his direction and looking at him.

He picks up his phone and then 'Here Comes the Sun' plays over the speakers.

'I didn't know you liked The Beatles. It feels a very white thing to like.'

He barks out a laugh. 'So rude. I was never a massive fan, but I've got into them lately.' He smiles bashfully and her heart soars. She has never really considered The Beatles before and would rather hear a different song, but doesn't say anything more about it. Kian returns to the canvas, concentration back on his face.

'So, tell me, do you always paint the girls you've been with?' she asks.

The side of his mouth turns upwards in a smirk. 'The girls I've been with,' he repeats slowly.

She remembers the painting she saw in here last time, which is now gone. He doesn't say anything else, which prompts her to say, 'Come on. I'm curious.'

He puts his utensils down, but does not walk towards her, the canvas a barrier between them. 'No, not really.'

It doesn't answer her question, but she nods anyway, accepting this. She doesn't know why she particularly cares. She thinks she must want confirmation that this moment between them is special, because she doesn't always get these things right – but this time it feels different.

He begins his painting in earnest now. He mixes red, blue and yellow together, so it makes a brown colour. Then he adds white and more yellow to make her skin tone. Lightly his paintbrush caresses the canvas. He is skilful in his approach.

They discuss the fallout from Rob Grayson's book being cancelled. Although Kian has the appearance of being unbothered, she can see excitement in his eyes. She feels bolder now around him, so asks him why he pretends not to care – and he says he thought if he pretended, it would eventually be a reality. She remembers that that's what she used to do at school. It's curious, she thinks now, how their roles are reversed. How it's often Kian giving Shirin advice, when before he leant on her – and part of her liked that.

To preserve her unsteady sanity, yesterday she muted Rob Grayson's name on all her social-media platforms. Over the past month she would see his name pop up – in a news article, Twitter thread, or one of his own tweets that someone she knew had retweeted and so it appeared on her feed, and it wouldn't quite derail her, but she would feel a heaviness inside her, like she is still bound by her past.

'Did your brother come over for Christmas?' she asks.

He nods. 'With his family, yeah. You can bet I got a roasting from everyone about doing my Masters and not settling down with a "real" job. Somehow they still compare me to Mehdi – only now I should be more like him, less "artsy" and more realistic. And when I mentioned my residency abroad, they lost their minds. They forget how miserable I was before, working a nine-to-five job in Manchester. And my parents can't talk – they left their entire family in Iran for England permanently, and I'm only talking about six months abroad.' He speaks quickly, slightly self-conscious when he finishes his rant.

She looks off past his shoulder and attempts to keep her face neutral when she says, 'Abroad?'

His hands still and they look at each other. His eyes squint slightly. 'Yeah, I told you about it, didn't I?'

'I don't remember,' she says slowly. 'Do you know where?'

'New York is my first choice. Berlin my second.'

Rather than spiralling and letting her mind linger on thinking, *Fuck, fuck, fuck, fuck, fuck*, she tells him that sounds amazing. Kian says he might not even get it anyway, and to change the subject he asks, 'So, when was your last relationship?'

She lets out a humourless laugh, the kind of laugh that is more to preface that you're not bothered about what you're going to say next, when really you are. 'Great subject change. I don't know – years ago. I've only really had one official boyfriend. I was twenty-one and had just graduated. We were together for two years. I've seen people since, but nothing serious.'

Shirin met Paul at Rye Wax on a night out with Hana, and their relationship was tumultuous. They consistently broke up and got back together again. She lost her virginity to him. It was this that made her cling to him and want to make it work. Hana calls him a softboi, which Shirin googled to find out means an artsy fuckboy. He fits the criteria. Paul is with a lifestyle influencer now, who has 104 k followers on Instagram, and Shirin respectfully hates them both.

'So you've not had a boyfriend since then?'

'No,' she says. 'But I don't think that's me being picky, like Millie often says. I'd say selective, rather.' She thinks if the person she is dating might eventually be inside her, it makes sense to be selective, and she says this, too, to Kian.

He bursts out in a surprised laugh at this. 'Jesus! Fair enough.'

'What I'd like to know is,' she begins, 'what really happened with Salma? You were vague before.'

His smile falters now, his hand gripping more tightly onto the paintbrush between his fingers. This alarms her. She wonders, startlingly for the first time, if she is a rebound. She had assumed that what this was between them was much more than that, even if it wasn't yet serious. She thought herself worth more to Kian than simply a distraction.

He looks up at her, his eyes a little darker, sadder. What he says next is in some ways worse. 'I broke it off because she suggested we try long-distance if I get my residency, and I realised I didn't want to do that, that actually I didn't want something serious right now. It didn't seem fair to her to continue things if I knew this, too. I don't think long-distance would work for me, if I do get a place, especially when I chose to drop everything for this course. I don't want to have any regrets, or wish I savoured the moment more. Does that make sense?'

'It does, yeah,' she says. Of course.

Tate Modern

Hana is late. Though this is not unusual, Shirin is conscious of people around her waiting too, their friends arriving and them leaving together. Nine separate people have completed this cycle, and she is still waiting. Each time Shirin texts Hana to see where she is, she says she's five minutes away, but when five minutes have passed, she says another five minutes. And on, and on, and on.

Her Maman Bozorg calls her while she is waiting. Whenever they speak it's hard to end the conversation, so Shirin lets the call ring out. Doing so elicits a pang of guilt because they keep missing each other's calls. She has quickly found herself back to being overwhelmed and busy at work, often working late into the evenings, which results in her forgetting to call her grandmother back. She resolves to phone her on the weekend.

Shirin is peculiarly nervous for this meeting with Hana now. She has never been nervous to see Hana before. Subconsciously, she realises now they have grown apart, without anything particularly dramatic having happened between them. Hana was irritated to hear that Shirin had acquired Abigail's book, though Shirin pitched it to seem as though it was less her idea than it actually was. They text less frequently because they have less to say to one another; their lives are too different. Hana's life, Shirin feels, is infinitely more fun and carefree. Shirin sees herself growing more dull as the years pass, her primary conversation topics being work and the issues there, which really, unless you're involved, is boring. Her social life is not particularly engaging, while Hana continues to go out most weekends (though she will tell Shirin that she is not, or she will tell her that she is but not extend an invite).

It is a particularly cold January evening. Despite the fur jacket Shirin wears – two sizes too big, from a vintage shop in Dalston – and multiple layers, she can feel the chill. Her ears, which habitually pop out of her hair, as though to see what is going on, are red and icy. She takes her hands out of her pockets to text Hana again at the same time as she sees her approach in the distance. Hana is wearing an oversized leather coat, a beret and pointed boots. She looks significantly cooler than Shirin.

'Sorry, sorry,' Hana says as she approaches, though she does not offer an excuse as to why she is thirty-five minutes late.

'You're always late,' Shirin says, in a jokey tone, though it does not match how she feels.

'I know, it's a chronic problem. You should know by now to be late yourself, then we'd both be on time.'

They enter the art gallery and have their bags checked upon arrival. The security guard probes Shirin's work bag, with the empty Tupperware wrapped in a Sainsbury's bag, using his security stick to dig to the bottom, past sanitary towels and Sharpies. He nods, satisfied. Hana comes with a mini cross-body bag, which is looked at very briefly.

They don't have a particular exhibition they want to see; Hana said she wanted to do something free. They wander the halls, barely looking at the paintings on the walls as they speak.

'So, you were in Paris for New Year's Eve?' Shirin says.

Hana looks at Shirin initially like she doesn't understand what she's saying, then in a flash nods her head rapidly. 'Yes! God, it feels like ages ago now. Valentia's mum has a flat in Paris and invited me along. Can you believe it? It was amazing. I really needed that break.' Shirin thinks Valentia is the one whose dad works for Chanel or Hermès. Somewhere impressive and luxurious, either way.

'That's so cool,' Shirin says, her voice empty. This urge to compare their lives emerges again. She wants to shake it off so she can move on with her life, but it remains a weight close to her back.

'They're all really cool. I'm so glad I met them.'

'I'd like to meet them sometime,' Shirin says, a half-fib. She has nothing inherently against rich people, but it is not their company that she would choose to keep. She works among too many of them, anyway. This thought of hers feels unnecessary, though she cannot muster any guilt about it.

'Yeah, maybe,' Hana says breezily. They pass a Picasso painting. Both stop for half a minute to observe, though Shirin is only pretending to observe. When did it become so awkward between them? Why do they have so little to say to each other? 'What did you do for New Year's Eve then?' Hana asks.

It was ten days ago now. Shirin has since returned to work. It was strange how she had forgotten the drudgery of her commute to work, the sticky bodies against hers, the way she can smell coffee on other people's breath. Perplexing how the mind quickly discards such memories. Though commuting hell aside, the office is quieter and much calmer in the New Year, post-Christmas. There is less urgency to every task, for now.

Shirin continues to work on Abigail's book with Florence. Though Florence now rarely responds to Abigail's emails, so it is Shirin who is answering queries, liaising with her agent, sending edit notes on the essays Abigail submits. It is as if now that Florence has the credit and praise, she no longer needs to work on the project. This suits Shirin, who would rather not work with her, but it makes Florence's motives so clear, so unopen to interpretation.

She tells Hana everything, toning down how much she likes Kian, while heightening how terrible her argument with Phoebe was. 'Um, what?' Hana raises her hand in the air between herself and Shirin and makes them stop by a floor-to-ceiling painting that is essentially painted black canvas with a tiny white dot in the middle. 'I never liked her.'

'Well, you never said so.'

'I thought she was your home-town friend, I didn't want to seem rude,' Hana says, pressing her lips together. 'But I knew she wasn't good. She always made you smaller when you were with her.'

Shirin has this urge to say, *Don't you do that?* But she isn't sure if that's fair. Maybe it isn't Hana that makes her do that, but it is Shirin who does it to herself. Maybe it is through being friends with people like Phoebe that Shirin thinks friendships need to be like that. She isn't sure.

'I don't know. It was just quite sad,' Shirin says. They've not spoken since brunch, though they still like each other's pictures on Instagram, which somehow is worse than if they had no contact at all.

'Fuck her anyway,' Hana says. 'Tell me more about Kian. How is it?' Hana has an expression like a Cheshire cat, and Shirin wants to fill Hana with exciting, good news, but the reality feels to her far from that.

'Well, he might be moving abroad soon. So, that's great.' Kian has told her that if he gets an arts residency placement, he will be leaving in early spring.

Hana rolls her eyes now, tells Shirin to enjoy the moment and not think about all of that. Shirin wishes she could. She wishes she could be the kind of person who falls into things head-first and thinks of the consequences later. But even if she was able to do that, it's different with Kian; they have a history. A history her friend knows little about. It feels too big to drop it in now. To have lost Kian once before, and now to have started something again only for it to end suddenly, would tear her apart all over again.

'What are you worried about?' Hana asks now, as though hearing her thoughts.

It makes her jolt to awareness, out of her spiralling mind. 'That I'll end up falling for him, if we continue to see each other, and get hurt when it ends. I'm not like you,' Shirin says. This is true, at least. 'Like, last week I went to his and we hung out and it felt so nice, so perfect. Then he painted me—'

Hana stops them again. 'Hold up. He *painted* you? That's so sexy.'

This makes Shirin smile, though she tries to mask it. 'I mean, yeah, it was.'

'I'm always debating whether I'd want a man who's a rich banker or a poor but sexy artist. You're living one of the dreams, Shirin. Enjoy it – everyone needs a fling every once in a while.'

'But it's too complicated. What we're doing is very stupid. You know I get attached to people.'

It is frustrating not telling Hana exactly what happened between her and Kian. She thinks if Hana knew she might understand, but she doesn't want to go into it. 'Life comes at us fast. If he makes you happy, even if it's temporary, I say you should go for it. You could die tomorrow!' Hana says, and Shirin rolls her eyes at the cliché, but Hana continues. '*He* could die tomorrow. Who knows? What will remain, though, is the fact that you, Shirin Bayat, are his muse.' Hana gives Shirin an irritating sarcastic look, and hooks her arm through Shirin's, and it is nice to walk arm-in-arm, like old times almost.

'I wouldn't go that far,' Shirin eventually says, though she lets herself imagine a world in which she is Kian's muse. Such thoughts are brief and short-lived – like the beginning of her relationship with Kian, she thinks.

*

That evening, Kian messages Shirin asking if he can come over. It is 9 p.m. and she has just taken off her make-up. The matching yellow pyjama set she is wearing clashes with her bleached hair; she bought it when her hair was a natural brunette. Her housemates are in their respective rooms, as usual, her own bedroom door locked.

Through the walls on either side of her she can hear murmurings from her flatmates. One on the phone, the other with her boyfriend over, and she can hear their laughter. Jane, the one speaking on the phone now, sent her a text earlier in the day, telling her to not have her alarm so loud in the morning because it wakes her thirty minutes earlier than she needs to. Shirin apologised, ashamed at both waking her up and being told off. In turn, though, she asked Jane if she could not speak on the phone late at night, to which Jane replied no, because it's her flat too. So it is confirmed that they will be actively avoiding each other even more than usual this week.

Now she looks at Kian's message again. She knows exactly what her answer will be, so her pondering is moot. A waste of time really.

Forty-five minutes later Kian is in her bedroom. Shirin has changed into leggings and a crop top to give the appearance of casualness. Kian is in navy cord trousers and a grey high-necked top. His hair is still damp from having showered at the gym just before he came here. He's wearing his clear glasses, though when they begin kissing, Shirin removes them and places them on her bedside table. His mouth tastes ever so slightly like a strawberry protein-shake. The imprint of his glasses remains on the bridge of his nose and she traces it with her fingertips, while he watches her with a doe-like expression. They have said very little to each other since he arrived, like they want to ignore that this is a bad idea.

Kian catches Shirin's hand and presses his lips to her knuckles, and despite the way this makes her feel, she asks, 'Why are you here?'

'Do you not want me to be?' he says, putting her hand down. His voice is steady, though his brown eyes are wide, giving him away entirely.

'Of course I do,' she says.

At this, he begins kissing the base of her neck, and her eyes shut of their own accord. It's so hard to concentrate, to think clearly and logically around him, especially when he is touching her, kissing her like this.

She pulls back. 'Aren't you worried we're only making things more complicated when you leave?' she asks slowly, finding some comfort in successfully avoiding his gaze, to stop herself crumbling entirely.

Kian catches her eye and holds it, and, with that, her resolve cracks. 'I'm not thinking about that. I might not even get a place. It's not guaranteed. But this,' and he takes hold of both her hands. 'All I know is that right now I want this – you. I feel so good with you, Shirin.'

Her name on his lips does things to her, which prompts her to ask, 'How long have you wanted me?'

'Since I saw you at my house-party. With your pink hair and cute dress,' he says, looking down at her now, making her heart beat quickly.

'Not before then?' she says, testing waters she needn't test, wanting to see how far she can go.

He only half takes the bait though, and lets out a small laugh. 'You know I fancied you at school,' he says. 'Everyone knew that.'

At this she frowns. To her this was never clear. She says as much to him now.

Kian shakes his head in dismay. 'It was a weird time. I was so distracted and angry about my brother and everything at home, but I definitely fancied you then. I could never tell if you liked me back though. And I didn't want to ruin our friendship if you didn't. Our friendship was everything to me then.'

A pang of uneasiness passes through her. 'I felt the same,' is all she can say.

His eyes darken and his lips part ever so slightly. 'About which part?'

'All of it.'

Round and round in her head are the implications of what he's just said. That he's always wanted her. And if she had known ... Rather than indulge in the past, though, Shirin gets up and stands over Kian, who is sitting on the edge of the bed. She puts her hands on his shoulders and climbs on top of him, so she is straddling him. He watches her as she takes his hand and puts his thumb in her mouth. His eyes flutter shut and he rocks against her. Soon their clothes are removed one by one; she reaches over for a condom and then he is inside her. She pushes her body down each time he thrusts upwards, and each time they meet she cannot hold back her moans. He holds her close against him, their breaths mingled together. He tells her he's only ever wanted her, and she says she is his. He asks her to repeat this over and over again.

After, he stays the night and holds her in the dark. She thinks she might love him but doesn't say it. His hand is wrapped around her waist and she clutches it.

'I struggle to fall asleep,' she tells him.

'What do you think about?' he asks.

She sighs. 'Everything I've done wrong, or just bad things.'

He pauses, doesn't say anything for a beat or two. 'What bad things?'

It's easier to speak candidly in the dark, facing away from him. She shuts her eyes. 'That day we got suspended. The way I was pushed around. How often that happened back then.'

She keeps her hands on top of his and he squeezes them. 'The way you were treated was really fucked up. It wasn't fair. They'd say it was abuse if it happened now, you know,' he says, his voice low.

She frowns. Abuse feels dramatic, like they didn't do it to everyone who was different. She says this to him and she feels Kian shaking his head behind her.

'Let yourself process it, Shirin. You deserve to.'

'I don't know how,' she confesses.

'It might take time, but I'm here for you,' he says. 'Talk to me about it.'

His body against hers is comforting and solid, and she leans into him. 'Thank you,' she says.

Inhaling his scent, she resolves that they're in too deep now. Either way, she is going to be hurt, it's just a case of it happening now or later. Because she is human after all, she chooses later, to enjoy Kian now.

Herne Hill Market

On a Sunday morning Kian and Shirin walk down the road from Kian's house to Herne Hill market. They rarely stay at her flat. His housemates are seldom in and, if they are, there is still enough space that they do not feel on top of each other, like they do in Shirin's flat. The past month is a blur, though Shirin has tried in vain to make time slow. It is much harder to stop time when it is enjoyable. They'll go out for dinner in Soho, on a long walk and coffee on Hampstead Heath, to the pub for Sunday lunch with their friends in Herne Hill, on a night out in Hackney Wick. There is no conversation about what they are, because they both know what they are doing is stupid. They find themselves drawn to each other, unable to stop whatever this is.

The disparity between Brixton and Herne Hill – which Kian lives between – is stark, despite them being only a twenty-minute walk from each other. Shirin often marvels at this in London; there will be old-school fish markets and butchers, and then down the road bougie coffee shops and independent bookshops. The market is just outside Herne Hill station and is bustling with people. The stalls sell food from around the world, and at each stall is a queue of people. Kian walks to his favourite coffee stall and orders two lattes, while she wanders towards the bakery stand. She gets them two large croissants, which are given to her in striped paper bags. While she waits in line she reflects on how, on the walk over here, she tried to take Kian's hand, but he walked with a bigger gap than normal between them, his jaw tense. When the market trader calls, 'Next!' he has to say it twice before Shirin notices it's her turn to order.

Today is a crisp winter's day, the sky cloudy. She is wearing a navy ankle-length coat, a brown scarf and mittens to defy the cold. She meets Kian back at the coffee stall and he hands her a takeaway cup, which she eagerly brings to her face, hoping the heat from the cup will provide her with warmth. Kian, conversely, is wearing only a grey hoodie and slim-fitting tracksuit bottoms. Whenever she comments on his lack of coat, he says it isn't that cold, that he doesn't feel it. At night, when her feet are icy, she likes to press them against his warm legs. He protests, initially, but then relents, and he is like her own hot-water bottle that she can snuggle into, while he wraps his arms around her. It is such a privilege, she thinks, to have someone to hold at night. When she lies next to Kian she sleeps soundly. She doesn't overthink; doom does not envelop her. This reliance, though, is concerning, considering they have only been together for a month now.

The night before, they went for dinner and drinks at a nearby Mexican restaurant. Kian seemed off then – less chatty, more sombre. Shirin asked him if everything was okay and he said it was, and that he was tired from boxing earlier in the day. When he'd first told her he boxed she'd been surprised; it was never something he took an interest in, and it seems so at odds with what his passion is – preserving his hands for his paintings. He told her it de-stresses him, and that he took it up when he was in college. Just those words – the implications of it all – lingered in the air. They stopped talking when he went to college and she to sixth form. Last night she almost asked him about it – whether he began boxing as an anger-management tool or whether it was because he felt like he needed to know how to defend himself – but she decided against it. There's a reason they haven't spoken about that time. A mutual agreement. Instead she asked him why he needed de-stressing, what it was that was bothering him. Across from her in the restaurant, his mouth tightened. He lifted his drink and kept it by his mouth. He opened his mouth like he was going to tell her what was wrong, but nothing came out, and instead he took a long sip and afterwards told her that his course is harder than he thought it would be, that he's falling behind and needs to spend more time in the studio. In return, she said her work was busy, too, and she wasn't sure why she felt the need to make a competition out of their work.

She wonders now, as they walk to Brockwell Park, if he was trying to say that she is the problem. They spend every other day together now – and it's mostly at his suggestion. When they had sex last night, he buried at his face in her neck as he moved, and she couldn't help but wonder if he was avoiding her eyes. Something was off.

They find a bench in the park that overlooks a group of children playing football in the distance. She leaves her croissant in the bag and sips her coffee. He doesn't eat his either.

'I have something I need to tell you,' he says, looking to the distance, his eyes narrowed.

'You do?' she says coolly, her heart thudding.

'I got offered a residency at a gallery in New York.' He is looking down now, at his takeaway cup, though her gaze is on his face, searching it for more information than he is giving her. 'And what they offered me is a little different from what I thought I'd get. It'll be for a year and it would mean I need to fly out in two weeks.'

She chews the inside of her mouth for a few seconds before speaking. Her hands grip her coffee cup more tightly. 'That's incredible,' she says. 'Congratulations.' She knows she needs to fix her face into a smile, to not look as devastated as she feels. Despite knowing this was coming, it still comes as a shock. 'When did you find out?'

'Last week,' he says. She nods, understanding now. 'I have to take this opportunity,' he goes on, his voice a little cooler, harder at the edges. She looks away from him.

'Of course you do,' she says, irritated now that he'd even think she'd ask him to stay, that she would ever want to hold him back.

He sighs, which prompts her to look at him. His eyes appear pained, though at the same time pitying, and she hates the thought of him feeling sorry for her. Or that, in this situation, it is she who should be the one that is deserving of sympathy.

'We were probably better as friends anyway,' she says, her words loud and ugly in her ears. They come out with such ease that she surprises herself, more so when she continues, 'We knew this time would come, and, like, I've been so busy with work, this has been a bit of a distraction for me.' She lets out a laugh, which comes out weak, but Kian barely notices. His face looks properly wounded now, which initially makes her feel sad, but then she experiences a horrible satisfaction that they both feel stung now.

What she said is partly true though. Her work is intense, though it has been seeing Kian that has de-stressed her, centred her when she went off-path. When Abigail's book was announced, it gained huge media interest, with Mariam claiming that Shirin was due a promotion imminently. Though now, sitting with Kian, thinking he'll be gone in just two weeks, the idea of a title change means much less. It all does.

Ahead of her, she sees a golden retriever running after a tennis ball on the grass. It is the kind of thing she'd point out to Kian, who would laugh and watch in amusement, but nothing is amusing to them now.

Later that night, when they are in bed and Kian is dozing, her head on his chest, Shirin savours the moment. She can hear his heart beating, loud and rhythmic. She wishes she could bottle this moment. His arms tighten around her, and he kisses her forehead. It is such a tender gesture that she can't help but wonder what they are doing. On the tip of her tongue are the words *Don't go* but instead she presses her lips together and closes her eyes.

The next two weeks pass quickly. They are intimate every time they see each other, everywhere – in the summerhouse, in his car, in her bathroom. It is like they are making up for lost time, not only this past year, but each kiss, each caress, is what they also longed to do ten years ago.

Shirin goes with Kian to Heathrow Airport. She watches as his back is turned and he walks through security, and only leaves when he is a tiny speck that she can no longer see in the distance. A tear rolls down her cheek on the Piccadilly line home. It plops with finality onto the lapel of her coat.

Team Updates

When Shirin returns home from Heathrow she struggles to enter her flat. The key won't turn. She knows she needs to jig it to the right side twice, before pushing hard to the left. But this time this method doesn't work, and it's only on her fifth go, when she is muttering and swearing, 'For fuck's sake, can something just go right for once?' that it clicks open. Her housemate Jane is coming down the stairs in her pyjamas as Shirin enters. 'It's a hazard,' she says. 'If someone was running after us and we had to get in quickly, we wouldn't make it. We'd be killed and dragged away.'

Shirin looks at her, not knowing exactly what to say to that. In the end, she says nothing. Her housemate trudges into the kitchen, and Shirin drags her feet up the stairs to her bedroom. When she checks her phone, she sees a disjointed email from her mum, which informs her that Maman Bozorg is in hospital with pneumonia.

The following Monday she receives an email with the subject *Team updates* from Allegra. She clicks on it idly. They're regularly sent these emails; someone is always leaving, joining, going on maternity leave or getting promoted.

Usually in the PR and marketing teams, which are constantly in flux. Her heart beats out of time, though, when she sees the name in bold and skims the body of the email:

> *We have exciting news to announce:* **Florence Ainsworth** *has been promoted to editor, effective immediately. Florence has shown herself to be an invaluable member of the editorial team, with innovative ideas and a can-do attitude. Notably, her acquisition of Abigail Underwood – the Windmill First Novel Award-winner and the Women's Prize-longlisted author – is such a massive book for us, and is in line with our mission to be more diverse and upmarket in the books we publish. We are excited to see more acquisitions from Florence. She will be handling many of Poppy's authors. Please do join me in congratulating Florence!*

At 10 a.m. Shirin and Lilian have their one-to-one catch-up. They always use the full hour, because Lilian is too busy for Shirin to ask quick questions throughout the week, and often they are things that only her manager can answer, so she stores them up in a list in her notebook.

There are two questions she wishes to ask Lilian. One: that she needs to take time off work to go to Tehran, to be with her grandmother, and can she use her annual leave to go? And two: does Florence getting a promotion affect her chances of getting promoted? The first is easier to word than the second, as she has twenty-one days of annual leave to use up anyway. When she told her dad about Maman Bozorg, he said he'd pay for her flight. One can say many things about her dad, about his character, but it cannot be said that he isn't generous with his money. He throws it around like it's nothing, lending money to friends who never give it back, so she has no qualms about taking money from him now.

She has been unable to sleep all weekend, thinking of Maman Bozorg, of how she hasn't called her in a while, that she is a bad granddaughter. Despite her mum's fraught email, it took her a full twenty-three hours to reply to Shirin's questions about whether Maman Bozorg is okay. She didn't answer the phone either. Shirin began to fear the worst. Hospitals in Iran are not always sanitary, and many of her relatives have suffered from infections after being hospitalised, which has caused them more harm than the ailment they went in with in the first place. She's trying not to think something like that could happen to her seventy-three-year-old grandmother. Eventually her mum replied to say that Maman Bozorg is getting better, but she is keeping a close eye on her. She said Shirin didn't need to come all the way to Tehran, that it wasn't necessary. Shirin isn't sure how her mum could think travelling to be with someone you love isn't necessary. She doesn't see her grandmother as a burden, though she wonders if that's how her mother sees her, and that's why she said that.

On Sunday, when her mum visited Maman Bozorg in the hospital, Shirin called her. She handed the telephone to Maman Bozorg.

'Shirin,' her grandmother said into the receiver, her voice quiet, when normally her talking voice is akin to a shout.

'Maman Bozorg, how are you? I've been so worried.'

'I'm okay, azizam, don't worry about me. It's nothing, I'll be okay.'

'You're in hospital, of course I'm worried.'

'I'm strong, Shirin jan.'

Hearing her grandmother's voice, even if it was raspy, reassured Shirin. Her mother's email had panicked her, made her think her grandmother was unable to speak, on ventilators maybe, and she'd feared the worst. That's the problem with her mother's poor communication skills.

'Inshallah, you'll get better very soon,' she said.

'Inshallah, inshallah,' Maman Bozorg said. 'How are you, azizam? Everything okay? You feeling better about work?'

Shirin let out a small chuckle. 'My problems are small compared to yours.'

'What talk is this? You're important, so your problems are important too.'

Shirin told her she was going to try and fly over next week. Maman Bozorg protested that it wasn't that serious, but when Shirin said, 'I miss you', her grandmother softened and said, 'I miss you too. It would make my year to see you.'

'I'll do my best,' Shirin promised.

Lilian and Shirin are in a meeting room. It is a two-person meeting room, narrow, with two plush velvet chairs opposite each other and a small coffee table between them. One side of the room is completely glass, and they see people walk past them. It is like a fish tank.

'So,' Lilian begins. 'How are you?'

Shirin always says, *Good, thanks. How are you?* She's not sure if she's ever said anything else in the last two and a half years she's worked at Hoffman. It's an odd question, she thinks, in a professional setting. No one really cares, and she can hardly say, *Shit, actually,* can she?

So, instead, she goes for a different, more tentative approach and says, 'Okay, but my grandma went into hospital on Friday. She's doing better now and they're going to release her, hopefully, but I wanted to ask, actually, if I could take some of my holiday to go back to see her?' She speaks quickly, as she often does around Lilian. It seems easier somehow to say it all in one go, rather than taking her time and enunciating her words. She is surprised that her eyes water as she speaks. Saying it all aloud, she imagines her Maman Bozorg in a hospital bed, frail and beautiful, wanting to be back home. There is nothing Maman Bozorg loves more than her own house; she is the most house-proud woman Shirin knows. Her children have asked her to move in with them, so they can take care of her better, but Maman Bozorg refuses, proclaiming she wants her own home, that she doesn't want to be a guest in someone else's.

Lilian's brows furrow. 'Oh, I'm sorry to hear that. When exactly were you thinking of taking time off?'

Shirin has her laptop on her thighs and pulls up the calendar app. 'I was thinking of going next Monday for two weeks. That way, I could get a flight on Saturday. I have three weeks' annual leave left anyway, and only two months to take it before it renews.'

Lilian makes a low sound, almost like a cat hissing. 'Usually we need more notice for annual leave. And don't we have an author event next Thursday? I think you volunteered to help with it?' This is not strictly true. Lilian volunteered Shirin to help with it. It is, of course, not paid, nor is their time in doing this extra work compensated.

'I could ask if maybe Florence could cover ...'

Again Lilian has a pained, pinched expression on her face. 'I don't think it would be right for you to ask her. Maybe you could go in three weeks? How does that sound?' Her tone is as though she is doing Shirin a favour.

'I'm just quite worried about my grandma,' she says.

'You mentioned that she's on the mend though? I would love to say yes to you going sooner, but we can't bend the rules, or else everyone will want us to. You understand that, don't you?'

Shirin wants to tell Lilian that her heart is in Tehran, and that she has this bubbling fear that if she doesn't go soon something bad will happen to her grandmother and she'll never forgive herself. Instead, deflated, she says, 'Oh, okay, thank you.'

Next on Shirin's list is *ask about promotion*, but when the moment comes, she is quiet. In her mind she is confident and assertive, but in work situations she is rendered mute. She bites her tongue and begins. 'I had a question about progression.'

'Hm?'

'I remember a few months ago you mentioned that I was on the path to getting promoted. I wondered, am I going in the right direction?' This isn't even the question she wanted to ask. But it is easier to skirt around the issue and hope Lilian understands.

She does not understand.

'Yes, indeed, I'm very happy with the work you're doing.'

Shirin smiles; it is a closed-lipped smile and of course she doesn't mean it, because really her heart is pounding anxiously. 'I mean, obviously Florence recently got promoted ...'

Lilian sits up straight, both hands on her lap, her large engagement ring shimmering in the light, the picture of formality. 'Yes, she did. Listen, Shirin, you shouldn't compare yourself to your colleagues. Focus on yourself.'

It is so vague and shaming, and she isn't sure what to say. 'Yes, of course. It's just that we have similar experience and have been working here the same amount of time, so I wondered ...'

'I'm not meant to say this, it's highly unprofessional of me, but the thing is, Shirin, Florence's situation is quite different from yours. She got a job offer elsewhere – and she is such an asset to the team – so we matched her offer. I'm being transparent because I know it can be confusing when someone in the same position as you moves ahead quicker, but we don't want to lose any of you, so that's what happened.'

'Oh, okay. Does that mean the editor position is still open?'

Lilian shakes her head. 'I'm afraid not. But we can discuss all this in your next review.'

Her next review is in May. Three months away.

Shirin says something non-committal and pathetic like, *'Okay, great!'* Inside she is withering.

There are so many things she wants to say, but she can't find the words to do so politely. She is defeated. When she speaks up she is not heard. She cannot use her allotted annual leave to see her grandmother. The promotion she was grasping for is no longer in reach. And Kian has left her. Everything that gave her joy, everything that she was striving for, is disappearing.

And then it is confirmed; two days after Shirin had planned to visit Tehran, her mum rings her in the afternoon. She never calls. Shirin gets up from her desk and only answers the call when she is away from her colleagues, down the corridor by the lifts.

'Your Maman Bozorg has passed away,' her mum says.

Shirin's body no longer feels like her own, her vision blurry. 'How?' she barely manages to ask.

'The stupid hospitals here.' Her mum's voice is shaking. 'She was doing much better, but then she got an infection. It happened so quickly – so, so quickly. I can't believe my maman is gone.' Her voice breaks.

When the call ends, Shirin goes into the toilets, into one of the cubicles, grabs a wad of toilet roll and buries her face in it. She cries silent tears, wanting to scream, wanting to bang her head against the door. She wishes, so badly, she could have said goodbye to her Maman Bozorg, that she could have told her in person that she loves her, before she passed away. That she had been granted permission to go to Tehran and see her sweet Maman Bozorg's face one last time.

Grief

Grief is a strange thing. Each hour is different. Shirin oscillates from hopelessness to anger; an absence of faith to praying solemnly for her Maman Bozorg; apathy to existential dread that makes her feel physically sick, but also out of her body.

She travels to Tehran for seven days. Lilian allows her this as compassionate leave, and Shirin wishes she had shown such apparent kindness sooner. The trip is a blur. At the funeral Maman Bozorg's children wail, pound the floor with their bare fists. Her own mother sobs into her handkerchief, head bowed, and Shirin holds her, keeping in her own sobs, letting singular tears slide down her face instead. Her grandmother's face is etched into the marble gravestone. In the picture she is smiling, her eyes crinkled, the rest of her face devoid of the wrinkles that decorated her face and showed that she had enjoyed life.

They stay in Maman Bozorg's house, though Shirin and her mother are in the same bedroom, Shirin on the futon once more. They cannot bear to go into Maman Bozorg's room. In the kitchen, the freezer is stocked to the brim with expensive meats that Maman Bozorg was saving;

Shirin's mum tells her with a forlorn expression that this was not an expected turn of events. When Shirin leaves Tehran she is glad; she has spent the week holding her mother up, and when she descends into London she allows herself to be, to crumble.

She receives deliveries of flowers from her friends, Phoebe included. They come in cardboard boxes through the letterbox and require her to cut the stems herself. Weeks later they remain in her living room, dead, exuding a pungent sewer odour.

Each day she returns from work and goes straight to her bed, eating family-sized pizzas under her duvet or a share-size bag of Tangy Cheese Doritos for dinner, or sometimes nothing at all. She takes Night Nurse before bed, but still wrestles with sleep and listlessness, thinking more and more that she wants to die, though she's not sure if she really means it.

She speaks to Kian sometimes over FaceTime. He'll be in a coffee shop, or on the move. One time he showed her Central Park and he looked truly happy. The smile she gave him then was almost genuine too. When he found out about her Maman Bozorg he offered to come back to London, and she told him not to be silly, that she was truly fine. She can be convincing when she needs to be, especially over the phone.

It is desperately lonely, this life that she leads. She badly wants someone to lean on, but everyone in her life is preoccupied with other matters. Their empty texts and online flower deliveries mean little; they don't fill the void inside her. She wishes she could speak to someone, get help, so she can leave this hole she has found herself in, but therapy isn't her reality. She is on an embarrassingly low salary, in a role that appears glamorous but is sucking away at her soul bit by bit.

After a month of this she visits her GP's surgery, experiences angry receptionists, uninterested doctors, and leaves with a printout about mindfulness and a three-month repeat prescription for sertraline. As she walks past Roman Road market, past the vendors selling clothes with the Topshop labels cut out, fabric and knock-off designer bags, she dries her teary eyes and decides she has to pick herself back up. No one will do it for her.

The first social event Shirin goes to after Maman Bozorg's passing is another one of Jasper's gigs in Brixton. The doorman checks her name on the list. As he scans the page, she finds herself and points it out to him. He crosses her name off and indicates for her to enter. The pub is loud with chatter before the show starts. She spots Hana across the room, her dark hair wavy, so shiny it looks like spun silk. Next to her a blonde head, which she assumes is Millie. As she weaves through bodies to get to them, she feels herself going funny. She is not ready for social interactions. It is different at work; there it is much easier to put on a façade.

When she draws closer, she sees Hana say something to Millie, then Millie turns and they both greet her, overly animated. Millie hugs her, this time not to be annoying, because she squeezes Shirin and whispers in her ear, 'I'm so happy to see you.'

Hana gives her a nod and says she looks amazing and compliments her on her outfit, saying her coat is gorgeous, and is it new? To which Shirin says no, she got it last year from Cos on sale. They both smile at her, clutching their drinks, like she is fragile and might break at any moment.

'Stop acting weird,' Shirin says, unbuttoning her coat. 'I'm honestly fine.'

Millie leans forward, rubbing her lips together nervously. 'But it's okay if you're not – it's been hard for you.'

Shirin shrugs. 'It's life, isn't it?' Not realising she's mimicking Maman Bozorg's words. She thinks she notices Hana watching her, though she doesn't say anything, doesn't add anything to the conversation. It has continued to be strange between them, their closeness morphing into awkwardness. Even over text, they have less to say to each other, so it fizzles out quickly. 'I'm surprised you actually came,' Shirin says.

'Well, you said his last one was so good,' Hana says. 'I thought I need to see Jasper in action myself.'

Shirin's eyes keep glancing at the door, like Kian will walk through it at any minute, which makes no sense at all. 'This is the first time I've been in Brixton since Kian left last month,' she says, thinking aloud.

They both give her pinched faces. 'Do you guys talk much?' Millie asks.

'We sometimes text, or FaceTime, but it's probably better that we don't too much. It's too confusing otherwise.' Her voice is empty, like she is trying to convince herself. What she wants to say is that she doesn't want them to talk too much because a year is such a long time; before long, Kian will find someone in New York and her heart will be broken again. She misses him in such a different way from all those years they were apart. There was so much hurt and anger back then, it clouded her longing for him, for their friendship. Now the happy memories make it even harder. That and the fact that Kian didn't once bring up trying long-distance with her, and it's something she's realised she wanted him to suggest, but didn't dare bring up herself, for fear of rejection. Because if he didn't want to do long-distance with Salma, and that was the reason they broke up, why would he want it with Shirin?

'Maybe when he comes back you guys can get together properly?' Millie says, as though this will cheer Shirin up.

She doesn't want any more false hope, which is why she shakes her head and replies, 'If he wanted us to be together, he wouldn't have been so opposed to long-distance.'

'But you didn't even ask him to do that yourself,' Hana adds, a bit too quickly, as though forgetting that she's meant to be tiptoeing around Shirin's feelings.

'He made it very clear he wanted to be free in New York,' Shirin says, before asking, 'Where's Henry?' – not that she is particularly looking forward to seeing him, but he is always at the centre of these events – and she needs to change the subject.

Millie rolls her eyes. 'We had a fight. We're always arguing lately … I was telling Hana, before you arrived, that I'm thinking maybe we aren't quite right for each other after all.'

Shirin leans forward ever so slightly; it is reflexive. She catches Hana's eye and it is gleaming, in a *finally* kind of way. With this news, she can be distracted.

'And I said she can do so much better,' Hana says.

'What do you argue about?' Shirin asks.

Initially it looks like Millie isn't going to respond, or if she is, she'll say something generic, but then she also leans in and says, 'He can be so toxic, you know. Puts me down, to make himself feel better when he's done wrong.'

Shirin shakes her head. 'Damn. You do deserve better. I always thought he was a bit ...'

'Let's just say it. He's an arsehole,' Hana interjects, waving her hand in the air. 'An arsehole with a huge dick.' Shirin gasps at this candidness and hits Hana in the stomach jokingly, while Millie bursts out laughing, covering her mouth. 'And you can't get annoyed at me for saying it because you shouldn't have shown it to us, that one time.'

When they first got together, Henry had sent Millie a dick pic, which she had shared with them both, not knowing that he would soon become a long-term fixture in her life.

'It is a pretty good dick,' Millie says, at first forlorn, and then they all burst out laughing again at the ridiculousness. It is the first time in a very long time that Shirin has laughed so effortlessly.

Fruit Flies

There are fruit flies everywhere. They dance in front of Shirin and her colleagues, travel close to their ears, their noses, their mouths, their eyes. Joanie says they like the moisture. An email was sent round by the facilities team detailing the fly problem. The staff are blamed for eating food at their desks and are told that Tupperware will be put on everyone's desks over the next few days and all food must be stored within these boxes. The cleaners have been briefed to throw away any food they see left overnight that is not in the aforementioned Tupperware.

When Shirin went to make her morning coffee, she saw that the flies had made their way into the coffee machine and were festering within the ground coffee. Rather than say anything, she went down to the café, where she paid £2.80 for an Americano instead. Now she has returned to the kitchen and sees one of the catering staff emptying out the coffee machine, throwing all the coffee into the bin.

'It's gross, isn't it?' she says.

He shakes his head, the picture of disappointment. She does not know his name, but sometimes sees him and they make small talk. He is passionate about the coffee machine, about filling it up. He tells her occasionally about the different kinds of coffee, or the mechanics of the machine. He is bald-headed, with kind brown eyes. 'I think there's mice,' he says. 'Dead mice somewhere in this building.'

Shirin frowns and cringes simultaneously. She has lived among mice in two flats before and their presence both times was the reason for her departure. It is their speed, their thin dirty tails, the way they can move through the smallest of spaces. If they were slow, less agile, she would begrudge them less.

'Do you think?' she says. 'That's even worse.'

He shrugs. 'The flies are here for a reason.'

She gives him a closed-lipped smile as she walks back to her desk, swatting flies away from her eyes in the process.

In the afternoon all Hoffman employees are called into their main event space. It is one of the rooms in which they sometimes have author parties, with spectacular grey views of London. At the front of the room is a podium with two large screens. Chairs are placed in multiple rows for the audience, and people are also sitting on the floor to the sides or leaning against the walls to watch the presentation. All the highlights for the year – the big books that they want everyone to be talking about – are pitched by various editors and publishers.

Twenty minutes into the presentation the CEO, David Hoffman, saunters onto the stage. David is a middle-aged man with a square face, thin defined lips, and he is wearing his signature thick black circular glasses. He frequently wears chinos and cardigans and dresses like a middle-class dad – today is no exception. He speaks with a confident lisp as he says he has a very special announcement to make. He says, 'Next slide please,' and that is when a headshot of Rob Grayson appears large on the two screens either side of him. Shirin is so taken aback by the image that her body jolts and she looks round, like it must be a mistake. People around her appear mildly confused, but do not match the abject horror on her face. Rob is looking dead into the camera, with a steely expression.

There are low murmurs around the room. David doesn't say anything for at least a minute, letting the speculation mount. Shirin's throat is dry and she shifts in her seat, crossing her legs, one over the other. She thought the room was a touch too warm when she initially entered, and now it is stifling. She has the urge to pretend none of this is happening; she wants to shut her eyes, put her hands over her ears and just pretend. That is the reason why she avoids Mariam's gaze next to her and keeps her eyes down on her chunky loafers.

'I, like many of you, couldn't avoid the outcry surrounding Rob Grayson's memoir being published – and then his deal being cancelled. It bothered me that the sole reason his publishers pulled the book was because of bullying and endless tirades by people who hadn't even read it. Objectivity is so important in our business. Our goal should simply be to publish great books. Does it matter really, then, who it is that we are publishing? Or maybe that's the point: it does matter. And we want to publish everyone, to embrace freedom of speech *for all*. Diverse, inclusive publishing also means publishing people whose opinions you may not agree with. That is the true definition of diversity.

'Rob Grayson is an inspiration. I met with him and I heard from him how he climbed up the social ladder – from being a working-class kid in Hull to being an internationally renowned comedian.

'So, if you've not already gathered, Hoffman will be publishing Rob Grayson's memoir, *Free to Speak*, this September. It's not the same book as the one that was first signed up. It's better. It's a book calling for action. It will make you think about everything we see online, and it explores how cancel culture is very real and harmful to our society. We plan to make this the book absolutely *everyone* will be talking about.'

Shirin's mouth is dry and her body feels like it is failing her. Her mind, however, is wondering: How? It's a non-fiction title and no one in her team has mentioned it in any of their meetings. It is impossible.

'Of course none of this would be possible without the work of Lilian Rees and Florence Ainsworth, who very speedily whipped the material into shape. So I'd like to give them a big thank-you. *And* I'm very excited to announce that Rob will be coming in next week to speak about his book and sign some limited-edition bound excerpts,' David says.

Everyone around her begins to clap. Shirin raises her hands to mimic them, but she cannot put her hands together. Every element of her life is like a domino, and one by one they are falling down around her, leaving nothing upright. She keeps working hard to put them back up. But, unlike the other times in which she's felt herself crumbling, it is anger that prevails now.

She looks at David, Florence, Lilian and at the headshot of Rob. She is seething. Shirin was not able to take time off to see her grandmother before she passed away. When she tries to sleep she can hear Maman Bozorg's voice when she said it would make her year if Shirin were to visit. Instead of another wave of sadness passing over her now, she is determined and strangely relieved that she has finally fallen out of love with her job. She has accepted it. She will never be respected in this job, or treated as an equal to her peers. So now she will do her Maman Bozorg proud and stand up for what she believes in. She will stand up for herself.

Rob Grayson destroyed so much ten years ago. She thinks more and more of what Kian said – that back then, Rob's treatment of Shirin wasn't taken seriously. She can see it clearly for what it is now, that she was abused; that's why she struggles to move on from it. Scars were left by him, and he got away with it. Well, she won't let him do it again. She won't let him succeed without a fight.

Too Far

Then

Kian had thought it would be fitting if it rained the day everything changed yet again, but no, the sun was shining radiantly, marking summer's arrival. That day everyone sat in the fields at lunch, looking up at the cloudless sky. Kian had kicked a football with Connor and the other boys and then they spent ten minutes lying down, their boot bags under their heads as they shut their eyes and soaked in the sun.

Something Shirin had said the day before had stuck with him. She was always trying to convince him to take his art seriously, and often he didn't believe her when she said he was talented or that he should pursue it. But they were making their final A-level decisions this week and, in one last bid, she'd told him it wasn't fair what his parents were doing to him.

'*They* haven't done anything,' he'd said.

'Are you sure? Or do you just want to think that?' she had said. 'They're projecting onto you – they want to make up for what happened to Mehdi with you, but that isn't how life works. Remember it's your life, not his, not theirs.'

He knew this, but hearing it said aloud, when he had started to doubt his decision, had changed things. He'd spent the rest of the day pondering the answer, and he'd woken up with something like clarity. Kian had risen from sleep realising it was true – it was his life, and if he wanted to study Art, he should. So it was on this day that he'd asked his form tutor to amend his selection of A-levels. She'd been uninterested as she'd amended his form, which had somewhat dampened the momentous moment.

After school, he went to meet Shirin. They sometimes took a detour on the way home from school and got milkshakes from a dessert restaurant owned by a Turkish man, who often chucked free things into their order because he said they looked like his children. It was a bit weird, but they always took it anyway.

She'd told Kian to meet her outside the Home Tech room, because she needed to collect the things she'd made earlier in the day. He had been in Science, which was at the opposite end of the school to Food Tech, and by the time he'd made his way to the cooking block the school was almost empty. Students tended to clear out of the school grounds rapidly. The school buses were across the field and always left ridiculously early, so everyone had to run across the field to make it. Kian didn't live too far away, so he would walk, though he often saw the agitated way Connor tapped his finger against the table when they were held behind in their final class of the day.

That day he was feeling content for the first time in a long while. He had heard that they would be releasing Mehdi from prison in two months, that his sentence was being halved for good behaviour. The end was finally in view.

As he walked down the long corridor to the Home Tech room, he heard them before he saw them.

'Are you *crying*?' Jordan said mockingly.

'Just leave me alone,' Shirin said. 'Please.'

'Oh, come on,' Rob said. 'It looked shit anyway.'

It sounded like there was a struggle, grunts and pushing.

'Maybe we should leave it ...' Tom said.

Kian turned the corner and entered the classroom, to see Jordan, Rob and Tom standing around Shirin, who had her head bent low. On the floor were a dozen or so smushed-up cupcakes.

The boys pushed her around in a circle like she weighed nothing, and she struggled against them, attempting to scratch their faces, but then Rob pushed her down on the floor, holding her hands behind her back. Jordan loomed over her, a predatory look on his face.

Kian didn't even think, really. He strode towards them, grabbed a rolling pin off one of the countertops and swung it towards Jordan, who was closest. It struck his head and he bounced away, hit the countertop and crumpled against it. Kian struck him a second time on his back, the impact making a cracking sound.

Tom's face was pink and he immediately looked terrified and ran out of the room, narrowly avoiding Kian in the process. Rob let go of Shirin to move towards him, but Kian had his hand already raised and punched Rob hard in the face, like Mehdi had taught him. Rob fell to the ground, his nose bloodied.

'Fucking leave her alone,' Kian shouted. He thought of all the nasty things Rob had said and done, and then kicked Rob in the ribs, which made him shrivel up, curling into a ball on the floor, rolling over the cakes he had ruined. He kicked him twice, three times, and in the distance he could hear Shirin saying, 'Stop,' but he couldn't.

He didn't see Jordan get up, and that was when Jordan grabbed him by his shirt and smacked Kian across the side of his face. Shirin shouted something and pulled Jordan off him. They were a fighting mass, limbs flying, yelling gutturally. They only stopped when the Home Tech teacher came in, shouting, 'What is going on?'

The physical damage to Jordan and Rob was much greater than the damage to Shirin and Kian. And when it was taken to Mr Rodgers, the blame was put on Kian. Kian had used a weapon on a student. Kian had bruised a student's ribs. Kian had taken it too far, just like his brother had done. When Kian tried to defend himself, to say all the things they had done to Shirin, then and in the past, Mr Rodgers raised a hand and said, 'This is the first we've heard of any of this. I gave you a chance, Kian. I thought you were different from your brother.' He shook his head, the picture of disappointment. 'I'm sad to say I was wrong. Violence at North Oak cannot be tolerated.'

Kian was given a one-week suspension from school, but they were near the end of the school year anyway. They only had to sit their GCSE exams, and so his mum made the decision to remove him from the school completely. To begin with, she was mad, shouted at him, threw her plastic slipper at him even.

A few hours later, though, she came into his room, sat on the edge of his bed where he was lying, and said she was sorry. 'I didn't listen to you when you said that school was bad,' she said. Kian shrugged, his eyes red, looking off into the distance, not meeting her eyes.

His dad came into the room and Kian expected him to go off too, but he agreed; said when he'd moved to the UK people had always called him names, and he had experienced great prejudice. Kian was even more surprised when his dad also sat on his bed, and his parents reminisced about coming over from Iran, how they wouldn't have changed it, but how hard it had been. They hadn't thought it would be hard for him too.

'I'm sorry,' Kian said.

'You were helping your friend,' his mum said.

'I know, but I took it too far. Like Mehdi. I was just so angry.'

His dad laid a heavy hand on his back. 'We take things too far for the people we love.'

Kian shook his head. 'It doesn't make it okay though.'

'You made a mistake, azizam,' his mum said. 'These boys, they sound like bad people. They bothered that girl again and again, and you wanted it to stop. You're human.' The justification sounded exactly like how they had justified what Mehdi had done – how far he had taken it.

'I had a choice though. We all have choices, I've realised. I could simply have pushed them off Shirin and gone to the teacher. I could have hit them once. Everything we do, even if it's for other people, is a choice we personally make. I really messed up.'

309

Suspended

Obviously there was shouting. It reverberated around Shirin's house, a tsunami of blame and shame. It mainly came from Shirin's dad, though her mum would sometimes interject. Words in Farsi, English, even Turkish. She was a disappointment. She was predictable. She was nothing like the daughter they wanted. What Shirin found most frustrating, apart from her dad's spit hitting her face with every shout, was that no one asked her what had happened. No one wanted to hear her side of the story. It was all about Rob, Jordan, Tom and Kian. The boys were the focal point, and she – the person at the centre of it all – was both ignored and unfairly punished.

'Suspended! My child is suspended from school for being in a fight?' her dad shouted, his face visibly red, bleeding into his bald head, so that it was also red. 'Why were you hanging around with these boys?'

'We told you no boys until you're older,' her mum added, from behind Shirin's dad. They hovered over her while she sat in the middle of the sofa, taking in their tirade. 'What are we going to tell people?'

'No, we never said that,' her dad retorted. 'No boys *ever.*'

'They were literally bullying me,' Shirin said. 'Kian was defending me – they were pushing me around.'

Her dad held his hand in the space between them. 'Kian? Why was this Iranian boy defending you? Huh?'

She frowned and spluttered the next sentence, 'Because he's my friend!'

'Girls and boys can't be friends,' he said. 'You should never hang around with boys – let alone boys like *him*,' her dad went on, to which her mum muttered something in agreement.

'Boys like him?' Shirin repeated.

Her dad let out a long breath, waved his hand in the air and told his wife to speak to her daughter. He threw himself on the armchair close by, dejected, like he was the one who was being pushed around and punished for it. Shirin was still shaking, her body a bag of nerves and adrenaline, and it was two hours since it had all happened. She kept her gaze down at the Persian carpet, at the way the red and cream of the pattern had faintly bled together because her mum had insisted it was okay to wash it with hot water.

'Kian comes from a bad family,' her mum said. 'We don't hang around with people like them.'

This was the first Shirin had heard of this. 'What? His dad is a dentist and his mum's a nurse—'

'His brother is in prison. They're violent people. You can't hang around with people like that. Look at what he did. Beating someone up with a rolling pin? We aren't animals. Now you're in trouble with the school, and they're saying they might get the police involved.'

'Those people are racist,' Shirin said, her voice almost a shout. 'They're always bothering me. Always calling me a paki, making things up about me, pushing me around, and I don't get why *I'm* the one in trouble now. Why no one cares about me.'

Her dad stood back up then and Shirin gulped, feeling the air shift. He gave her a long look. It terrified her more than when he'd been shouting at her.

'You need to be stronger than this, Shirin. We had it much harder. I'm going to tell you one more time: if you want to live in this house, you won't see this boy any more and you'll behave. Understand?'

She nodded and he left the room. With just her and her mum remaining, Shirin let out a breath. Her mum sat next to her on the sofa and was quiet for a moment, before saying, 'You need to remember your future, azizam. If you hang around with someone like him, he will get you in trouble. I didn't want to say it in front of your dad, but the school said your suspension might go on your record. It might affect the university you want to go to. You always said you wanted to go to a university in another city – don't let this boy be the reason you can't. Remember your future, Shirin.'

It was this that got it into Shirin's head that maybe they were right. The thought of being stuck with her parents, in this city with people who hated her, spun in her head. Kian meant so much to her, but she knew she would need to distance herself from him if she wanted to get out of here. She had to put herself first.

Meeting the Parents

There was a knock on the front door the day after Kian had been suspended. It was a Saturday, and both his parents were home. They were having lunch in the sitting room. His dad muted the television and gave his wife a look. It reminded Kian of the look they used to exchange when Mehdi had police and lawyers visiting the house. He feared the worst for a moment, but then remembered Mehdi wasn't there, and that they'd been told the police wouldn't be involved with the fight.

His dad got up to see who it was, and seconds later his mum followed to stand in the hallway. Kian remained in the living room, his plate of rice and chicken stew on his lap, untouched, as his ears pricked up to hear who was at the door. They were in the back room, so he could only piece together bits of the conversation. It was a man at the door, who had a thick accent like his parents. He heard words like 'people like him', 'bad influence' and 'stay away'. It was only when he heard 'Shirin', though, that he put his plate down on the coffee table and moved to the door. His mum was by his dad's side, the front door half open. The man was almost shouting and Kian's dad was speaking just as loudly back, both talking in Farsi now. Kian could understand Farsi pretty well, though he struggled with certain phrases.

'He was defending her,' his dad was saying. 'As a friend, nothing more.'

'You're meant to be a Muslim family. What is this about the school saying they "hang around" together? The school telling me to be careful. My Shirin is a good girl – a good Muslim girl – so tell your dirty son never to contact her again.'

His dad said, 'Goh too saret,' and Kian knew it was something insulting, because Shirin's dad exploded at this, but was met with a door in his face. When his parents turned, they saw Kian standing there, clutching the living-room doorframe, his face pale.

'Stupid baboon,' his dad said. 'That man is a laughing stock in this city, and he says *we're* a bad family?'

His mum was rubbing her husband's shoulder, though her own face was furious. It softened slightly when she said to Kian, 'He is right though. You should probably leave that girl alone now. They suspended her, as well, from school.'

'What? Why would they do that?'

'Probably to make a point,' his dad said, before muttering something unflattering in Farsi.

'I need to speak to her, see how she's doing …'

'No,' his mum said. 'We said you should leave it now, Kian. We're lucky the police haven't been involved.'

'Leave it? She's my friend,' he said slowly, like they did not understand him.

'Maybe make friends with English girls,' his dad quickly retorted, to which his mum elbowed him in the stomach. 'Her family are strict with her. She's a girl – it's different for them.'

Kian couldn't believe what he was hearing, but rather than argue with them, he went straight to his bedroom. He logged into MSN and prayed Shirin would be online – but she wasn't. He knew it was risky, but he called her mobile. On the second ring she answered.

'Hello?' she said.

'Are you okay?'

There was a silence on the phone for a few seconds before she said, 'Yeah, I'm fine. You probably shouldn't call though.'

'Your dad just came round to ours.'

'What? Seriously?'

Kian was pacing his room, too pent up to sit down. 'Yeah, he was shouting the odds, said you were suspended? Which makes no sense – you were the victim in all this.'

'Only for two days. Mr Rodgers said he had to make it clear that violence isn't tolerated.' She said this quietly.

'Your dad said we couldn't see each other any more.'

'He was so mad last night. Said I brought shame onto the family for being involved in a fight. Then, when he found out we were friends, he got even madder. I kept saying we're *only* friends, but he said boys and girls can't be friends. Even my mum was on his side. It's the only time they are united and it's when they're telling me off.' Her voice caught, and Kian could see her so clearly then – he knew she was crying.

'Shit! I'm sorry.' The silence on the other end of the line was deafening. 'Shirin?' he said.

'Kian, why did you have to take it so far? You could have just pushed them out of the way or something. I kept telling you to stop. It was really scary. And now we're suspended and it could go on our records. Our records, Kian. You know how important it is that I get out of here – what if unis see, and we can't get into any good ones? What were you thinking?'

He felt outside himself then. He shook his head, though of course she couldn't see him. 'I got so mad. They're always bothering you. I only wanted to help.'

'I just … You turned into something else then. I've never seen that side of you before. You didn't need to take it that far.'

Kian thought of his brother, and how resentful he had grown towards him – and how he himself was no different from Mehdi after all. 'Maybe we should keep a distance for a little bit,' he said. 'Until it cools down.'

There was a long silence. 'You mean not see each other?' she said.

'Yeah.'

'That makes sense. I don't think we're good for each other,' Shirin said, before ending the call.

And that was that.

He sat his GCSE exams in the sports hall, and in some of them he knew Shirin would be there. He looked around the room, and each time he spotted her she was either looking away or, if she had been looking at him, she quickly diverted her gaze elsewhere. After each exam he did not linger, as the others did outside to discuss the test. It had been agreed between his mum and Mr Rodgers that he'd sit his exams but did not need to attend any of the final-week classes, which he was relieved about. He went to a different college, instead of the school's sixth form.

Shirin messaged him once, weeks after their phone call. She apologised and said she hoped he was doing well, and that she missed him. He wanted to reply, to say he missed her too, but what she had said had imprinted itself into his mind. It confirmed everything he'd thought about himself: that he was no good for her. So he didn't reply. She didn't message again and neither did he. They cut their ties effortlessly – that was how it looked from the outside at least, but he never stopped thinking about her, rehashing what they had said or wishing things were different.

Back Yourself

Now

'We need to stage a walkout,' Shirin says. Around her are a group of Shirin and Mariam's trusted colleagues – the ones who take part in the monthly Diversity and Inclusion open forums because they care, not for pretence. Before her now is Mariam, Kate (a white editorial director in the children's division), Derek (an editor in the audiobook team, who has just complained that everyone gets him mixed up with Femi, a Black man who hasn't worked in the company for three years now), Naomi (a publicity manager) and Ross (a Scottish designer who often wears tweed). They are looking at her like she is speaking another language.

Shirin stands, walks around the meeting-room table to the front of the room, where the whiteboard projector screen is, though there is nothing being displayed. She feels like a character from an adventure movie, trying to rally her troops for battle. But the reality is they're a group of ethnic minorities, gay people and/or allies, who are tired of publishers promoting racist fascists.

'We have to do something. Some of us might have to work on this book,' Shirin continues.

Kate is wearing deep pink lipstick that is well applied and rubs her lips together nervously. 'I'm here to support and be led by you all,' she says. Kate is the type to go on about her white privilege often, which is a little annoying, but she is well-meaning.

'It's bullshit, to be honest,' Naomi says. 'I was told I'm doing his PR. I have to pitch his shite book to the press, when he once spent fifteen minutes taking the piss out of Indian people. I'm fucking Indian, for fuck's sake.' In her anger her Birmingham accent becomes more pronounced.

'Shirin is right, we need to do something – a walkout in protest to show we're mad and won't take it,' Mariam says. Shirin remembers Mariam saying that ever since she was little she has been going to Free Palestine protests with her family, and though Shirin has never been to a protest before, because the thought usually makes her nervous, it is all she wants to do now. To shout for change.

'Listen, I want to, you know I do, but I have rent to pay,' Derek says. 'I'm tired too, but let's not be too hasty. We need these jobs – what if they fire us?'

Shirin and Mariam look at each other. Mariam gives Shirin a look as though to say, *Don't tell them yet,* and Shirin nods, like, *Fine.*

After they found out Hoffman will be publishing Rob Grayson's book, Mariam and Shirin convened in the stationery cupboard. Mariam stood there, a concerned look on her face. 'Something isn't right. Are you okay?'

Shirin explained everything. Things she'd never told anyone about Rob. It was an exorcism. To speak out about the trauma, to let herself cry as she said the words and removed the toxicity from her body. She told Mariam about Rob, Jordan, Tom and Kian. Mariam knew Shirin had been seeing Kian, but didn't know the extent of their past.

It wasn't just school that she talked about, though. Once she began speaking, she found it hard to stop. Mariam didn't interrupt, didn't really move at all, except to rub Shirin's back. Shirin told her how nothing in her life is how she envisaged it being, that even her friends don't have her back, don't get her. When she mentioned her argument with Phoebe, and how she'd seen Tom again on New Year's Eve, she expected a visceral reaction from Mariam – one that she feared. She imagined Mariam would call Phoebe trash, as Hana had done, and be done with it, but instead she let Shirin finish. Shirin realised it was so rare to be heard. There's one good thing that has come from Hoffman at least: she's got to know Mariam.

When she finished, she leant against the shelves. It was uncomfortable, with different sharply shaped objects jabbing into her back. She stayed in that position, relishing the slight pain, pushing further into it. Mariam laid both her hands on Shirin's shoulders. 'Mate, why have you been keeping all this in?'

'I thought I could hold it together. But it's too hard. Like, they gave Florence the promotion because she had another offer, not because she performed better. Then my grandma – if it wasn't for Lilian, I could have seen her one last time, you know?' She felt the tears coming and breathed in deeply, but they fell anyway. 'I don't see anything here for me any more. They publish racists. A racist who abused me. I can see that now – that it was abuse. It wasn't normal and it still affects me now. I just think I didn't want to admit for a while what it was.'

Mariam took Shirin's hand in hers. 'I truly am sorry, Shirin. If you like, I can teach you how to pray for your grandmother – for everything. It's too much for you to shoulder. Maybe if you leave it to Allah, you'll feel more at peace?'

Shirin squeezed Mariam's hand, found it hard to speak, but managed to say, 'I'd like that, thank you.' Because she would. She has felt so faithless for the past year, so outside the religion that she knows. She wants to connect with God, but isn't sure how to.

'And you've got me, you know,' Mariam said. 'I am always here for you to talk to. You don't have to keep it in any more.' Then she told Shirin, 'I've been interviewing for new jobs.'

Shirin's back began to hurt, so she stood straight, both because of this and because of what Mariam had said. 'Seriously?'

Mariam nodded. 'Have you heard of Green Tree Press? They're a new publisher founded by a Palestinian woman.' Shirin had seen articles about them online – and a billboard for one of their books in Hackney Wick. 'I just did the last interview for a marketing manager position. I didn't want to tell anyone in case I didn't get it, but I have a good feeling. I know publishing is shit everywhere, but this feels different – I've never even had a manager who's a person of colour, let alone a Palestinian like me.'

'Wow,' Shirin said. 'I really hope you get it. But also, don't leave me here alone, please.'

'I love you, Shirin, but from what you've told me, you need to take control. You can leave Hoffman too. We're not trees; if we don't like something we can, and should, move.'

'I'm pretty sure that's an Instagram caption.'

Mariam smiled. 'I mean, it is, but I'm serious. It's true, and you know it. Publishing has its problems, but I think anywhere else would be better than here. They make you think they're ethical and they brainwash you, but really Hoffman is the worst publisher of them all. Like, I know HR is never on our side, but especially here, they're as bad as our managers.'

It's true, the HR representative at Hoffman Books is sketchy. She once told Shirin in the kitchen that she was going on a Tinder date and, to be polite, Shirin asked for more details, to which she showed Shirin a picture of the aforementioned date and said she only dated Black men. She is white. Shirin was speechless for a moment and eventually replied with, 'Oh, okay.' She reminded Mariam of this now, to which Mariam made a sound between a cackle and a groan.

'It's all smelly,' Mariam said. 'I'm getting out of here. For your sanity, you need to as well. And I'm going to help you.'

Later that day, just before 5.30 p.m., Shirin got a Teams message from Mariam saying:

I got the job! Now it's your turn x

*

So Mariam has less to lose than the rest of them. She has already handed in her notice.

'What we need to do,' Ross says tentatively, 'is get a lot of people in on it, if we don't want to risk our jobs.'

'That shouldn't be too hard,' Shirin says. 'If we all get, like, five people to join us, that's enough, right?'

'We can definitely get more than that,' Naomi says, leaning back.

'Yeah, easy,' Mariam says, stretching her clasped hands out, like she is preparing for a fight.

'Okay, I'm in,' Kate says. 'If we can't fight fascists in our own workplace, where can we?'

Everyone looks at Derek, whose nostrils are flared in stress. 'Okay, let's do it,' he finally spits out.

There is momentary jubilation, before silence comes. 'So what do we actually have to do?' Shirin asks.

'I think I know,' Derek says, surprising everyone with his new-found enthusiasm. Then their heads are bent low as they explore exactly how they will successfully orchestrate a company-wide walkout.

In the evening Shirin messages Kian:

My company are publishing Rob's new book.

He FaceTimes her immediately. She is walking from the bus stop to her flat and raises the camera to her face, checking herself out in the camera image, smoothing her hair down, before accepting. In the call, she can see the various ex-council housing in Bow behind her as she makes her way to her own building.

Kian's face takes up most of the shot, though it looks like he's at a coffee shop. There is a low hum of chatter, and what she imagines is a coffee-machine steamer whirling. Though she might be imagining that detail.

'Shirin,' he says, his face lighting up. This is the first time they've spoken in weeks and, despite all that has happened, her heart still swells when she sees his face. He leans the phone against something, so that he can sit back in his chair. 'How are you doing?' he asks with a pinched expression.

'I'm angry, but to be honest it's the clearest I've seen things in a long time.' She turns the corner and there is a group of kids at the bus stop taking up the pavement, so she skips into the road to go past them.

He shakes his head. 'It's so fucked up that they bought his book in secret, after everything that came out.'

'We're staging a walkout,' she blurts.

His head moves closer to the screen. 'Really?' He breaks into a smile.

She nods manically. 'We're doing it in two days. Rob is going to come into the office to talk with the CEO at an event, and we're secretly spreading the word to people we trust that when they begin to talk, we'll all get up and leave. Mariam is making placards and talking to journalists about it. I've been speaking to people I know at other publishers to see if we can get their support. It's all mad, but it's nice to actually do something about all the shit that's happening, rather than let it defeat me, you know?'

She is approaching her flat now and struggles to balance holding her phone while rummaging inside her bag for her keys. She puts the phone in her pocket. As usual there is a struggle to open the door and when she manages to open it, she bounds up the stairs into her room and firmly shuts the door. Her breath is caught from the short run and she pulls out her phone. 'I'm back.' In the phone she can see herself, her nose pink, her eyes excited.

'I'm so proud of you,' Kian says. He bites the inside of his cheek like he wants to say more, but doesn't.

'You know, I blocked out a lot from school – about how much I hated it, how I simply put up with things happening to me and didn't stand up for myself. I blamed myself a lot for what happened to us, like if I was different or had said something to someone about it sooner then none of it would have happened.'

'Shirin, what the fuck? No. You didn't do anything to deserve any of that.'

Her stomach is uneasy. This is the closest they've got to talking about what actually happened, and she is holding her breath. 'I'm just sorry. I always wanted to say that, and I've avoided it for so long, but I am.'

'Sorry about what?' he asks.

'I'm sorry about so much. I'm sorry about the things I said to you. At the time I was so fixated on the idea that us being suspended could ruin my chances of leaving Hull that I panicked. I wasn't kind to you – especially knowing now that you blamed yourself for your brother going to prison. I'm sorry I got you involved with Rob and the others in the first place. I'm sorry you were suspended—'

'How was that your fault?' Kian interrupts. He is holding the phone closer to his face now and he looks mad. She opens her mouth to speak, but he continues anyway. 'It's not your fault, Shirin. Don't apologise.'

'I always thought you hated me. You didn't reply to my text, and I figured you'd get in contact if you wanted to and you never did.' Her voice is small now, and in many ways she feels fifteen again, heartbroken that she has lost her best friend, and the only person back then that she felt her truest self with.

He lets out a breath, his face panic-stricken. 'I remember feeling like I had become Mehdi, and that you thought I was some angry kid who got you suspended. And our parents didn't want us to see each other any more. I guess I thought it would be easier for you if I left you alone – that it would be better for you, in the long run. You were the most important person in my life, Shirin, and I felt like I failed you.'

'Kian, you could never fail me. Hanging out with you back then kept me sane. I've realised all my friends at school weren't true friends to me, but you were. I don't know what I would have done if I hadn't had you back then.'

He smiles and says, 'Likewise. Even after all these years, sometimes I'll think about the times we would hang out, and I'm just so thankful we met when we did. I was so sad about my brother, and I think I pretended I wasn't a lot of the time. You were the only person I could be myself around back then. When we stopped talking I felt a bit like a martyr – like me not fighting for you, not getting in touch with you, was for the greater good. But really, Shirin, it was one of my biggest mistakes.'

A Walkout

Shirin enters the Shard's revolving doors in chunky sandals and a summer dress. It is unseasonably warm for March. In fact on her way to work she saw a BBC News report that it is the one of hottest Marches on record in the UK. People online are saying it's a result of climate change, joking that they'll enjoy it anyway, even if they feel bad about it. It is a sign, Shirin thinks, that they are having a heatwave in March on the day she is part of something so monumental to her career, to her dignity.

Mariam sent her a voice-note earlier in the morning to say she thinks at least forty people will take part, and that some magazines and newspapers have agreed to cover it. Shirin didn't realise how well connected Mariam is. Though, actually, it is unsurprising, because at every publishing event people seem to know Mariam.

When she heard about the sheer number of people taking part, the potential publicity scandal of it, Shirin's instinct was to shy away, thinking maybe they are taking it too far, that this is too big for her. But then she thinks of the past year, of blow after blow, and of Rob Grayson being the final knockout punch – but only if she lets it be. Change doesn't happen on its own. And change isn't comfortable. That's the whole point.

She taps her employee card to trigger the gate to open and eyes the security guards by the doors, imagining they are looking at her with suspicion. She is being ridiculous.

At 10.55 a.m. they will all go to the event room, as though they are attending the compulsory talk between David Hoffman and Rob Grayson. Then, when David introduces Rob, and just when Rob begins to speak, they will all silently get up and leave. Mariam has created placards with slogans like 'NO BIGOTS, MORALS BEFORE £££' and 'DROP ROB GRAYSON'. Across the road from Hoffman is another publisher, and Shirin has received messages from some of them to say they will join the protest during their lunch break, in solidarity. Various newspapers also share the building with them. It is a prime place to stage a protest.

She remembers, when she first joined Hoffman, being so amazed to work in the Shard. She feels a strange nostalgia now for this corporate building, for this role at a company that has made her so miserable. Last night, she thought long and hard about her decision. She is now taking stock of each little thing, because that's what you do when you realise you won't see something again. It is like a final kiss with a lover – bittersweet – and she savours it like a keepsake of this time in her life that wasn't pleasant, but she thinks was necessary.

There are numerous people waiting to get into the different lifts. She recognises some of the people from her floor outside lift H. David's PA, whom she always sees around but has never spoken to, is talking to an author. The author is wearing a long beige trenchcoat, despite the blistering heat outside. Even for aesthetics, it seems a strange choice.

When the lift lights up, the PA turns to everyone and asks if they mind if she and Rob go in it separately. It takes Shirin a moment to actually process the words that have come out of her mouth. The others nod, and she is stood there thinking: Surely not. The PA steps into the lift, and that's when Shirin sees Rob. He is wearing sunglasses, which he removes once inside and folds over the neck of his dark T-shirt.

For two seconds they make eye contact – Rob and Shirin. His head turns to the side in slight wonder, his lips almost smiling, like he has seen an old friend. He looks strangely unimpressive and rather small, unlike the pictures online. In photographs he is always onstage, alone, so she imagined him much taller. She is so shocked that initially her face remains impassive, frozen in place. Her heart, however, is beating quickly, so fast now that she has to turn away from him. Bile, in the form of the coffee she has just drunk, threatens to rise, and it is the only time she has ever had such a visceral reaction to seeing someone. She swallows hard, placing her hand, which is now cold, against her clammy neck. But despite her bodily instinct to flee, she turns back to the lifts and, unsurprisingly, Rob is looking right at her, still. The way he looks at her is like he has forgotten everything, but when Shirin doesn't return his smile, when she looks at him with a steely expression, she sees his façade slip. She feels strength then, a power she always thought she did not have. She is face-to-face with this weak bully, and she is not the same person she was back then. She will no longer cower away from him. Too much has happened for her to do that now. Then the lift doors shut and, just like that, she is no longer face-to-face with Rob Grayson.

'Tell me again that this will go smoothly,' Shirin says to Mariam in an empty meeting room. Her heart is still beating fast, her mouth impossibly dry. She takes a long sip of water, her hands shaky, which results in her missing her mouth, water dripping down her chin, which she quickly wipes off.

'Yes, of course it will! Don't panic, Shirin. Now is not the time to panic.' Mariam has her hands on her hips, looking down at Shirin as though to say, *You can do this – don't let me down.*

'What if it's only you and me who get up? What if everyone else backs out?'

'That's not going to happen. And even if it did, would that be the worst thing?'

Shirin is about to say, *Yes, because we'd get a reputation*, then she wonders why that matters now. They didn't care when Maman Bozorg was in hospital, and then she never got to say goodbye to her. They also didn't care about giving her a fair shot at promotion. And now they're publishing a racist who made her life a misery. Her desire is to quit anyway, so what does it matter? 'I'm nervous. Like, so nervous I need to use the toilet every five minutes.'

Mariam puts her hand on Shirin's shoulder. 'Me too, Shirin, me too.'

When they leave the meeting room they pass by the kitchen. The coffee-machine man is shaking his head as he empties another batch of spoiled coffee.

'What's happened?' Mariam asks.

'I knew it,' he says. 'I knew it was mice.'

The grey aluminium fridge that contains all their packed lunches and individual dairy-free milks has been pulled out of its spot, and the cleaners tell them they need to leave the kitchen.

The walk up the stairs to the event room feels as though it takes both for ever and no time at all. The stairs to the floor above are spiral and wide, and walking in front of them and behind them are all the other staff from their level. Normally there is loud chatter when such a horde moves together to the events floor, but there is a hushed atmosphere now, a marked change that you'd only really notice if you knew what was about to happen.

By the time they get there, the only seats available are the ones at the front. The seats are black plastic, with metal legs, and the back rest curves to the shape of Shirin's spine as she settles in. There is no one on the stage yet, but the screens brandish the cover of Rob Grayson's book. It has all happened so quickly – to have the cover already produced, proofs already printed, this has clearly been in the works secretly for a long time. It is like they knew what they were doing was wrong and waited until it was too late to go back before they announced it.

Mariam's arm is pressed against Shirin's, partly because the chairs are so close together and also, Shirin thinks, as a gesture of support. They are one. They can do this. Looking around, they see their colleagues holding coffee in teacups, and mini pastries balanced on their knees or on the side of the saucer. It is rare that such events get catering, though it usually incentivises people to arrive early, so as not to miss it. Normally Shirin and Mariam stock up on the almond croissants and custard tarts, washing them down with the bitter coffee provided.

Suddenly there is a hush, and people stop talking. David strides up to centre-stage in tailored trousers and a crisp white shirt, open at the neck to expose his dark chest hair. Shirin only really sees him at such events when he is addressing the whole company. He sometimes talks to the junior members of staff at the Christmas party, making dad jokes and buying them rounds of drinks. Though she has not been blessed with his presence in this way before.

He stands by the microphone in the centre, though behind him are two low-backed armchairs, with a coffee table in between. On the table is a jug of water and two glasses. He begins with a preamble about how excited he is to introduce Rob, that he has admired his work for a long time and that they really are privileged to have him with them today. Shirin cannot concentrate on exactly what he is saying because her brain is whirling from thought to thought.

Growing up, when she aspired to be an editor, she never considered the political role she'd have to play in her job. But she can't just let it go – even though she tries not to, she cares too much. She cares about the readers, like herself, so desperate to see themselves in books. For the younger generation wanting to get into an industry they're passionate about, but always being the minority. There are so many reasons she needs to do this, and this is what she reminds herself of when her body wants her to flee rather than fight.

There is weak applause and then Rob Grayson stands before everyone. He has removed his trenchcoat and wears a plain T-shirt with *Prada* in red across the front, pinstripe trousers and chunky Balenciaga trainers. It is a terrible outfit. His stubble is strawberry-blond, his hair mousy, and short on the back and sides, long on the front. He looks almost inoffensive, but then he also deceived her ten years ago. David pats him on the back as they hug. It is such an unnecessarily chummy display of affection that Shirin struggles not to look away.

She realises she's been holding her breath when Mariam nudges her with her shoulder. It is then that she exhales slowly. She touches the locket she is wearing – the one Maman Bozorg gave her – and hopes she would be proud of what she's planning to do.

David sits down on one of the chairs on the stage and crosses his leg, looking up adoringly at Rob. Rob takes the mic from the stand, puts it in his other hand and paces the stage cockily. He's on the right-hand side, looking down, then up, at the crowd when he begins.

'Wow, this is—'

And that is when Shirin and Mariam stand up. Her heart is beating painfully in her chest now, her hands impossibly clammy. Because they are at the front, they don't see Kate, Derek, Naomi and Ross stand in unison too. And then Joanie.

Even Toby from the post room. And then half the room also stands up. They don't immediately leave, they stand there in solidarity for about ten seconds, before turning. When she sees the sheer number of people joining them, more than a hundred of them, Shirin's eyes prickle. It is a moving sight.

As they leave the building, she presses Send on her drafted email to Lilian resigning from her position at Hoffman, with immediate effect.

New York

Spring sun streams into his studio, the shadow from the window panels creating aesthetically pleasing patterns on his white desk. Kian has been staring at the blank A3 piece of paper in front of him for the last forty minutes. Each time he thinks he knows what he will sketch, he collects his 3B pencil from the table, bends his body to begin, and then it is gone. His mind is not on his work. Understandably, really. Everything re-emerging with Rob Grayson has Kian thinking about the past. He opens Twitter and, among the noise, there are articles about the walkout or think-pieces about what freedom of speech really means when the speaker is a racist. He sees pictures of Shirin at the front of a crowd, raising a placard, shouting into a megaphone. It is the most confident he has seen her in public. It is the version of her that he always saw within her privately; he is glad she has allowed the world to see this side of her.

He is thinking about the aftermath of his expulsion. He tries not to consider what could have been, but the past year it has been impossible not to. He thinks about all the things we want to tell the people we love, but don't. He saw the world so differently at sixteen, and he wonders now what else he got wrong. He gets up from his desk and heads out to a coffee shop, intending to add further caffeine to his body, which will no doubt exacerbate the jitteriness already coursing inside him.

Later, on his way back from the coffee house, his takeaway cup in one hand and his phone in the other, he calls Mehdi. It is midday in New York, early evening in Manchester where his brother lives. It rings and rings, though Kian is persistent and stays on the line until Mehdi eventually answers.

'Hello?' Mehdi says.

In the background Kian can hear his nephew and niece babbling away, although their voices fade off into the distance, as he imagines Mehdi going into another room.

'Hey,' Kian says. 'What you doing?'

'Watching *Peppa Pig*,' Mehdi says with derision. 'Fucking *Peppa Pig*. I've seen this episode at least twenty times.'

He is laughing and Kian chuckles too. This is his brother's life now – so far away from his difficult youth. Mehdi is a good father. Better than Kian expected he would be, though such thoughts feel unfair. He is incredibly patient with his children and speaks to them like they are adults, with a level of respect that prompts them to reply as though they are adults too, or at least as close to adults as toddlers can be.

'How's things?'

Kian crosses the road, jogs to the other side and leans on the brick wall outside his studio building. The conversation feels more private out on the New York streets, rather than indoors. He watches people pass with such determination; everyone has somewhere to go and walks as though they're late. He takes a sip of his cappuccino. It is bitter. More because he has already had three coffees today and his tastebuds are tired.

'Alright, alright,' he says. 'I've been thinking about when we lived in Hull.'

'What about it?'

'There are things I never said to you, back then.' Kian shuts his eyes when he says this. It is painful – shockingly painful, really. He assumed he was over all of this, that if he wanted to, he could speak about his past with more ease. He thinks of all Shirin has done to confront her past, and what scares her – the kind of advice he has given her, which he hasn't followed himself. It is this that propels him to continue. 'I always felt guilty about you going to prison. When you were in there, but even more so when you left prison and struggled to find a job. I've always felt like it was my fault.'

His brother blows air out of his nose, the sound audible through the telephone. 'What you on about? It wasn't your fault. It was all me.'

Kian shoulder has loosened; he hadn't realised until now how tensely he was standing. He downs the rest of his coffee. 'You went down defending me—'

'I would have gone to prison regardless, Kian. I was doing some bad shit. If it wasn't that fight, it would have been something else,' Mehdi says. 'Listen to me when I tell you that I never for one minute blamed you.'

Relief floods him. 'I always wanted to ask. Why do you think you acted out, when you were younger?'

Mehdi lets out another laugh. 'Well, this is unexpectedly deep. I was just angry. Where we lived, in that time, it was racist and people bothered me. I made the decision – one I regret now – to be "hard" and to show people they couldn't mess with me any more. I got in with the wrong group and, when you're in it, it's difficult to see what's right and wrong.'

'Ages ago, when you had a bruise on your back ... was that what started it?'

Mehdi sighs on the end of the phone and takes a moment before replying. 'Things happen how they're meant to happen. This was all Allah's will. I've found Islam now, and while I wish I could undo the hurt I caused others, part of me thinks it all happened how it was meant to happen. It shaped me. Kian, man, stop thinking about the past. It's all okay now.'

Kian hears his niece Yasmin asking Mehdi who is on the phone.

'Let me speak to my niece then,' Kian says, a smile in his voice, his body shaky from the weight that has finally been removed.

When he returns to his desk, he is less restricted as he sketches, though his mind often returns to Shirin. After all this time, she is still at the forefront of his mind. He is more than 3,000 miles away from everyone he loves – and he thought an adventure was what he needed, but now he is not so sure. He wants to hold Shirin, to feel her against his body, instead of their video calls, which are not the same. But he does not say any of this when he texts her. Instead, he simply tells her that she is amazing.

Hull

Shirin is back in Hull, at her dad's house, in her old bedroom. The single bed feels smaller than it used to, and when she tried to sleep last night, her body kept sliding off the edge. So she slept with her back pressed up against the wall, and it was bizarrely comforting. Her phone pings constantly with messages from Mariam or her former colleagues, updating her on news articles covering the walkout.

The walkout wasn't exactly front-page news, but it did feature on some online news sites. *The Bookseller* had it on their home page, with a picture of Mariam and Shirin holding their placards high and proud, with the headline:

HOFFMAN EMPLOYEES WALK OUT FOLLOWING
ROB GRAYSON ACQUISITION

Shirin wrote a long feature article about the protest, about publishing prominent fascists in general, for *HuffPost*. It went viral. Shirin's DMs are flooded with people writing to convey their support for her, as well as people who think she is scum and should go back to her country if she doesn't like it here. She responds to the latter by either liking their messages or taking screenshots and posting them to her feed with no caption. One of the people writing the vile messages works for American Express and people are calling for his employer to sack him.

The actual events during the protest were a blur. Now, when she tries to recall it, she can only remember snapshots. Like the sheer size of the crowd. People she had seen in the kitchen, who she never thought would care enough about something like this, stood among them, shouting even louder than Shirin and Mariam. Them waving the placards Mariam had made them in the air, which said 'DROP ROB GRAYSON'. Another colleague's sign said 'WHY ARE YOU PUBLISHING A RACIST?' Ross had a megaphone – though it is unclear where he got it from – and he was shouting, 'To the left, to the left, send Rob packing!' It didn't quite have the ring to it that he thought it would, but they went along with it anyway.

Passers-by, mainly tourists and office workers around London Bridge, stopped and observed. Some held their cameras up to video the protest. Southern and Thameslink staff occasionally came out of London Bridge to join in the chanting, too.

Shirin had never been to a protest before. Let alone been at the front of one. She had always wanted to, but something about being so present, in a crowd, had always made her nervous. With Mariam by her side, though, her nerves were alleviated, and the power and rage of the group radiated within her and propelled her to continue.

Two days after the walkout she informed her landlady that she'd be leaving her flat and told her to keep her deposit in lieu of her month's notice. A van and a storage unit were booked, all her stuff quickly boxed up and moved.

She isn't sure why she didn't leave sooner. Both Hoffman and her flat. Once she changed one thing in her life, it was surprisingly easy to let everything else go. Lilian responded to her email resignation with a simple: *That seems best*.

And that had been it. Shirin knows Hoffman Books will swiftly replace her with another person of colour, eager for a chance to shine in the industry they love, and the cycle will no doubt continue.

In the middle of the day, when Karen and her dad have gone out for a walk, Shirin is watching daytime TV. She is surprised by how different she feels now. She did not realise the weight of everything she was carrying. Though she still feels a sense of emptiness, like without all the heaviness from before, she is realising how unfulfilled she is. Her medication is working at least, and she is trying out the mindfulness app that she rolled her eyes at when both Kian and her doctor had recommended it. She switches the channel to watch *Who Wants to Be a Millionaire?* and spends the day blocking trolls from her social-media accounts.

Phoebe pops round later that afternoon. Shirin's dad and Karen are back in the house, and earlier Karen made a pointed comment about Shirin staying in *their* house. 'How long do you think you'll be here for then?' She was unpacking her Asda shopping, huffing each time she lifted one of the bags from the floor to the kitchen table, to sort the groceries into the cupboards. Shirin had offered to help, but Karen had told her to not be silly and that she wouldn't know where anything went anyway. Shirin wanted to say that actually, she'd lived in this house longer than Karen had. That the kitchen looks exactly the same as it did when she was a child. The cabinets white and shiny, the countertop black marble.

'Not long, just until I can find a new job.'

'Right, okay, love,' Karen had said and had continued unpacking. Shirin had gone into the living room to find that her dad had changed the channel to Sky Sports. He lay on the sofa, like he did when her mum was here, his bare feet dangling off the end.

Now Phoebe is standing by the front door, and Shirin takes her keys from the side table and goes out with her. They go for a walk, which reminds her of being fifteen again, and how they'd meet halfway between their houses and go on long walks, stopping off at the takeaway to get cheesy chips to share. She always imagined that when she was an adult she would feel so different – like she had her shit together and knew what she was doing. It's rare she says this aloud, because she cringes at people talking online about how hard 'adulting' is, but she has to agree: it is hard. You never really feel like an adult, and now she has reverted to being a teenager, living in her single bedroom, in her home town, jobless.

Last night she retrieved one of her old journals from when she was in sixth form, from a shoebox at the back of her wardrobe. Recurring among the pages was Kian's name. She wrote of how she longed to message him again, but thought he wouldn't want her to, convincing herself that it was better, easier, that they didn't speak. She relates to her younger self now, thinking the same thing, eleven years later: that she misses him, that she wishes he was here, that things were different.

'So you just quit then?' Phoebe asks her now, as they cross the road. Anlaby Road is a long stretch. They're doing the walk Shirin used to do to go to primary school and, if they walked even further along, secondary school.

'Yeah,' she says.

It's hard to talk to Phoebe now – they are detached from each other. It is a sad feeling losing a friend. Their conversation is stilted. There is a gulf between them, though she isn't sure if Phoebe even recognises why this is. The heatwave is over and it's feeling like March again, though the trees are gaining leaves; spring is on its way. Shirin wraps her arms around herself, hoping that doing so will insulate her body heat within her jacket. Phoebe is wearing a thin blazer, like it's not chilly. Perhaps it is the true Northerner in her that means she can take it.

'Aren't you meant to be at work?' Shirin asks. It's Tuesday afternoon.

'I'm "working from home".' With her fingers, Phoebe puts air quotes around the words. 'And I wanted to see you. I'm sorry I didn't pop round on the weekend. I was at a friend's hen-do.'

Shirin shrugs and says, 'That's alright.'

At Shirin's resigned tone, Phoebe gives her a pointed look. 'What's up with you? Things are weird – you're not talking as much.'

'The last few weeks have been a lot,' Shirin says.

Phoebe makes a guttural sound, a cross between a sigh and *urgh*. Shirin looks up and, rather than appear annoyed, as she imagined Phoebe would look, sadness crosses her face. 'I've been thinking about the café, and I feel really weird about it. I didn't mean to upset you. I just sort of snapped. If it's any consolation, I was on my period. But sometimes you make everything about you. And I really do think you need to let go of the past. I'm not saying this to be a dick – I'm saying it as a friend.'

It takes Shirin a moment to replay Phoebe's words in her head. Back then, she would have nodded along, murmured something like, *Yeah, okay*, because Phoebe had apologised at least. But Shirin has been through too much now. She is not the fifteen-year-old girl who longs for a better future, accepting bad treatment, even if it's masked as something else. It's one thing to let go of the past, but to do so you need to accept it, not flippantly brush it away as Phoebe always encourages her to do.

'Phoebe, with all due respect, this is not okay,' she says through gritted teeth. Her legs continue walking, though they stop when Phoebe's do.

'What?'

'I've given you so many chances now, but you're not a good friend to me. Or maybe we just aren't good friends to each other. I was bullied, abused, and you were there while it happened, and you are gaslighting me by pretending none of it was real, that I have no right to be upset.'

'No—'

'Yes. This isn't up for debate. My experiences aren't up for debate, and never will be.'

It is that easy. She turns and leaves Phoebe standing there, her mouth slightly open in shock. By the time Shirin is back home, she feels a peace that comes from knowing she likely won't see Phoebe again. She will not call or text her and they will lose contact. She's realised she is a different person from the one she was as a teenager, and it's unrealistic to expect their relationship to continue after all this time. That's the thing about friendships – they don't all last for ever, and that is okay. Or, as they say on Twitter, ending a friendship needs to be normalised. When she is with people like Mariam – and Kian – Shirin feels so *good* afterwards, like she has been heard and supported. It has taken her a while to realise that, with Phoebe, that isn't the case. They are only friends because they always have been, and if they met as adults, they would never choose to be. She goes straight to her bedroom and sends Mariam a voice-note about what happened.

Mariam's voice-note back says, 'The excuse about being on her period … that is a *tired* and, to be honest, very weird excuse. When we're on our periods, we don't become monsters. I'm sorry you went through that on top of everything else. You deserve better – and good on you, for standing up for yourself.'

Shirin replies, thanking Mariam for everything, truly, because without Mariam she sees that her life would have been much darker.

She knows she could have been a better friend to Phoebe, but similarly Phoebe could have been a better friend to her.

Maybe that's the point. The fact that they weren't is a sign that they're not meant to be, and that's fine. Now, though, in getting her friendships in order, she needs to speak to Hana.

While Shirin would rather throw herself out of a moving car than deal with confrontation, she knows she needs to have this conversation with Hana. Once you focus on sorting out your life, it becomes addictive.

It is almost midnight. Her dad and Karen went to bed not long ago, and she's migrated from her bedroom to the living room. In her room she had just done a dua for Maman Bozorg, using a book Mariam gave her, which lists different prayers. It is a comfort, even if she has to speak the English translation.

Keeping Up with the Kardashians is on now in the sitting room, and Shirin is inspired by Kourtney's confrontation with Khloé about something minor. They argue, but then they hug and there is a segment about how family is family, and how Khloé didn't realise she had hurt Kourtney.

Shirin messages Hana:

Are you free to talk?

Hana sees the message and then Shirin's phone is ringing, and the profile picture she saved for Hana flashes on her screen. Hana is only nineteen in the picture, and it was when they went to Greenwich Park for the first time, the background showcasing summer and the succulent green grass. It seems a much simpler time, though it didn't feel that way in the moment.

'Hello?'

'What's up? Is everything okay?' Hana says.

Shirin shuts her eyes tightly, which makes what she says next feel marginally less difficult. 'I feel like we're not close any more.'

'What are you—'

'I've been feeling hurt because you seem to have all these new friends, who you prefer to hang out with instead of me. Which is fine, but then you say we're best friends and always want to reminisce about the past, and it makes no sense to me. I've been struggling lately, and I never wanted to say it, but I think I really needed you. And I don't want us to just continue drifting.'

'Shirin, that's not it at all. I really am sorry about your nan. I didn't realise you needed me. But about you thinking I don't want to hang out with you – that's not it at all. I ...' Hana pauses, like she isn't sure how to say what she wants to say next, until she lets it all blurt out. 'I've been feeling really shit lately. I didn't want you to see that side of me. You seemed to be doing so well in your job, and everyone seems to have their shit together. And, of course, they do, as we're nearly thirty. But I don't. I was hanging out with people that I thought would help me get a job in fashion or something, and I'm not going to lie – I got caught up in their lifestyle. But I do miss you, Shirin. I miss us. You can tell me when you're annoyed at me. I'd rather that than you pretending we're okay when we're not.'

'I miss you, too. And I'm sorry, as well. I think everything has been so much that I let us drift apart and I didn't let you know how I was feeling sooner. I find it hard saying how I'm really feeling, but I know we should be able to tell each other. To clarify, though, I don't have my shit together. *And* we're not nearly thirty. *God!* We have three years left – and it's not like we'll drop dead after we hit thirty anyway. It's simply a new phase of our lives.'

Hana lets out a small chuckle. Then Shirin tells Hana exactly how her life isn't put together. She tells her everything. Of course Hana knew she was part of the protest, but she didn't know of Shirin's close connection to Rob Grayson. Shirin expects Hana to derive some glee from this, some camaraderie that things aren't going well, but instead Hana says, 'Fuck, I'm sorry, Shirin.'

It seems Shirin didn't give her friend enough credit, and that's on her.

They spend the next hour catching each other up properly on their lives. Millie has offered Hana a PR assistant's role at her company, which she plans to take. 'I think I romanticised having a dream job,' she says.

'I know what you mean. I definitely did that too.'

'Like, can a job really be the dream? You're still working.'

'Yeah. Like, my dream is to not work and live a life of luxury,' Shirin says.

'*Exactly*. And I need to let uni go, I know. It just felt like the time in which everyone was equal, and now I've found myself falling behind everyone. It's embarrassing.'

'It's not embarrassing, Hana. There isn't one set path in life, and that's okay. You're still objectively the coolest person at every party, I hope you know.'

'I mean I *do* know that, but thanks for vocalising it.'

Shirin can hear the smile in Hana's voice, which makes her own lips perk up too.

The phone call is cut short when Karen comes into the living room to tell her to keep it down. Despite Karen's steely expression, Shirin feels weightless after speaking to Hana. She is almost giddy that she has her friend back, that she was able to say everything she felt and be heard.

This moment with Hana – and with Phoebe – marks a change in all her relationships. She has been so scared of telling people how she really feels, of calling them out on the things that they've done that hurt her, of opening herself up, for them to do the same to her. But now she thinks she values herself enough to do that. She's realised that if she does not set the precedent for her relationships, and what she will and won't accept, then she will never have the kinds of relationships she truly wants. She always wanted to avoid confrontation; she thinks because it was easier to be quiet at school. It meant you were not seen, and were less likely to be picked on that day. But actually, confrontation is important. It is part of a healthy life, like eating kale. You might not like it at first, but it's good for you in the long run – and you might end up quite liking the taste, once you're used to it. She hopes so anyway.

A Comeback

When Mariam had asked Shirin if she wanted to live with her and her housemate, Fatma, it had come at the perfect time. Mariam's nightmare housemate was finally leaving and it had coincided exactly with Shirin's move back to London, which had made her think it was fate.

She took the Hull Trains service down to London, her journey mirroring the one she'd taken when she was eighteen, leaving for university. Her luggage in the overhead rack and behind the seats by the entrance, travelling now, as she did then, with a sense of hope and possibility. It had taken her two months to find a new job. She'd needed two weeks back home to decompress, but had very quickly realised she couldn't stay with her dad and Karen long-term. Especially when Karen's kids had visited on the weekends. She wanted her life back in London, but not the same life – a different one.

She'd got an interview at a small literature organisation funded by Arts Council England. The role was a mixture of editorial consultancy and project management. Shirin had heard of the organisation before, though, and liked their ethics – it matched her own, which she now realises is paramount. They have always supported under-represented authors in London and offer discounted, accessible writing workshops for everyone. Their offices are based in Deptford, south London. She had only been to Deptford once before. Her interview was on market day, so the streets she walked through to get to the office were bustling with market traders, selling everything from vintage Levis to fresh fish, to battery-operated robot toys. She had a good feeling about it all, which is rare for someone as cynical as Shirin.

She waited outside the offices, in a café, for half an hour before the interview. The café had a bookcase with a sign that said BOOK SWAP. HELP YOURSELF. She idly picked one up, not really looking at the cover, and returned to her table. She sipped her coffee and flicked through the book to ease her nerves. Fairly quickly she realised it was by an Iranian author. *Refuge* by Dina Nayeri. The cover had pomegranates scattered on the front. Another sign, Shirin decided.

Her interview was in an airy room, with plants on the bookcases that lined the walls. The interviewer, Sophia, told her two shelves were dedicated to the writers on their programmes who had gone on to have their books published. Sophia was a middle-aged white woman, originally from Darlington, with a very kind smile, a full fringe and bouncy yet thin brown locks. She got straight to the point, and when Shirin answered her questions, she leant in to listen properly. This, Shirin realised, was probably the bare minimum, but it was the first interview in which she didn't feel like she had to put on a façade to impress the interviewer.

The inevitable question came towards the end, when Sophia asked, 'And why did you leave your role at Hoffman Books?'

Shirin had of course rehearsed her reason many times in her head, though she thought if Sophia had done an inkling of research on her, she'd know why. She had planned to say, *Because I wanted to work somewhere more fulfilling,* but instead she said, 'Because they are publishing a racist.'

Sophia smiled, nodded in approval and asked, 'Is it true you were the organiser of the walkout?'

Shirin's cheeks coloured. 'One of.' She corrected herself then, by holding her head high, rather than diminishing something she was proud of, and said, 'Yes.'

'I think that's bloody brilliant. Go, you!'

Shirin got the job on the spot: a first in her career. She treated herself to a korma from the vegetarian Indian restaurant next door. The building blocks were set in motion for her return to London – and her new life.

Soon after, she moved in with Mariam and Fatma in leafy Brockley in south-east London. Their house is airy and multi-storeyed, with a green tiled bathroom that is so aesthetic Shirin cannot believe she gets to call this place her home. The living room and kitchen both have dining tables and ample room to walk around. When Shirin expressed delight at this to Mariam, her friend responded with, 'God, you really were deprived before, weren't you?' The rent is more, but Shirin's realised she forfeited so much of her happiness for cheaper accommodation that she spent most of her time away from her flat anyway, spending more money outside, in the process. And, most importantly: nothing, as of yet, is broken in the flat. The key slides in like a dream. The shower is high-pressured and the hot water lasts for *three* showers in a row without growing cold. All the hobs are functional. Luxury indeed.

Both Fatma and Mariam are practising Muslims. Fatma is British Turkish and works as a dentist in a surgery in New Cross. She has a strong Geordie accent, and as soon as she met Shirin she made her feel at home. It is an environment Shirin didn't know she needed until she was in it. Every Thursday they have a movie night and order a takeaway. They have captured the delicate balance of not hanging around with each other too much, but still seeing each other regularly.

Shirin has always wanted to learn more about Islam and asks Fatma and Mariam the questions she never asked her parents, but always wanted to. They are patient, non-judgemental of her curiosity about a religion that her parents never fully taught her.

This time, for their Thursday movie night, Shirin invites Hana along. It is initially a strange meeting of two worlds, but quickly Hana, Mariam and Fatma are making jokes with each other, like they have known each other much longer than fifteen minutes. They're waiting for their vegan fish and chips from Brockley's Rock when Mariam turns to Shirin on the sofa to ask, 'Whatever happened with Kian?'

Fatma and Hana, from the sofa to the right of them, look at Shirin, and then six eyes are on her.

'Nothing, really,' Shirin says.

'You don't speak any more then?' Mariam asks.

Shirin and Hana look at each other briefly, and then away again. With everything that has gone on in Shirin's life, she's barely had the capacity to even think about Kian in that way. Though, if she's being completely honest, that's a lie that she tells Hana and herself. She thinks about him most of the time before she goes to sleep, but they are fantasies in which he has come back to London and there are no longer 3,461 miles between them (yes, she has looked it up).

'He won't be back in London until at least the end of the year, and I've decided it's better if I don't hold on to him any more. For my sanity,' Shirin says.

The doorbell buzzes, breaking them from the conversation, and Shirin is the one to go to get their food, successfully avoiding speaking more about it. She realises, though, that she cannot have it all. It is greedy to want everything in your life to be perfect. Impossible, in fact, because life doesn't work like that. To be content, to see the good in life, is all that Shirin wants. What she has is enough – for now at least.

The Roaring Twenties

People are calling it the Roaring Twenties. The decade of glamorous parties and people living their best lives. However, it begins with continued devastating forest fires spreading around Australia. Then conflict between Iran and America, resulting in an abundance of crass World War Three memes and lost lives.

It is now February 2020 and they are all at Millie and Tommy's house-warming party. In a shock discovery, Henry was caught texting other girls, which prompted Millie to finally break up with him. She had only been seeing Tommy for three months before they decided to move in together. Millie claimed, 'When you know, you know.' While Shirin is not quite sure about that, she is glad her friend has moved on from her toxic boyfriend. Millie and Tommy have moved into a one-bedroom period flat in Forest Hill. The kitchen they stand in is narrow, illuminated by soft, warm lighting. Cool jazz beats through from the living room, vibrating the walls of the kitchen, where Shirin is standing now.

'We're old now, aren't we?' she says. Her hair is now dark brown and she – like everyone at the party – is dressed up. She wears a red midi-length dress that is tight on her waist and flows out at the skirt. She glances up directly at Kian for the first time that night. He is leaning against the kitchen cabinet, a beer in his hand, his eyes downcast. He wears a white shirt, tucked in, and navy trousers. A strange, familiar feeling encircles her. She wants him to look up, to smile, to disagree with her – anything, truly – but he is detached from her, from the conversation. They have not had a chance to speak yet, and he is all she has been able to think about since she saw him walk in just before dinner. Her nerves are jacked.

'Well, that depends on how you look at it. Is twenty-eight old?' Jasper says.

'We're old for being in our twenties, but in the grand scheme of things, I think we're still young. We've still got a young person's railcard,' Millie adds.

'Yeah, but it's the new twenty-six-to-thirty railcard, because, as millennials, we're not well off,' Jasper says.

'It's nice, though, isn't it, being older? Like, in our early-to-mid-twenties I felt like I had no idea what I was doing. I was bashing away at what I thought I should be doing, but it feels a lot calmer now,' Shirin says.

Millie nods thoughtfully. 'True, yes.'

Hana is pouring herself a glass of red wine, her back to the group, when she says, 'God, uni was fun, though, wasn't it?'

Shirin smiles – because while Hana still reminisces about university, there has been a marked change in the past year. It is no longer romanticised as the best period of their lives. It was only a segment. The best is possibly yet to come.

'Shirin, do you remember at uni when you freaked out because a psychic said you had a third eye, and you thought that meant you had powers?' Jasper laughs. 'Any time you were high, you'd give predictions about what would happen in our future.'

'How could I forget?' she says absent-mindedly. She steals another glance at Kian, who at that moment looks back at her. He holds her gaze for a moment before they both look away. Her heart begins to beat more speedily.

'I'm just going to the loo,' she says, leaving the group.

She joins the short bathroom queue, leans her back against the wall and breathes out deeply. *In-out, in-out, in-out.* She is much more grounded now, but despite all this, Kian arriving – again unpredictably – has shaken her up. She has had so much time to think about what she wants, has imagined this moment many times, but when it is presented to her, she does not know what to do.

'You alright?'

She starts at this. Opens her eyes to find Kian next to her.

'Yes, fine,' she says. Something about him being so close to her breaks the façade she has kept up all night, of pretending that he is exactly like everyone else in the room. She lets out a held breath.

'What are you doing here?' she asks. Someone leaves the bathroom and it is her turn. 'You can go,' she says to the person behind them – a friend of Millie's that she does not know very well.

Kian scratches his neck, and she notices he is wearing her old hair-bobble around his wrist. She averts her gaze quickly, but she notices him noticing her noticing it. He looks like he finds the fact amusing for a second, before shaking his head.

'My residency ended,' he says.

A lot has happened in the past year, though it doesn't feel as though a year has passed since they last saw each other.

'I know that,' she says. 'I just wasn't expecting you to be here. I always thought you were more Henry's friend than Millie's.'

They have not spoken properly in months. Not intentionally – at least that is what Shirin tells people. She thought it was self-sabotage, really, to continue talking to someone you have feelings for but with whom it can never work because of the miles between them.

'Yeah, well. There was a reason I wanted to come tonight.' He squints down at her, his eyes a deep brown. He has grown a well-groomed beard and it makes him look much older, but also softer somehow. He then bites his bottom lip, ever so briefly, as though considering his next words carefully. 'Do you want to go for a smoke?'

She nods and they go outside together.

Millie and Tommy's flat, like many in London, does not have a garden or a balcony, so they sit on the steps in front of the converted house. The winter air is sharp. Ahead of them, across the road, is a small patch of grass, cordoned off with high steel gates. They see a fox running, foraging in nearby bins for food, its body lean and its tail plump.

'I feel sorry for foxes,' she says, to fill the space. 'They're always starving.'

'Yeah,' he says. 'It's shit.'

He lights up his cigarette and they are both avoiding each other's gaze. It is as though once they look at each other, they will be laid bare – each fearful that what they are feeling will not be reciprocated.

'Have you been following all the stuff about Iran and America?' Shirin asks suddenly. It has been bothering her, but anyone she speaks to about it does not seem to care.

'It's fucked up,' he says, shaking his head.

'Did you see the memes? People joking online about it?'

He nods. 'It pissed me off.' He had a long Twitter argument with someone about it, in fact.

'I'm glad it annoyed you, too. I feel like if you're not Iranian, you don't get it. People think it's funny.'

There is a silence, then they both begin to speak at the same time, and that is when they turn to each other, lock eyes for the first time.

'You go first,' he says.

'No, you,' she says.

Kian smiles, blows out a puff of his cigarette to the side, before beginning. 'I've been thinking a lot about the past, and the things I've been holding on to. And I'm so glad we bumped into each other at my house-warming party. I just want to say thank you, I guess.'

'Thank you for what?'

'For being you.'

It is objectively one of the kindest things someone has ever said to her, though Shirin is unsure what to say in response. She settles on, 'I'm glad we saw each other again too.'

The fox has made its way to the end of the road now. It is merely a speck against the night-time darkness.

'I keep thinking, though,' he begins, pausing to gulp. He looks nervous. Nervous and handsome. She wants to touch his face, to soothe whatever anxiety is bubbling away inside him. 'What happened with us this time around? Why didn't we make it work?'

She is taken aback by this and looks down at her feet – at the scuff on her pointed-heel shoes – and eventually settles on, 'I don't know.' The words are not quite truthful. She has come a long way, although, like most things, resetting your mind is not an overnight change. Much like with her depression and anxiety, she is looking inwards to manage it, but it takes time. 'I thought you didn't want to do long-distance.' It is hard saying these words, being honest with the people she cares about. She feels herself vulnerable, opening herself up to be hurt.

He shakes his head, a frustrated look on his face. 'I was scared.' This makes her look up at him. 'I left everything in my life for this adventure, to focus on my art, and it felt like I only had these few years of my course to do it in. So when I found out I got my residency, I was surprised by how much I wanted to decline it and stay here, with you. I almost did, but doing that after we'd been together for only a month ... it felt crazy to me. I didn't want to hold you back. And, maybe selfishly, I didn't want to hold myself back. But all the time I was there all I thought about was you, even when we weren't talking. My heart was here, with you.' He gives her a small sidelong smile. She is struck by how Kian's beauty has refined over adulthood, that he has grown into himself, and she has not stopped being drawn to him over the past twelve years.

His honesty makes her bold enough to say, 'I wish I had said something then. I was scared too – scared to say how I felt, in case I got rejected. But I've not stopped thinking about you, either.'

'We've both been stupid then,' he says, still smiling, hope rising within him. 'I sometimes think how different our lives would have been if we hadn't stopped talking – not just this past year, but back then. If we'd told each other how we felt, back in school.'

Shirin's brows furrow. She looks different now from how she did when he saw her a year ago. She is slower in her movements, more considered. There is an absence of chaos that he hadn't even realised was there before. She reaches up and takes his cigarette from him, draws a long drag, before handing it back to him.

'I don't think we would have been good together at school,' she says. 'We were held back by so much. I prefer adult us, right now, to be honest with you.'

He smiles but doesn't say anything, realising she's right. And while they cannot do anything about their past, they have power over their future.

'So,' she continues. 'You're here for good?'

'I think so, yeah.'

'I'm glad.'

Kian lets out a long breath before saying, 'I don't want to regret not saying this. I don't want this to be another thing I look back on and wish I did differently.'

'How do you mean?' Shirin looks up at him then, really looks at him, which makes his mouth run dry.

'I want this.' There's more he wishes to say, but he's hoping he can convey everything in what he is not saying. She puts her hand gently over his, the hand that isn't holding the cigarette. Hers is warm and soft. 'When I left for New York I wish I had told you how I really feel about you, that I didn't want us to stop seeing each other. So I'm telling you now, Shirin. I want us to try again this time, properly – all in.'

'I want that too,' she says, heart soaring, her lips curled up in a smile.

He thinks she looks her most beautiful when she smiles like that. It is infectious and soon his expression mirrors hers.

They sit on the steps for a while, watching the cars pass in the night. Whereas before they were haunted by their past, they lean into it now, acknowledging that it led them to be here, together.

Acknowledgements

This book was written predominantly during the lockdowns of 2020–2021, and if there was ever a point in which a writer needs support in their solitary profession, this was the time. So, unsurprisingly, I have many lovely people I would like to thank.

My endless thanks, firstly, goes to Emily Griffin, my editor at Century. Your support and guidance has been truly – and I mean *truly* – invaluable. The second book syndrome was real with this book, and your calm and wisdom helped shape it into the book it is now, so thank you so much. It wouldn't be what it is today without you.

I would also like to thank so many other people who worked on *People Change* in various wonderful ways: Niki Chang, Roisin O'Shea, Rose Waddilove, Ceara Elliot, Amelia Evans, and Marie-Louise Patton.

A special mention, too, to the Society of Authors and the Authors' Foundation for providing me with funding to write this book. I took a six-month sabbatical from my full-time job in 2021 to completely redraft this book (numerous times, I should say), and the funding that was provided enabled me to do so with less worry and I am so grateful for that.

This book, among many things, is about friendship – and I also wanted to thank all the special people in my life that listened to me spinning around in circles about the plot for this book. There are at least three entirely different versions of this book, and it's through rambling conversations about big plot issues, or what kind of music Shirin and Kian would listen to, that we are here today! So thank you to all my wonderful friends, though especially Matty Thompson, Grace Crannis, Hannah Brewin and Harriet Martin. I can remember specific moments in lockdown, during walks or long phones calls, hashing out various potential scenarios in this book with you all. I hope you can see the little and big moments in which you shaped the book through these conversations – from whether Kian should be in New York at the start or London, to whether Shirin would really be smoking in the middle of cross-country (as you will know by now, that was sensibly changed!).

Thank you to Tice, Kira, Riley, Jarred, Sophia and Koyer – you're the best writing group a girl could ask for!

A special mention to Nicola Webb – my first ever work wife when we were at Mills & Boon. It was such fun remembering our time together as assistants, meeting by the book bins to rant, chat and/or spiral. My fondest memories of my first proper publishing job are due to you! And similarly, Asmaa Isse, my work bestie from when we worked together at Puffin. I'm glad we had each other in 2020 when the world turned upside down, and love how we've encouraged each other to be our best selves since. It's through being friends with you both that Mariam was born. I appreciate you both so much – and feel lucky to continue to be friends with you both, beyond work.

For my debut novel, *The Mismatch*, I was so touched by fellow authors offering their kind words to help readers find my book. Thank you to Libby Page, Zeba Talkhani, Huma Quershi, Sophie Cousens, Abbie Greaves, Lauren Ho, Haleh Agar, Beth Reekles and Helly Acton. It means so much to me, truly. And if you liked this book, and you haven't already read their books, I urge you to!

And finally, thank you to you – the reader. Thank you for reading this book.